Although *this* Tour takes place in the near future, it would be almost impossible to write about a Tour without making passing reference to famous riders of past years. But every character in the story is fictional. None is based on an actual person, past or present. The names of the teams are also invented, as are many of the locations.

LEGS

Liz Cochrane

ORIGINAL WRITING

ISBN: 978-1-906018-12-2
A CIP catalogue for this book is available from the National Library.
Printed by Biddles Ltd, King's Lynn, Norfolk.

Published by Original Writing Ltd, Ireland, 2007.

TOUR DE FRANCE
STAGE 13

Dino Nardini

'Remember: I want Ribero blocked.' Dino Nardini rode up along-side three of his team.

'Yeah, Dino. We know. You already told us twice,' said Bruno.

Bruno's tone was patient, but Dino didn't like the sideways look that went along with it. It was the kind of look you give someone who might be losing the plot.

'So maybe you'll understand this is important,' Dino snapped. 'It's a narrow road. I want the team to fan out in front of him. Don't give him space to get past you.'

'Won't be easy. He's a helluva fast climber.'

Dino couldn't argue with that. Paco Ribero had beaten him up the Alpe d'Huez—a double-points victory, which brought the little bastard too bloody close in the contest for Best Climber. Along with the title went the cash prize that Dino desperately needed. About to give the guys another warning, he heard Bruno ask: 'What about Vauban?'

'Not so important. He'll be no threat in the Pyrenees. Martens is more of a danger.'

Bruno made a choking sound, halfway to a laugh. 'You want us to block *Martens* as well? You have to be joking!'

'I'm not bloody joking,' Dino snarled. 'I never joke about winning points. Points are money.' And his team would get its share, so he demanded their obedience. 'Block Ribero. Got that?'

He never used to be this tough on the guys, but this year was different. Things had changed; things the guys didn't know about. Nobody knew, except Fiarelli, and Dino had to keep it that way. He sensed that, out of his line of vision, Bruno was exchanging meaningful glances with the other two but, as they passed the signboard marking two kilometres from the start of the climb, Dino breathed deeply and tried to clear his problems from his mind. Right now he had to focus on being first at the top.

Jo Bonnard

The TV and radio unit was always positioned near the finish line. In one of the booths, Eltsport's English-language commentator, Jo Bonnard, heard the countdown to a commercial break. She sat back, drank from her bottle of water and thought about the race so far.

∽

The Tour had started on the west coast of France, from where one hundred and eighty-nine cyclists had set off eastward. Jo had reckoned that perhaps ten of them had a realistic chance of outright victory. There were twenty-one stages, each a race within the race, over varied terrain. On flat roads, the sprinters achieved incredible speeds in death-defying finishes. The climbers led the way on mountain passes. But all riders shared one dream: to survive the three gruelling weeks and get to Paris.

The first six stages had been flat and fast, with two mass pile-ups on narrow roads, but only four riders injured and out of it. In the Alps, slogging up mountain passes and careering down hairpin descents, ten more had come to grief. Now they were crossing Provence, frying in the heat, and yesterday another rider was liquidated by stomach trouble. Today's flat, transitional stage took them through vines and sunflowers, heading west. Tomorrow's stage would be a steady uphill grind into the foothills, and then would come the long, hard climbs in the Pyrenees. For a few more riders, those climbs might well put an end to the dream.

Jo had been keeping an eye on her stopwatch. One minute to On Air. She smoothed her short blonde hair under the band of her headphones and listened for her cue. Her youthful looks had scarcely changed since she started out as a teenaged cub reporter, more than twenty years ago. A touch of cynicism had come with maturity, yet her enthusiasm was undimmed. This sport was her passion, and The Tour was the jewel in its crown.

As her countdown ended, she flipped her microphone switch and began her commentary again: 'We're approaching the only climb of the day—four kilometres up the face of an escarpment—so of course the camera has focussed on Chiali's team captain, Dino Nardini. There he is, in the white jersey with big red dots that distinguishes him as the current Best Climber. Dino is a magnet for the cameras, and so are his famous fans—the girls who follow their idol everywhere.'

The motocamera had slowed to film a group of those girls. They were all wearing *I love Dino* T-shirts and screaming his name. The cameraman had a close-up action shot of an obviously bra-less girl running alongside her idol. Jo stifled a giggle and a remark about sexist photography as the girl came to a panting halt, but the riders sped onwards and the camera had to follow.

'Around Dino, in the lime-green jerseys,' Jo said, 'are three of his Chiali team—his personal buffer zone in case there's a collision. We can see that Dino's talking to them. A pity the camera's not wired for sound, but I guess he's giving them a pep-talk before he hits this climb.'

Already Dino Nardini was standing on the pedals. His team-mates had dropped back, their protective job over for the moment.

'There he goes,' Jo said, 'but he's not going to get away that easily. His rivals have been alert for this. They're after him! Jonkers in the race leader's Yellow Jersey, with Charreau just behind him, and now here's somebody else sneaking between two of the Chiali riders. It's Harry Vallon in the dark blue jersey of the AFA team. It's surprising that Vallon, who's not a great climber, should go after Nardini.' She leaned forward, peering at the screen. 'But Ribero is

3

well and truly blocked in the main bunch. He simply cannot get around the Chiali roadblock. So now we know what Nardini was telling his three bodyguards. They dropped back to where two more Chialis were waiting, and now all five have spread out across the width of the road. This is a new tactic from Chiali, quite different from the old US Postal method. Remember Lance Armstrong's 'blue train'? They perfected the tactic of riding in line-ahead, so that anyone trying to get to the front had to overtake them all. Nevertheless, wherever Ribero tries to break through, there's a Chiali rider in his way.

'However, the Chialis are so intent on blocking Ribero, others are breaking through. There goes Bob Rothman and with him is Marc Martens, both in the red-gold-black jerseys of the Mr Chip team. And another little chase is developing. I can make out two more dark blues from AFA—Jacky Bernard, a good climber, and his team captain George Ferrer. With them is David Vauban of Intapost, and the three are trying to latch on to Rothman's group. Vauban's riding hard and should easily bridge the gap. Bernard is looking back over his shoulder, waiting for Ferrer to follow his wheels. Ferrer's still chasing…' Jo paused, frowning. 'No, he's not. He seems to have had second thoughts and slipped back into the main bunch.'

What on earth was George Ferrer doing? That kind of indecisive move would get him nowhere. During the previous week, his evident self-doubt had lost him several minutes. But for his popularity, he might also have lost the support of his team.

'Bernard has reached the first steep bend,' Jo continued. 'It has a gradient of twelve percent. That's one-in-eight, if you're accustomed to ratios. Nardini is still in front, with quite a bit of daylight between him and the pursuing groups. The first and second groups of chasers seem to have merged and, even as we watch, they are splitting up again. Behind Nardini there's only one small chasing group—Vallon, Martens, Vauban and Jonkers, in that order. Bob Rothman shepherded Martens past the Chiali block and into the chase, but now he has dropped back into the second group.'

Lucky Marc Martens, Jo thought, having a mentor like Bob Rothman. Not every former champion would take on a protégé and ride selflessly for him; but that was one of the reasons why Bob, the quiet American, was so highly respected by everyone.

A helicopter shot showed the pack fragmented into little clusters of ten or a dozen riders. The front groups were frantically trying to catch up to the leaders while the back markers were fighting to hold their position, hoping not to fall too far behind. Jo's eyes stretched in astonishment. A collective frenzy, like some bizarre infection, had made the pace extreme. She had no time to wonder who had initiated this madness, because the picture had changed again.

'This is the picture from the first camera, almost at the top of the climb. Dino Nardini is about ten metres ahead of Harry Vallon.' Suddenly she banged a fist on her knee. 'Watch Marc Martens! Pushing a mighty big gear, he's catching up with Vallon, gaining ground all the time.'

The absolute power of Marc's riding had a throat-grabbing quality. This was racing! This was the spectacle and drama that she loved. Her voice rose in excitement. 'Look at him go! Marc Martens passes Vallon and keeps going away, making it look like Vallon is glued to the asphalt. Now David Vauban also starts to sprint. He lacks Marc's power but he's one of those lightly built riders whose ability to accelerate on steep gradients marks them as pure climbers...the summit line is in sight...and Nardini sails across it, easily first by about ten metres. David Vauban's still speeding and he's pulling alongside Martens...but Martens pushes just that little bit harder...and crosses the line just ahead of him. Harry Vallon faded into fourth place and won't be too happy about that. He started the chase, but he's one-paced on climbs.

'Now comes an easy downhill run, so I guess most of the groups will join up again before the next sprint, about fifteen kilometres down the road.'

∿

Jo's prediction was correct. The long, sweeping descent was taken at a relaxed pace and, by the time the riders reached the flat ground, all of them had reunited to form a compact bunch. But she could not have predicted how the intermediate sprint would play out.

'Tom Dash is first to break clear,' she said, 'but once again George Ferrer emerges from the pack to try his luck—this time against Dash, the demon sprinter. Following Ferrer is Jan Claes, the sprint specialist of Mr. Chip. But now Vallon goes for it as well!'

5

She gaped incredulously at the sight of Harry Vallon, from Ferrer's own AFA team, riding *against* his team captain, instead of with him. Was this some novel variant of team tactics; or was it simply Vallon, self-compensating for missing the points on that climb? He wouldn't beat Dash; that was sure.

'Dash is first across the line, Claes a metre back, Vallon third. Ferrer is fourth, *but* the points go only to the first three.'

In her headphone, Jo heard the countdown to a short commercial break and switched off her microphone, glad to let her annoyance with Vallon subside. She had read yesterday's press handout from the AFA team manager: *Despite rumours,* it said, *there is no dissent within the team who are all riding in support of their captain George Ferrer.* Oh, really? A manager should have known better than to blow such transparent smoke in the eyes of the media. There certainly *was* dissent, in the person of Harry Vallon.

The first time Jo interviewed Harry, she'd seen how he capitalised on his resemblance to the young Paul Newman. She reckoned he must have studied Newman's movies to copy the mannerisms, but Harry's sexiness was phoney, and his arrogance surfaced all too often. If Harry didn't watch out, his sneer would become permanent and spoil the Newman look.

She had to admit that Harry was a good rider; but when he'd won the eleventh stage, his after-stage interview had been an exhibition of such overwhelming conceit that it was easy to see why the team was fed up with him. They'd done most of the work, and not a word of thanks from Handsome Harry. No way they'd support him. On the other hand, they liked George Ferrer whose dark jaw and thick black eyebrows gave him a brooding appearance, quite at odds with his good nature. George was a scatterbrained romantic, liable to forget things, but so amiable that even the youngest riders took fatherly care of him.

George had been a constant stage-winner in his glory days, but his star was setting and his wife Paula, a former podium girl and now a top model, was looking for someone with a higher profile. On account of Harry Vallon's victories earlier this year, Paula apparently saw Harry as the potential winner of this year's Tour and had been blatantly following him around for months. According to the grapevine, they'd been caught in bed together in Italy, almost under her husband's nose. The lads in the team, far from being amused, had been downright puritanical about that; and from then on their dislike of Vallon had grown.

Nevertheless, George had finally realised that his adored Paula had used his name to promote her own modelling career. Small wonder that George, his life and his mind in turmoil, was making so many tactical misjudgements.

The advert break ended, and Jo rapidly brought her concentration back to the action on screen. The pace remained fast but steady until, with just over one kilometre to go, five of the Chiali team manoeuvred into line ahead.

'The Chialis are getting into position to give a lead-out to their powerful, explosively fast sprinter, Tom Dash. He is fifth in the line, and will sit sheltered in their slipstream until, one by one, his lead-out men will peel off and Dash will make the final sprint. Now they go under the kilometre banner and the Chiali line is going full speed on the left of your screen, and...Ah-ha! They won't have it all their own way. Look at the other side of the road where Mr Chip has three men in line. But that's it. Not *one* other team looks organised.' She was always disappointed when a stage ended scrappily. 'Different team colours are scattered all over the place, so it's down to those two teams to fight this out.

'Five hundred metres, the Chiali line is reduced to two—Dash, being led out by Salvatore. On the far side of the road, Martens peels off and Jan Claes goes it alone, hands low, sprinting fast. And there goes Dash! From this head-on view, he and Claes are neck and neck. This will be close...Wow! How close can you get? I can't say who won. We'll have to wait for the photo finish.' This would take some seconds. She had time to add an explanation: 'Even in slow motion, the overlapping of bikes makes it too complex for the human eye to make out the placings, but every bike has a mini transponder that registers its time to thousandths of a second as it crosses an electronic beam. Here's the replay now.'

Aimed across the line, the photo-finish camera showed that Dash had beaten Claes by the width of an ultra-slim racing tyre. The rest of the pack came hurtling across the line in a mob that the computer sorted into order, and then the stage results came up on the screen. Tom Dash and Jan Claes got the lion's share of the bonus points. Vallon was sixth, Martens seventh. Dino Nardini was well up the list in tenth place.

This would change the overall classification. Jo waited silently while the computer made the calculations by adding everyone's total time to date and then deducting the time bonuses.

A few seconds later the list appeared, showing that Jonkers still had the Yellow Jersey, but by only nine seconds over Charreau. Harry Vallon was now third, Marc Martens had moved up to fourth place, while Nardini's bonus points had promoted him into sixth position.

Dino Nardini was a talented climber and, barring disasters, he would assuredly win a hatful of points in the Pyrenees. But did he see himself with a serious chance of winning The Tour? Stage 19 was a flat time-trial that would call for endurance and power riding. Jo doubted that Dino possessed these qualities. And yet Pantani, previously reckoned a 'pure climber,' had ridden a dramatic time-trial that gave him victory in the '98 Tour, so one never could tell.

When the podium presentations had been made, Jo closed the day's broadcast and strode, trim in jeans and a cool green shirt, to the Press Room—today the badminton hall of the local sports club. She went first to collect the usual handouts from her pigeonhole, but was surprised to find it empty. Janine, the super-efficient Press Officer, found her a plug-in for her laptop, right next to Susana the bouncy Spanish reporter who was the only other press-accredited woman on The Tour.

Jo began to copy the stage results and bonus points into her files. It was time-consuming work, but necessary. In this male environment, a woman had to keep at least one step ahead of the men.

At one point she looked up to find she was being watched by two of those men—the journalists who'd once been in line for her job. They immediately looked away, sniggering. Jo ignored them.

She had been writing about cycling for longer than she cared to remember. Her first exclusive interview had been with Paul Breton, and when she had seen the name Danny Breton on the Intapost team list, she had been mildly shocked. Danny was Paul's son, and Jo had faced the fact that he represented her second generation of riders. It was not much consolation that, in this year's Tour, Danny was the youngest rider.

In her youth, Jo had seen the cyclists as older men, but some years ago she had caught herself thinking of them as boys. Now she carefully referred to them as 'the riders,' 'the cyclists' or 'the competitors'—words with no trace of age-ism. But how did they see *her?* From Girl Reporter she'd gone to Big Sister, but now...Maybe she had become Aunt Jo.

She got on well with most of them, treating them not as riding machines or rolling adverts for their sponsors, but as people with lives beyond cycle racing. They trusted her and talked to her off the record. As recently as last week, Cedric Charreau had confided his worry that his pregnant wife would give birth 'too early'—meaning before the end of The Tour. They told her of their joys, ambitions and disappointments. Reminded of today's main loser, George Ferrer—now down to eighth place—Jo sighed and went back to filing the overall race positions.

After thirteen days, the best riders' times were close. Less than eight minutes separated the first ten competitors. The two leading riders, Jonkers and Charreau, had lost key lieutenants, injured in Alpine crashes, and consequently their time advantage had gradually been whittled down. It seemed that their days in the lead were numbered, and their main rivals were Harry Vallon and Marc Martens. And what about Dino Nardini? The Pyrenean climbs could well move him up the rankings, but these last few days he'd worn a hunted look. His riding—in fact, his whole demeanour— had an air of desperation. Jo decided that, if she were asked to bet on a likely winner from the current top ten...she wouldn't.

STAGE 13

Evening

Harry Vallon

In the dining room of the hotel where the Anglo-French Airtrain team, or AFA, was lodged, eight of the cyclists were replacing calories in unusual silence. Only Harry Vallon was talking, but nobody was paying attention to his tirade. Instead they were casting glances at the door, waiting for George Ferrer to join them.

An hour ago, George's wife Paula had turned up unexpectedly and they'd all heard her sounding off at full Neapolitan volume. Paula had no problem getting past the hotel's security. She had a famous face and a high-handed manner, so nobody had questioned her right to come in without a pass.

Vallon sat with his back resolutely to the door. He didn't give a toss if Ferrer was starving or sulking. Harry's only concern was how to get the team to ride for *him* instead of Ferrer.

'I should have had somebody to relay me on that climb.' He directed a blue laser glare at Jacky Bernard. 'You're supposed to be a climber. Where the hell were you?'

Bernard took his time about answering. Small and light-boned, he had the serene face of the priest he had thought of becoming—might yet become when his cycling days were over. 'I was riding with George,' he said, his voice calm. 'He's had a few bad days but he's regaining his form, and he *is* the team captain.'

'Jesus Christ!' Vallon exploded, deliberately offending Bernard.

'You should have been riding for me! The whole bloody lot of you should be riding for me. I'm in third place—no thanks to any of you idiots—and I'm six minutes ahead of Ferrer.'

'George can catch back six minutes in the mountains,' Bernard pointed out quietly.

'In *your* expert opinion?' Vallon treated him to a sneer. 'Well, if you think loyalty to our fucking useless captain is more important than cash, *I* don't! I'll win without help from any of you stupid bastards, but just don't expect me to share the prize money with you.'

Another long silence followed, broken eventually by Nat Arnold. He looked sulkily at Vallon. 'It was your own fault. You started that climb too fast.'

Arnold, tall, gangling, and mournful-faced, was work-shy. A blame-shifter and compulsive complainer, he was convinced his lack of success was everyone else's fault. Arnold took sides with nobody but himself. 'Today was supposed to be an easy stage,' he grumbled, 'and we finished up riding at a crazy speed. It's not fair to expect us to...'

He shut up as the door opened. Everyone but Harry turned round, but it was the team manager Harvey Jones who dithered, neither in the room nor out of it. He asked: 'Where's George?' Answered by shrugs, he said, 'That damned Paula!' and went off, muttering.

Harry Vallon's startlingly blue eyes were bright with malice. 'Jones would do better to worry about the team, so-called, and bloody well *order* you to ride for me.' He added with an offhand shrug: 'Paula is George's problem.'

'Nothing to do with you, eh?' Arnold again.

Harry raised his eyebrows. 'Jealous?'

Arnold was halfway to his feet when Jacky Bernard tugged him back, telling him to keep quiet.

Harry's sneer was back in place. 'George's wife screws around and he does nothing about it. If Paula climbs into my bed, why shouldn't I take what's offered to me?' He stopped talking. Everyone was looking at a point above his head.

George Ferrer stood behind him.

Seven mouths gaped in astonishment as George, wild-eyed, yanked Harry Vallon from his chair, spun him round and slammed a fist into his face.

STAGE 14

Jo Bonnard

Jo reckoned she had plenty of time to watch the start. Today's route was on minor roads that formed a ragged C shape on the map. A major road linked the points of the C, and was marked in the Route Book as an alternative for the press cars. By using it, she would easily make it to the TV unit at the finishing line where she was due on air at three o'clock.

Carrying her toolkit of notebook, mobile phone and laptop, she made her way to *Le Village Départ,* the marquees erected daily at each starting point. Jo surveyed the usual scene of apparently aimless milling about. The atmosphere was always an odd mixture of boredom and anticipation, and a brief chat with a few of the competitors was a good way to gauge the mood of the day.

Teams arrived, managers hovered anxiously, an over-amplified voice introduced the riders as they signed in and had their numbers checked—a process that took more than an hour. Reporters and photographers stalked the star riders. Invited VIPs stood about, looking either self-important or bewildered, and everybody freeloaded at the sponsors' expense.

Local wine was on offer in the inevitable plastic tumblers, but Jo had long ago decided that warm wine made a bad start to anyone's day and contented herself with coffee, dispensed by a pretty blonde girl got up as an unconvincing Brazilian peasant.

A cluster of bright green shirts marked the arrival of the Chiali team. Over the crowd-barriers, screaming girls beseeched Dino Nardini for his autograph. He was instantly recognisable in the Polkadot Jersey of the King of the Mountains—the popular title, more glamorous than the official Best Climber. Even without the Polkadot Jersey, Dino would attract attention. The boy had charisma.

Would Dino have made her heart flutter when she was twenty? Jo very much doubted it. She'd always been put off by egotism. No denying he was eye candy, but his Latin-lover charm was too unsubtle for her taste.

He saw her, removed his high-tech shades and came over to her, giving her the famous, big-brown-eyed smile and a *Ciao*. Then, his smile slipping a bit, he said, 'I read that article you wrote about me. Some of it's…okay.' He rocked spread fingers. 'Some, I wasn't so sure about. My father says its ironic, but…' a swift look round at the craning spectators, 'what would a boy from the back streets know about irony?'

'I haven't a clue,' said Jo tartly, 'not being a boy from the back streets. And neither are you. If you don't know about irony, your father wasted his money on your expensive education.'

Why did he persist with the humble-beginnings myth? He'd created it years ago in order to appear just one of the lads, but nowadays everybody knew he was the son of a rich industrialist.

Dino's smile stayed firmly on his mouth, but faded from his eyes. 'You write nasty things so nicely; but even the nice things, you make a little nasty.'

Jo registered his obvious anger. 'I've done you no harm in the cycling world.'

'But what about my fans?'

Ah! So that was what bothered him.

'Don't worry. They still love you.' She smiled. 'And they'll still buy your T-shirts. You're worried about your company's sales figures?'

At once Dino's finely shaped lips tightened, his eyes became ice cold and muscles hardened in his handsome face. Then equally quickly he reconstructed his smile. It was as though a draught of Arctic air had briefly invaded the sunny Mediterranean.

'No,' he said defiantly. 'And next month I'm going to change the logo to *Dino, King of the Mountains.*'

'You're very sure of yourself! Ribero's only five points behind you.'

Dino's chin went up. 'Ribero got most of his points on the low-category climbs.'

Jo raised eloquent eyebrows. 'Low category? The Alpe d'Huez?'

'I had mechanical problems.'

The excuse had a familiar ring but she simply reminded him not to discount David Vauban and Marc Martens, both of whom were only two points behind Ribero.

Again the dismissive shrug. 'Vauban's okay up to eighteen hundred metres, then the altitude gets to him. Martens...strong, but not a pure climber. As for Harry Vallon...' Dino made a throwaway gesture.

Jo hid her puzzlement. Vallon was certainly a contender for the overall victory, but was by no means a threat to the Best Climber award, which was Dino's only realistic goal. Or was it?

Before she could ask what the remark signified, Chiali's manager Enrico Fiarelli came towards them, obviously looking for Dino. Jo had no wish to talk to Fiarelli. She glanced at her watch. 'Better make tracks. Have a good stage, Dino.'

She watched him wheel away. Something in her article hadn't pleased him. It had been syndicated beyond the specialised cycling publications, even to a women's magazine, such was Dino's fame. It was recent, the text stored in her laptop's memory. She sat at a café table and accessed it. Which paragraphs had annoyed him?

Dino Nardini's well-publicised romances with film stars, pop stars and tycoons' daughters have made him the most famous cyclist in the world. People who know nothing of cycling recognise his face. His dark eyes smoulder from the coffee adverts. His dazzling good looks sell those designer jeans...

The pity is that the cycling fraternity, equally dazzled, seems unable to see him clearly. He has been dismissed as a showman and publicity-seeker by those who should know better. Pushing the gears on a steep gradient takes a lot more than good looks...

The famous T-shirts, printed with his handsome face in a heart-shaped frame, adorn the palpitating bosoms of the girls who wait by the roadside to scream his name. He loves them all. Every T-shirt they buy is a small contribution to his bank account. Not only does he own the copyright of the logo; he owns the factory that makes the shirts. Smart thinking...

A cyclist's career is short. He'll be burned out in seven years. Maybe his detractors are envious of his fame. More logically they should envy his clever exploitation of his undoubted talent. And they should never forget that he's not just a dishy dreamboat. He's one helluva bike rider.

What, in that, had turned the sun briefly to ice? She'd emphasised his undeniable ability in the world's toughest sport. She had first talked to him six years ago when he was a new professional aged twenty-one. But this was her first inkling that Dino's character had a dark side concealed behind the smiling, public face. Did he feel she had spoiled his playboy image by pointing out that he was a businessman? What had she just said to cause his loss of cool? His anger had flashed when she mentioned his T-shirt Company. Did he want his ownership of it kept quiet? Why?

~

So much for having plenty of time! Jo had watched the riders set off and then gone to her car to discover a flat tyre. She knew better than to expect any offer of help. Equality was equality. Knowing how to change a wheel was one thing, loosening wheel nuts was another. She had wrestled them off, changed the wheel, and then she'd had to wash her filthy hands and change her grimy shirt; and now she was going to be late.

The traffic was barely moving. What was causing the hold up? Craning from her window she got her answer. Roadworks! Surely the organisers knew about this? Why hadn't they issued an update about this alternative route? She picked up her mobile phone and called the Press Office.

Janine answered. 'But you *were* notified, Jo,' she said, sounding vexed. 'I put the notices in all the press pigeonholes, including yours.'

Those two sniggering clowns in the Press Room... 'I believe you, Janine. I know why I didn't get it. It's not your fault.' Into the 21st century, the male chauvinists were still trying to stymie her.

A man with a Stop-Go board waved on another batch of traffic. Jo missed the cut by two cars. Closing the window against the smell of hot tar, she tried to tune in to Race Radio, the short-wave broadcast that came from the lead car. It gave updates on the progress of the main contenders, announced falls, notified team cars about punctures or mechanical problems, and also relayed riders' requests for more water, food or medical help. The commentary boxes and all official cars were equipped with receivers but, at the moment, Jo's receiver produced nothing but static and she guessed she was still out of range. She hated not knowing what was happening out on the stage, so she tuned the car's conventional radio to a French commentary and heard that four riders had gone ahead of the pack. Two were from Chiali: Tom Dash and Nicco Salvatore. The others were AFA's George Ferrer and Nat Arnold.

Jo shook her head in bewilderment. What was George thinking about? Was he thinking at all? Making his bid far too early in such a long stage, he had no chance of staying in front.

George Ferrer

George Ferrer sighed as a voice beside him said: 'This is bloody stupid.' Of course it was Arnold, complaining as usual: 'What's the idea, killing ourselves for bugger all?'

'We're in front,' said George, 'so we stay here. There's another sprint coming up.'

George kept his eyes fixed on the road ahead, trying to blot out the image of Paula's beautiful, angry face. With one hundred and eighty kilometres to go, he knew they couldn't hope to stay in the lead, but he had to try something...anything.

'You're crazy.' Arnold glanced over his shoulder and saw that his signal had been relayed to the team car. It drew level and Harvey Jones leaned out, his bald head shining, a water bottle in his hand. Arnold grabbed it. 'You going to tell this maniac to ease off?' he shouted.

'You're still two minutes ahead of the peloton.'

'Only two? This is a waste of bloody time and energy.'

Jones handed out another bottle. 'What's your problem?'

Arnold drank and took the second bottle. 'Ask Ferrer. He's the one with the problem.'

Jones eased the car forward and handed water to Ferrer who took one swig and shoved the bottle into his frame clip. Jones became agitated. 'You have to drink.'

Ferrer said nothing and pedalled on doggedly.

Salvatore, the muscle man of the Chiali team, rode up alongside Arnold who shook a drop of sweat from his long nose and started again for his new audience: 'What the hell are we doing out here?'

Salvatore, permanently cheerful, replied in his rough-and-ready English. 'Me? Contenting my sponsors. Small group, lots-a time on TV, lots-a publicity for Chiali logo. Next day your wife shop, she buy Chiali wine. Why? She see me plenty. She like me!' He flashed a white-toothed grin and blew a kiss at the motocamera filming this leading group. 'And I get a bonus,' he added.

'You *what*? Shit! I wish I rode for Chiali. AFA doesn't do bonuses,' said Arnold. 'And anyway, I haven't got a wife.'

George Ferrer ignored them. He was going for the next sprint. Salvatore and Dash had got the first one, forcing him into third place, worth only two points. Points were time and points were money. The team got its share, but every second was a second, every euro a euro.

Paula, tossing her hair and throwing accusations into his face: *My earnings are higher than yours.* But what a hell of a shock when she said she was pregnant! Too late for an abortion, she'd said, and she wanted a divorce. Talked about another marriage. Was it Vallon's child, as she claimed? Not his own, that was certain.

Arnold passed him to take over the relay at the front. 'Two kilometres to the sprint.'

'Lead out and peel off at a hundred metres. Right? This one's mine.' He hoped.

Sweat ran into his eyes, the salty sting blurring his vision. The soaked padding of his obligatory helmet squeezed like an iron band. On the plus side, the zoom lenses no longer took lingering close-ups of his balding head. He rubbed the back of a hand over the rasping black stubble on his jaw. Going bald and having to shave twice a day—the cameras loved it!

Not far to the sprint line. Better drink some water. Hell, it was lukewarm already. He poured the rest of it over the back of his neck and for a moment his mind cleared. This was damned stupidity. He thought of what Jo Bonnard had written about him only a year ago.

> ...*Ferrer the wily fox, biding his time, using all his experience to wait for the moment to pounce and be across the sprint-line before the huntsmen have even thought of a tally-ho...*

Look at Arnold with his tongue hanging out, giving an impression of maximum effort that fooled nobody. So why was he, the wily fox George Ferrer, out here with only that moaner for support? Trying to prove something to Paula?

Divorce. No hope of getting back together. But if she thought she'd get half of his money she was in for a shock. The two sports cars and the powerboat—all written off. As for the house on the lakeside, they'd hardly ever lived in it and last year's floods had turned it into a disaster area. He'd never bothered with insurance...

She'd thrown herself at him four years ago when she'd been the stunning podium girl who handed him the flowers day after day. Up, down and across Italy, he'd been a winner of stage after stage. How many? He'd lost count. Just kept winning more flowers and kisses from that beautiful girl.

'I kiss better than this when nobody's watching,' she'd giggled in his ear between camera-conscious smiles.

And the day he'd won the first sports car, she'd been sitting in the passenger seat, laughing and saying something about driving off into the sunset. And he, high on victory and besotted by her beauty, had done just about that.

Fool! It hadn't occurred to him that she'd calculated the media exposure she'd get as a kissy-kissy girl, regardless of who she kissed. But he'd fallen for her and he'd been single...a nice bonus for the wannabe model.

She'd just used him; used his name to claw her way up her career ladder. Oh, how proud she'd seemed—Paula Ferrer, wife of champion cyclist George Ferrer. Now she called herself Paula di Luca. Top model. She didn't need him now, but if she wanted money she'd better save it from her famous earnings.

The sign flashed past marking the start of the sprint. Damn Paula! She was wrecking his concentration. And Arnold was behind him. What was the lazy sod doing there?

Salvatore and Dash were on his back wheel at the 500-metre post.

400 metres. Shouting crowds lining the street; a blur of faces, open mouths yelling.

300, and Dash's front wheel drawing level...200...100...The line flashed under his wheel. Had he done it, or had Dash been ten centimetres in front?

He didn't know and suddenly he didn't care. He sat up and freewheeled as Arnold came up complaining that Dash had blocked him.

As the hunting pack thundered up and surrounded the group, Ferrer tucked himself behind Jacky Bernard's wheels. He'd save his strength for tomorrow—a mountain stage with two long, steady climbs of the type that suited him. He'd catch up some of the time he'd lost to that rotten bastard Vallon. For a moment he had a beautiful vision of winning tomorrow's stage, and then reality kicked in. *Beat Nardini? Dream on, George.* But going over three climbs, he'd beat Vallon, for sure.

Jo Bonnard

Jo combed her fingers through her hair, lifting it briefly clear of her sweltering head. The sun struck through the window, roasting her arm. The air-conditioner was stuttering because the car was at a standstill again. She reached for a map to use as a fan and caught sight of her overheated reflection in the rear-view mirror—wide green eyes, wide mouth and short, straight nose. Not bad...apart from the sweat-damp hair. She pulled a face. *The things I suffer for my passion!*

∾

Her passion for cycling dated from a school holiday with a group of friends. Riding their bikes through the byways of France, they'd been halted at a junction to let The Tour go by.

Suddenly, here came the cyclists! A blur of brightly coloured jerseys, bent backs, shouts, humming wheels and a buffeting wave of air that seemed to suck her up in their wake, leaving her stunned and feeling—as she wrote later—"like St Paul on the road to Damascus." From that moment she was hooked.

What kind of wonderful bikes were those? Who were those supermen that had rocketed past her? Could they really pedal for hours at such colossal speed? She bought *L'Equipe* and every cycling magazine she could find, devoured information, and planned her next holiday around three stages of The Tour. She'd written about her experience and sent the piece to one of the magazines. Because cycling was a man's sport, she reckoned no one would look at an article written by a girl, so she signed it, not Josephine, but Jo Bonnard.

It had been accepted, and Jo had scrapped her plan to teach languages, opting instead for an intensive course in journalism.

~

She was jolted back to the present by her mobile phone. The caller was Tony, her producer. He was in the Luxembourg centre, but knew she wasn't in the commentary box, and he demanded to know why. She explained why, and assured him she'd get there in time. She was only six kilometres away.

Tony was responsible for selecting the images for the TV screens, and for controlling the timing and advert breaks. 'Thirty-five minutes, a commercial, then you're on air,' he warned. 'Are you getting Race Radio?'

'I can hear it, but not clearly. Reception's bad today. Plenty of crackle.'

'Atmospherics, probably. The forecast says there are thunderstorms building over the Pyrenees.'

So that's why it was so stiflingly hot. Damn thunderstorms! If the helicopters couldn't go up, the pictures would be terrible. Helicopters received the images, sent by a microwave link, from Motocameras—photographers riding pillion on motorcycles. Those helicopters also had onboard cameras that provided spectacular overhead shots of the riders streaming across the countryside. The choppers provided a relay link to a fixed-wing aircraft circling high above. The plane sent the pictures up to a satellite that bounced them back to the vast dishes in Luxembourg. From there, Tony transmitted the best images to his commentators, and to viewers in Europe and beyond.

This year her commentary was being re-broadcast by a TV channel in the USA where first LeMond, and then Armstrong and Rothman had created an ever-growing audience. But without the helicopter relay, picture quality was unreliable, to say the least.

Through the static, Race Radio announced that Bob Rothman had been 'distanced,' which meant that he was trailing off the back of the race. Then the tinny voice listed the twenty riders in the leading group. They included Rothman's young protégé Marc Martens.

Marc, a big fair-haired Belgian, had corrected her two years ago, saying that his name was pronounced Mar-*tenz*. He was an all-terrain rider and incredibly strong, but headstrong as well. At one time, his impulsive chasing after futile breakaways had made his performances erratic. Now under the tutelage of the experienced Rothman, Marc was riding with more tactical intelligence. In early season races he'd had a respectable number of stage victories. Jo liked him. His podium and interview style gave the impression that this was his job and he couldn't understand what all the fuss was about.

Not so good was the news about Bob Rothman. Were the heat and distance too much for the American veteran? Or was he just going through a bad patch?

Bob Rothman

Bob Rothman felt like he was riding through syrup. He'd gone through a bad half-hour. Sweat pooled above his collarbones and spilled down his chest. However many litres of water he'd taken in, they weren't combating the loss of body fluid. The burn of oxygen-starved muscles was familiar, but this accelerated heartbeat and the sensation that his legs were made of Jell-O was a new experience. He couldn't keep up! Rider after rider passed him, like he was riding on rollers, getting nowhere.

In his car-to-riders earphone he'd heard Willem de Groot, his *directeur,* telling Max to drop back and give The Old Man a slip-stream. Rothman smiled when they called him The Old Man, and today he guessed they had reason.

Thirty-four years old. Should have quit last year but he'd reckoned he was still pretty fit. But this was too much. Never again.

Armstrong had cast a giant shadow, but only two years ago Rothman had topped the rankings. Two years ago he'd been The Chief, showing the way to the new kid Martens. Now Martens was the phenomenal Whiz Kid, and The Chief had become The Old Man. A helluva team for nicknames, this. The team's sponsor was Mr Chip—a Belgian company that made potato chips—so they referred to themselves as the Belgian Fries. Not French Fries, but Belgian...get it? Big joke, huh?

Shit! Was he dreaming or what? He hadn't seen the team car come alongside until de Groot shouted and handed him more water from the cool box, along with a carton of Frutactiv, a drink so sweet it made you thirsty. But it was loaded with glucose so he swallowed it down with the water as a chaser. Now he'd have to hang on in there, and wait for his strength to return.

Whiz Kid Martens! The boy rode like a sweetly tuned engine, powering along, never tiring—a mean machine with no fear and no feelings, but inexperienced and impulsive. What was the kid doing now? Planning to dive off the front and half kill himself before tomorrow's mountain stage? Well, right now somebody else could nurse him. Today Bob Rothman was too tired. But if his legs held out he'd make it to the finishing line, hopefully not too many minutes behind the leaders. Nobody was making a serious attack off the front...yet.

Marc Martens

Willem de Groot had retired from riding three years ago and was now *directeur sportif* of the Mr Chip team. After breakfast this morning, his riders had swung their chairs side-on the table where he'd spread out the big map and explained today's tactics. 'It's an undulating route, starting with a Category 4 hill climb. Two intermediate sprints early on. The final six kilometres are a four-percent uphill drag.' He looked at the sprint specialists: Seamus Patrick, the quiet Irish boy, and Jan Claes, 'the Flanders Flyer' with thighs like tree trunks. 'How do you feel, lads?'

'I'm fit, but I want protection from Dash the Crash,' Jan said, referring to Tom Dash, Chiali's aptly named star sprinter.

Dash the Crash had earned his nickname as, time and again, his tactics of cutting in, weaving and elbowing had brought down other riders. He was the most disliked rider in the pro peloton.

Marc Martens propped his heels on the back of Jan's chair and said, 'It's psychological.'

Jan Claes swivelled his shaved head. 'What's that supposed to mean?'

'He knows you're scared of him. You're so busy watching him, you lose your own line.'

Jan dislodged Marc's feet with a shove. 'How often have *you* tried to dodge his elbows?'

'Me? I'm just your lead-out, giving you a slipstream. But when I peel off, I can still see you looking at Dash all the time, scared shit-less, trying to keep out of his way.'

'That's enough,' de Groot cut in. 'We're not here to throw out insults.'

Marc looked aggrieved. 'I'm only talking facts. Everybody's chicken-scared of Dash, so they all keep looking at him. That's why they get in each other's way and go down like skittles.'

'Dash is dangerously aggressive, and you know it,' de Groot gave Marc a hard stare. 'For the prize money, Dash would knock down his own grandmother.' Dash had been disqualified a few times on the slow-motion replays. Other times he'd been lucky when the judges gave him the benefit of the doubt.

Willem tapped a finger on the map. 'Now, team, here are the tactics for the final sprint: Jan goes for it, with Seamus and Marc as his lead-out men. The rest of you, line up and try to keep the other teams off the front of the peloton.'

Marc Martens sat up straighter and asked, 'What if there's a break-away group?'

'Depends who's in it. I reckon the high-placed riders will sit tight today. Some ambitious types might try it, but you can let them go.'

Marc, as usual, argued the point. 'If there's an early break, some-one should chase it. I'll do that.'

Bob Rothman looked at him across the table, tolerantly amused. 'Hey, Whiz Kid, we're into the mountains tomorrow. Why burn yourself up today for no good reason?'

'No good reason? I'm lying fourth overall!' Marc's fair skin flushed with anger. 'Going off the front and winning points for a high place on the stage...seems reasonable to me.'

Rothman smiled. 'Oh, sure, very reasonable. All you have to do is ride away from the rest of us. Go ahead and stay ahead, all day and every day, so you win every stage. Simple as that.' He spread his arms in the exaggerated shrug of a stage comedian. 'Why ain't nobody never thought of that before?'

Everybody laughed except Marc who muttered, 'Well, why not?' He hated being got at.

Rothman shook his head sadly. 'Because it can't be done. Not even by you, Whiz Kid.'

Marc continued to look stubborn, and de Groot intervened before a pointless argument developed. 'The Tour is not won by an occasional stage victory. The secret is to stay amongst the front-runners every day, so you never miss out if the peloton splits. Stay near the front, okay? When you get to the last few kilometres you can make your own decisions.' He checked the time. 'Right, team, let's go'

Jo Bonnard

A policeman spotted the official sticker on Jo's car and tried to direct her through clogged traffic. With twenty minutes to her deadline, Jo pushed back her hair that was now dripping sweat onto her forehead. Ah well, she'd never thought this would be a stress-free career.

She thought back to the time she'd applied to follow The Tour as an accredited journalist. It had taken nerve because, until very recently, no women had been allowed anywhere near The Tour. She'd met with a sports editor who'd been astonished to discover that Jo Bonnard was a girl. Years ahead of his time, he gave her a chance regardless of her sex. Very few people had shared his views on sex-equality. She'd been an object of hilarity, but she'd known it was a man's world and there was no point in becoming bitter at the condescending laughter. Open hostility and obstruction were something else, and she'd once thought of giving up. But she wasn't a giver-up, so she became determinedly self-sufficient in the all-male environment. It had not been easy, but her love of the sport kept her going.

In her second season came her lucky break—an interview with Paul Breton. Something had clicked between them. The interview had sparked into instant friendship, and then something more than friendship.

Paul, winner of almost every race on the calendar, had provided introductions that cracked the wall of prejudice. Her dispatches came alive, and her editor praised her and extended her contract. She had a lot to thank Paul for. She'd been eighteen, and those had been heady days.

~

Sprinting from the parking area, she reached the commentary box with one minute to spare. Her French colleague Dufaux had run the equipment checks for her. She muttered, 'Thanks. I owe you,' and clamped her headset over wet hair, watching her monitor screen as a commercial break ended. Race Radio crackled in one earphone. Tony, her producer, sometimes spoke in the other but, after three years in this job, Jo was used to it. She heard her countdown, did the intro, and began her commentary.

'We're looking at the pack of riders who have less than fifty kilometres to go before they reach the end of today's stage. They're in a tightly packed bunch, which means nobody's in a hurry. No wonder! It's fiercely hot. There's nothing wrong with your TV picture. That shimmer is caused by waves of super-heated air. The air temperature is thirty-seven degrees, over ninety if you think in Fahrenheit. The road temperature is higher and the asphalt's melting in places. Heavy going for the riders.'

The picture on Jo's monitor was the one the viewers saw. It had switched to the lead motocamera, called Moto 1, running ahead of the bunch, with the cameraman twisted round, facing backward to film the action.

'In green is Chiali's powerhouse, Nicco Salvatore. He looks like a body-builder with those muscles. Hi there, Nicco!' she laughed, as the big Italian grinned and waved at the camera. 'He's a happy character who always seems to be enjoying himself, laughing and joking no matter how tough the stage.

'Now the speed's going up and the riders are organising themselves into a line. Watch how the front-runners take turns to relay each other. At the speed these riders are travelling, the leader creates quite a slipstream that sucks the others along. That's not to say they can rest. It's just less hard work at the back.

'The red-and-white jerseys are the Intapost team, and this is one of their French riders, David Vauban, who's a good climber. He gives us a smile as the camera zooms in, as always, on David's famous ear-studs. They seem to be his trademark and he has a collection of them; various sizes in silver and gold. They are, in fact, St Christopher medallions. The Patron Saint of travellers, right? Well, the cyclists all do plenty of travelling. They're in races all over Europe, scarcely a day's break from February to October. It's a hard way to make a living.

'This is Chico Montes, who's Spanish,' she said as another Intapost rider appeared on screen. 'You don't think of Spaniards as being blond and blue-eyed, do you? But Chico's from Galicia in the north-west of Spain, where his colouring's not unusual.'

She'd have guessed Chico's origins as Scandinavian. She often wondered if somewhere way back in his gene pool there had been a shipwrecked Viking.

The next rider, however, was everyone's image of a Spaniard, with his black hair and deep, dark tan. 'This is another of Intapost's Spanish riders: Paco Ribero, the pint-sized former Mountain Bike Champion, whose fan club is reputedly the biggest in Spain. Judging by the stampede that greets his every appearance, he's a national hero to girls, boys, men and women of all ages. He has a cheeky, pixie grin, like a little leprechaun...or whatever's the Spanish equivalent.'

What inane waffle she was talking! Jo shut up and watched as Paco Ribero rode up beside Chico, and the two proceeded to carry on a laughing conversation. In this heat, how could they maintain that speed and still find breath to chat?

She knew why the team was making a huge effort. Intapost Parcel Delivery Service, the company that sponsored them, had announced a re-structuring of its advertising budget, leaving the team short of money and in need of another sponsor. Jo knew the manager well, and he'd told her that talks were ongoing with GSG, an insurance company, but he had asked her to keep quiet about what he called 'delicate negotiations.' She was aware that GSG's advertising manager would be easier to convince if the team's colours appeared regularly on TV screens, and front-runners got most TV time. Money made the riders' wheels go round; but mechanics, masseurs, drivers and medics were all part of the team, and their jobs were likewise at stake.

~

With less than twenty kilometres to go, Jo took advantage of an advert break to drink from her bottle of water. The viewers saw the ads, but her monitor continued to show the action. This was the longest stage of The Tour: two hundred and forty kilometres, with a strength-sapping finish the riders would hate on such a hot day. From here to the finish was an uphill drag. Not a mountain, just a long slog.

Tony had fed in the picture from Moto 4, seldom broadcast as it covered the tail end of the race. Intapost's second team car drove into the shot. The driver, steering one-handed, was handing out water to Danny Breton who shoved three of the *bidons*—rigid plastic bottles—into his back pocket, and two more down the back of his jersey. To take these to his team-mates up the line, he'd have to ride fast through the pack, weighed down by all those kilos of water. As Jo watched, he passed George Ferrer and handed a bottle to him. This act of kindness was against the rules and would usually have earned a sanction—a few lost minutes for both riders—but, in conditions of extreme heat, such rules were waived. Still, not every rider would hand out water to someone from another team; but that was typical of Danny. He was a sportsman in both senses of the word.

The camera focussed on another car, and this time it was the Mr Chip *directeur* Willem de Groot having a word with Bob Rothman. According to Race Radio, Bob had been 'distanced,' but it seemed that he'd now caught up with the tail of the pack.

The countdown interrupted Jo's thoughts and she recommenced her commentary of a Moto 2 shot.

'Intapost has several talented climbers and we're looking again at Paco Ribero, the best of them. A few days ago Ribero, the ex-champion mountain biker, was first over the Alpe d'Huez, thirteen seconds ahead of Dino Nardini. It'll be interesting to see how their duel goes tomorrow when we have two First Category climbs and a *Hors Catégorie,* which means it's atrociously long and steep.

'For viewers who may be new to this sport, let me explain that climbs are categorised by numbers. Categories Four and Three are supposed to be the easier ones. Unless you train regularly on your bike, you might zigzag up them, *very* slowly. Category Two, you'd probably get off and push. A Category One climb is steeper and longer, often twenty kilometres or more, and therefore very tough. But *Hors Catégorie* means Beyond Category and also beyond description. Watch tomorrow and you'll see for yourselves.'

A picture switch to a helicopter shot.

'You can see patches of the same colours forming as team members get together. The red-and-white of Intapost stands out well. It's a very international team whose ranks include the Swedish former champion, Nilsson, Mike Gregory who's American, David Vauban and Danny Breton are French, and there's the Spanish contingent we saw earlier. If you wonder how they communicate, it's mostly in French. They have a French *directeur sportif*—Guy Lacrosse who rode in The Tour when I was a cub reporter...Seems like only yesterday...

'Actually, most riders speak several languages because they don't always stay with the same team, and nowadays there's usually a mixture of nationalities within any team. But French is the main language of cycling, with words like *peloton,* meaning squad, now used by everybody for the main pack of riders. There's also *domestique,* a rank-and-file team member whose job is to assist his leader or leaders. They fetch water bottles, called *bidons,* from the team cars at the back, and take them to their team-mates up the line. If there's a head wind, the *domestiques* will ride in a *chevron,* like geese in flight, to conserve the strength of their star rider by giving him a respite in their slipstream. A *domestique* has a hard life and almost never gets any glory.'

The monitor flicked again to a shot from Moto 2 running alongside the peloton. Set faces, no smiles and a lot of sweat.

'I don't know about you, but just watching them is making me suffer. The sun is like a branding iron on their backs. Waves of heat are coming off the road. They've already been riding for over five hours with no breaks, no half time, and no rest. They eat and drink as they go along, and they keep this up for three weeks. So far, today's average speed is only about forty kilometres an hour. Yes, I did say *only*. That's below average, in fact. Imagine doing that for five hours in sweltering heat! If you want to know how it feels out there, you could try riding your exercise bike in the sauna.'

The camera swung to a close-up of Harry Vallon. Jo stopped talking and peered at her monitor screen. Vallon appeared to have a gash under his eye.

In her earphone, Tony's voice said: 'Short commercial, seventy-five seconds, starting in six, five...'

Jo slid open the glass partition separating her from Dufaux. She scribbled a note and passed it to him: *Did Vallon crash? A cut under his left eye?*

Dufaux shrugged and passed the note to Hans, the German commentator. He also shrugged and passed it along the row to Biagi, the Italian member of Eltsport's commentary team. Eventually the paper came back to Jo. Scribbled in three languages were: *Not that I heard, No idea,* and: *Ask him yourself.*

Maybe she would do that later, given the chance. Jo folded the paper and tucked it in her shirt pocket.

The stage hadn't far to go now. Leon Jonkers, the race leader in the famed Yellow Jersey, was isolated; no team mates around him. There was a trio of Chiali riders at the front, but right beside them were three red-yellow-black jerseys of the Mr Chip team—Seamus Patrick, shaven-headed Jan Claes and Marc Martens. The trio were discussing something. Jo wondered if they were poised for a sudden move.

Marc Martens

Marc wove his way to the front of the pack, just like Bob Rothman had taught him. Calmly, unobtrusively, passing one rider at a time and spreading no shockwaves, he tucked himself behind the first ten riders. A glance confirmed that Claes and Patrick had followed him. Jonkers in the Yellow Jersey was just ahead, and Marc was less than a minute down on Jonkers's overall time. Should he put on a spurt now? Old Man Rothman had warned him not to waste energy on useless breakaways. On the other hand, at this morning's tactical briefing, de Groot had said they could make their own decisions in the last few kilometres. How many made 'a few'?

Marc knew very well that patience was not his best attribute, but he had learned to appreciate Bob's advice, so he'd wait a bit. The Old Man was a great tactician, no doubt about it, and he was back there, keeping en eye on him.

Marc knew that another man was watching him—Dirk, his friend who'd sent the text message to his mobile phone this morning: *Working early shift so as to watch you on TV. Today's stage is made for you.*

∼

Dirk, now Police Captain Dirk Leyden, was the man who'd got him into cycling nine years ago when Marc was a tearaway kid heading for trouble—like being stupid enough to filch a packet of cigarettes in full view of the shopkeeper. He'd thought it was a kick when the man came running after him, panting 'Stop! Stop, you little thief! I saw you!'

A few passers-by had made half-hearted grabs, but Marc had spotted an old bicycle propped outside the bakery. He snatched it, flung a leg over the saddle and took off, scattering the pedestrians, while a woman in an apron shot out of the shop screeching 'Hey, you! That's my bike! Come back, you!'

Marc dodged amongst the evening traffic, closing his ears to the car horns and angry shouts. Then he'd looked back to see he was being chased by a cyclist on a racing bike. Oh boy!

Marc shot between a van and a car, and sped round a corner. Another glance over his shoulder. The racing guy was still chasing, but already Marc was halfway up the steep hill of St Nicolas that came near the end of the Liège-Bastogne-Liège race. He'd watched it a couple of times, but he'd no idea the climb was so hellish steep. He began to feel the effort. The woman's bike was a heavy old boneshaker, three gears only. He sat back in the saddle, powering the big gear, making like he was Miguel Indurain. Again he glanced back and saw he was getting away from the guy in the racing kit. This was great!

Near the top of the hill several roads branched off. Marc took the road home and next time he looked round, the racing guy was nowhere in sight. *Yeehah!* It was the best fun he'd had for ages.

Short-lived, though. His father had gone ballistic and had made him return the bike immediately to its owner. But the shopkeeper had reported him, and Marc had finished up in juvenile court. Not funny. But the returning of the bike had softened the heart of the lady judge who issued only a stern warning.

He'd emerged from the court with his parents and the appointed lawyer who led them over to a stranger, saying, 'This is a friend of mine—Dirk Leyden. He's interested in young Marc.'

Marc's mother drew him back protectively and asked the man if he was a reporter.

'No,' he replied. 'I'm a cyclist, in fact.'

Marc's father said, 'You mean, like Eddy Merckx?'

'In my dreams!' Dirk laughed. 'But, yes, I'm that kind of cyclist, in a very inferior way.' He turned and asked, 'Where did you learn to ride a bike, Marc?'

'What's it to you?' Marc Martens, tough guy, talked the tough talk.

Dirk answered that at face value. 'To me, it's a matter of great interest. I'm the guy who chased you up the hill last week. You saw me, didn't you?'

Marc's lip curled. 'Was that you on the race bike, with all the gear, the crash helmet and all?'

'The very same.' Before Marc could crow, Dirk handed out the compliment. 'And you, with no gear and a beat-up old bike, left me standing.'

Robbed of his next line, Marc had been confused, and Dirk addressed his parents. 'This boy's got great legs. He's a natural bike rider and he's strong. The team I belong to has a youth programme. We train and encourage young riders, and enter them for junior races. The talented ones go on to senior events. A few get good enough to turn pro. Maybe one of them will be the new

Eddy Merckx....Maybe not, but they all get a lot of fun out of it. Interested, Marc?'

Finally Marc nodded and said, with a standard show of indifference, 'Yeah. Maybe. Why not?'

∽

...And now, nine years later, Dirk Leyden would be watching on TV as that same Marc Martens was riding steadily towards the front of the Tour de France peloton. *Thanks, Dirk. You're the best.*

Marc saw the banner marking five kilometres to the finish. Was he going for the stage victory? He lacked the explosive power to be a true sprinter. His strong point was endurance but...you never know. He looked across at Jan Claes. 'What about it, eh?'

'Too soon.' Jan said. 'Better wait for the 2k marker.'

'Why? Can't keep up a fast pace for five?'

Claes ignored the taunt. 'Bloody right I can't. Look at who's behind us.'

Marc looked. Three Chiali riders—the big guy Salvatore, Bruno, and of course Tom Dash. An idea formed. 'If I go off on my own, Salvatore will come after me. He can never resist it. That'll leave Dash short of a lead-out man.'

Jan Claes considered for a moment and then nodded. 'Okay.'

Marc turned to Seamus. 'You stay with Jan, eh?'

A nod, then, 'Right. Off you go.' From Seamus Patrick, it was a long speech.

Marc laughed. 'Right. I'm off.'

Jo Bonnard

Jo thumped a fist into her palm as she watched Marc explode off the front of the race. Streaking like a soul escaping from hell, Marc was seventy metres up the road before Salvatore flicked his gear and set off after him. Bruno put on a burst of speed and then dropped back, evidently obeying team orders to stay with Dash. By the time the other riders woke up to what had happened, Marc was almost out of sight.

The motocamera speeded up to film this sudden move. A close-up of Marc filled the screen. His face was expressionless, his body immobile. He almost never stood on the pedals. Like his idol, the great Miguel Indurain, he sat low on the saddle and his phenomenal legs powered him along.

The camera swung round on the now distant figure of Salvatore who was standing on the pedals. As the 2k marker flashed by, four other riders detached themselves from the front of the peloton—Bruno, with Tom Dash right behind him, and Seamus Patrick leading out the stocky figure of Jan Claes.

Then the static camera on the finishing line gave a head-on, full-zoom view down the straight road to where Marc had reached the red pennant that signalled the final 1000 metres.

By the 500-metre board, Salvatore had been caught and swallowed by the following mass of coloured jerseys and helmets. At 200 metres, Bruno and Patrick peeled off. Suddenly there were only three riders—Marc, with Claes tucked behind him, and Dash, racing for the line.

Jo's voice rose in excitement. 'Dash is going flat out, closing up on Claes and...Oh, no! Dash is riding on a diagonal line, forcing Claes almost into the crowd-barrier. That was a nasty move. Now Dash cuts across again! Martens just avoids a collision but he loses vital metres...And Dash crosses the line, hands clasped above his head in victory. Claes was a wheel's length behind him, Martens third.'

The scene was replayed in slow motion. 'That was really not on!' Jo said. 'Surely there will be an objection to the way Dash rode. With only three men contesting the sprint on a wide road, I can't see the judges allowing those tactics.'

She watched the next shots of the peloton rolling in, and then a photographer got in amongst the vans and officials and pointed his camera at Marc who stood with one foot on the ground and a hand on Claes' shoulder as he talked to him.

A microphone appeared in the shot and someone asked an inaudible question.

Marc replied, 'I'd heard that Dash was a dangerous rider.'

'And now?' a voice prompted.

'Now I've apologised to Claes.' With no further explanation, Marc wheeled slowly away.

The interviewer appealed to Claes who said, 'No comment,' and followed Marc.

The hand-held camera swung on Dash. He'd removed his crash helmet and stood, red hair in sweaty spikes, arms akimbo, grinning up at the giant screen where the provisional results had just flashed up. Then the screen went blank. When it lit up again, DQ, *Disqualified* had been inserted after Dash's name.

Jo was fairly exultant. 'I should think so! That was blatantly dangerous riding.'

The grin vanished from Dash's face. The microphone was thrust towards him. He spat and uttered a dozen words before he turned on his heel and barged through the clustered reporters.

'Tom Dash has only himself to blame,' said Jo, 'but seemingly he isn't prepared to admit it. However, the stage goes to Claes and—by a margin of *four seconds!*—Marc Martens has the Yellow Jersey! Everything will change tomorrow, of course. The sprinters' days of glory will end in the Pyrenees, but Martens is now in the lead and he has a slender chance of hanging on to that jersey. It will depend on how well he climbs.'

Marc Martens

Later, in the team bus, Marc found a new text message on his phone. Dirk again: *That's my boy! Bravo, Marc!*

STAGE 14

Evening

Jo Bonnard

The forecast thunderstorm had materialised. Not long after the stage ended, huge clouds swelled and merged, blotting out the sun. Their bloated undersides darkened from grey to dirty purple where lightning flickered. Rumbles of thunder echoed amongst the mountains. Then the rain came; at first in huge drops that exploded, cratering the dust and evaporating instantly on the baked ground. Then their drumming became a roar and water engulfed the valley.

Jo was scheduled to spend the night in a hotel in Les Chalets, a two-hour drive in normal conditions. She was supposed to share one of the Eltsport cars with her outsized Italian colleague Biagi, but he had opted to travel with Dufaux and Hans. Jo had shrugged off another piece of male chauvinism. If they chose to cram three men and their luggage into one car, well that was fine by her. She liked her independence.

Right now, however, she'd have welcomed a co-driver. Deafened by the percussion of rain on the car roof, she guessed that the storm would be worse up in the mountains. Visibility was terrible.

This was the Trois Têtes climb—a steep road with tight bends that called for cautious driving. Luckily, the cars provided for Eltsport were automatic drive vehicles. The engine-note sounded like second gear, third at best. She threaded the wheel through her hands on a sharp left-hander and immediately had to spin it again as the road hairpinned to the right. Imagine riding a bike up this road!

She had driven over dozens of mountain passes, but tonight she felt the gradients in her body, as though she were straining her own muscles to pull the vehicle up and round the endless series of bends. She imagined herself on a bike, forcing her legs to push the pedals—climbing, labouring to reach the next bend, and the next, and the next. On the insides of the hairpins, it was like climbing a wall. The outsides were easier—but longer. More turns of the wheels, more turns of the pedals, more pain in the screaming leg muscles. Maybe better to climb the wall and shorten the agony.

How must it feel to ride such a climb, and two more, all in one day?

The road levelled off. Ahead she saw a hotel with a car park where some vehicles stood glittering in the rain. She pulled in and sprinted for the building, clutching her jacket over her head. The receptionist was on the phone, dealing with what sounded like a cancellation. Jo crossed her fingers.

Ten minutes later she was on the phone to Tony. 'Tomorrow's going to be grim. The cloud base is six hundred metres! We'll be lucky if the plane gets up through this. The choppers certainly won't. In fact, we'll be lucky if the stage isn't cancelled, or at least shortened.'

'Oh, come off it, Jo,' he scoffed. 'They don't cancel for rain.'

'This isn't just *rain*. There could be rock-falls, bridges washed out...It's frightening!'

'Stop panicking. It will probably have improved by morning.'

'It had better!' Jo clicked off her phone.

Now to call the small hotel in Les Chalets. Someone might bless their luck at getting the room she was about to cancel.

~

Next morning, Jo set off early to reach Les Chalets, the new little ski station where the day's stage would finish. It took her three hours, the last of them at crawling speed behind the three huge vehicles that were the mobile laboratory units. The signposting gang must have worked all night in the downpour, because the route markers were already in place.

38

Today's stage snaked up mountains, along valleys, and briefly crossed the Spanish border. Pictures always broke up in rainstorms, and Jo wanted to see the terrain she would have to describe from memory. But the scenery—'magnificent' according to the guidebooks—was invisible, and most of the time her fingers were tense on the wheel as she took one blind corner after another.

On the giddy, twisting descent from El Puño to La Portette, she was grateful for the mist that prevented her from seeing over the edge of the recently constructed road where only a steel crash-barrier marked the left-hand verge. On the right was a sheer wall of rock. The road was like a ledge hacked out of the mountainside. The surface was good, however, with newly painted white lines at the sides and a double line in the centre.

Just before La Portette she emerged from cloud. Below and to her left, a river raged over a tumble of boulders. Just as well not to have seen that from higher up.

And they're going to come down this drop on bikes!

To tackle a road like this in a storm, the elite cyclists had to be a breed apart.

STAGE 15

Dino Nardini

In the start village, Dino waited until everyone had left the catering marquee before asking for take-away coffee, de-caffeinated of course. The pretty waitress smiled and said, 'Anything, any time, Dino,' fluttering her eyelashes at him. Then her hungry eyes began to rove, licking his body. He could read her mind. *She'd love to run her fingers through his black wavy hair. What she'd give to rub the massage oil onto his smoothly muscled legs! And those tight Lycra shorts left nothing to the imagination, did they?* With an obvious effort she shifted her gaze and concentrated on pouring the coffee.

Horny girls. They were everywhere, screaming his name from the roadsides, standing at the starts and finishes, begging for autographs and photographs, eating him alive. But they bought the *I Love Dino* T-shirts—Fiarelli's masterstroke of marketing—and they were filmed and photographed wearing them. Dino's girl fans had become a part of the cycling scene. Girls were important to his media image, so he gave this one the XL version of his smile, picked up a ballpoint from the counter and autographed the inside of her arm. He'd read that one girl had had his autograph tattooed over. Great publicity.

He went out holding the Styrofoam beaker and turned the corner, out of the girl's sight. He stood under the awning, looking through a curtain of rain toward the crowd barriers where the fans huddled under umbrellas. Otherwise The Village looked deserted; no riders in sight. They had signed in and must now be sitting tight in their team vehicles. No pressmen, no cameras either. For once that was good news. He looked around again, but there was nobody near enough to see his sleight of hand with the coffee beaker. He then put it in the back pocket of his jersey, together with the Frutactiv carton that he checked again to make sure it wasn't leaking. Surely he'd get a chance.

He had to get rid of Ribero, that little bastard who'd taken the Alpe d'Huez victory; and also to get rid of Martens who was climbing too bloody strongly. Tough luck on them, but he had to be *sure* of beating them. He desperately needed the Best Climber prize money for Gina. Because of Gina, all the glitz had suddenly been stripped from his life, leaving him raw and angry. It was so unfair! Unfair to Gina, his better self knew, but his conflicting ego whispered *unfair to me*. He enjoyed his playboy lifestyle but he would have to give it up. He couldn't kid himself that nothing would change, because the playboy image was a media money-earner.

He must win the prize; must get that money. We must be ruthless, he'd said; and so, he and Fiarelli had come up with a great plan. But putting the plan into action had proved much more difficult than they'd thought.

At last a chance had come his way this morning at the meet-the-press breakfast buffet when he'd taken care of Martens. Now for Ribero. All he needed was a chance. He'd like to get rid of Harry Vallon as well—that bastard with his perfectly healthy...

A howl of feedback, quickly corrected, came from the public address system. Then the bell summoned the riders to the assembly area. Dino collected his bike from the mechanic and checked the gear cassette, chain and brakes. There were two bottles of water in the frame clips. He dumped the contents of one bottle onto the wet cobbles, reached under his rain cape for the Styrofoam beaker, and carefully refilled the bottle with the de-caff.

The second bell sounded and he got into the mass of rain-caped riders, but Ribero was on the far side of the mob. Fuck it! Dino never seemed to get near him. Never once in the whole fucking Tour had his and Ribero's teams been booked into the same hotel.

A bevy of suits climbed out of two large cars. The VIPs had arrived for the ribbon-cutting.

At Dino's shoulder, Harry Vallon's voice said, 'Hope to God they skip the speeches, a morning like this. I hate to get soaked.'

'Rainwater's good for your skin.'

'Huh! You don't know the amount of acid in a litre of rain.'

Dino smiled. Harry was freaky; but here was one of the chances he'd been hoping for. He reached down and took the bottle from its clip. 'Have some hot coffee.'

'You know I never touch coffee.'

'It's decaffeinated, stupid!'

'Oh. Right. Thanks.' Vallon drank the lot. 'Age of miracles—no speeches. Now we can get moving.'

Willem de Groot

They'd been on the road for ninety kilometres when a voice came scratchily over Race Radio: *Fifty-three, punctured.* That was Marc's number! Willem de Groot swore. 'Of all the bloody places...' His car was at the foot of the climb, on a narrow road with deep ditches on either side. The intervening vehicles would pull over as best they could, but he'd have to weave through a swarm of TV and stills-photo motorbikes to get up to Marc with a replacement wheel.

Glittering steel rods of rain slashed through the beams of the headlights. Ahead, the climb snaked up into clouds that were suddenly lit by a flicker of lightning. A crash of thunder followed almost immediately, and the rain pelted down with renewed force.

Willem called on the intercom set for Max, the nearest team member, to catch up and give Marc a lead back to the second chase group—after they'd changed the wheel, of course. Per, his chief mechanic, sat in the back of the car amid a welter of spares. He had readied two wheels, not knowing whether it was a rear or a front tyre that had gone.

Suddenly, Per exclaimed, 'There he is!'

Willem was shocked. He'd thought that Marc must be much farther up the climb. He knew that three riders had broken clear to go ahead of the pack, but Marc should at least be in the first group chasing them, not down here amongst the *domestiques!*

Marc's drooping figure, soaked to the bones, simply stood there shivering, holding his bike, apparently oblivious to the TV and press photographers who'd stopped to capture the drama.

Per jumped out and ran to him. The rear wheel, he saw at once. 'Why the hell didn't you get the wheel out, at least?' he roared, working the quick-release lever. Marc could have—should have—done that; saved vital seconds. Per fitted the new wheel and rapidly checked the alignment of brakes and gears. Marc remounted stiffly and Per ran with him, giving him the push necessary to engage the sprocket on the slope, before sprinting back to the car.

Marc Martens

Half blinded by the rain and overwhelmed by the cramping pain in his stomach, Marc became aware of Max's voice shouting something about catching up. In his earphone, another voice—Willem de Groot's—told him to latch on to Max's wheels. 'Yeah,' he said. 'I'm trying to.' But he was simply answering the voice, forgetting he must speak directly into his tiny microphone.

Max dropped back again and rode beside him, shouting, 'Come on, Marc! What's the hell's the matter with you?'

'Don't know. Go on.' It was an effort just to turn the pedals. Getting his mind and voice to work as well was too complicated. Beside him, Max fumbled under his rain cape and brought his microphone close to his mouth. He said something—Marc neither heard nor cared what—and then rode ahead. After a few moments Max looked back and gave a resigned sort of shrug.

Bob Rothman

Farther up the hill, Bob Rothman heard the exchange between Max and de Groot. He tucked his chin down to speak into his microphone. 'Hey, boss, what gives with the Whiz Kid? You want I should drop back for him?'

This was quick decision time. He was in the first chase group but his overall position was nothing to bust a gut for, whereas the Whiz Kid...What the hell was it with him? You puncture, you get a new wheel, and you catch up. So it wasn't just the puncture.

De Groot came in. 'Bob? Sort him out, if you can.'

Rothman slackened his pace and riders passed him, heads down, squinting through the rain. Then Max was alongside, shouting, 'Marc is like a zombie. Can't get going.'

'Get on the back of the chase group and stay there.'

Max would provide a wheel to follow, provided he, Rothman, could lead the kid back up to the chasers. A zombie? Why the hell? Some physical problem he'd omitted to mention? The knee injury from the Paris-Nice playing up again? More likely, as too often before, the dumb-head failed to eat. No matter how often he was told to take on more energy before starting a climb, Marc 'forgot,' or he needed both hands to control a downhill run, or some goddamn excuse.

Rothman cursed as a couple of team cars, the second *commissaire* vehicle and a motocamera swished past, showering him with spray. And here came Seamus Patrick—a sprinter, for godsake, a no-hoper on a climb—and Marc struggling to keep up with him.

As they came abreast of him, Bob took one look and yelled with incredulous fury: 'What the hell gear are you using? Change gear, dumb-head!'

Marc looked down at his gears, flicked the lever once, but didn't so much as glance at Bob. His face remained a mud-splattered mask of misery, his eyes slatted against the rain. Marc was moving like a malfunctioning robot that might do as ordered, but with no understanding behind his actions.

'And again!' Bob ordered. 'Jeez, are you sleeping or what?' And as Marc flicked the gears again, he snarled, 'Now get on my wheel and stay there!'

'I can't.' The kid's voice was barely audible. 'Too cold.'

Bob thought of the Garfield sticker he'd had for years: *Friendly persuasion is okay, but nastiness gets better results.* Nastily, he snarled again. 'So shift your ass and get warm!'

A sound like a whimper, and Marc made small, momentary effort.

Over his shoulder, Rothman continued snarling. 'You rode away from me yesterday, you young punk, and now look at you!'

Seamus was still with them. 'Sure, you could always get off and walk,' he remarked mildly in his gentle Irish accent. 'Provided you don't want to abandon, that is,' he added as an afterthought.

That got a reaction at last, Bob saw, even if it was only a grunt. Maybe the soft approach might work after all. He nodded to Seamus who addressed Marc again. 'Jaysus, come on! Sooner we get there, sooner we'll get dry.' And Marc made an effort to open his mouth wide, sucking in oxygen.

Jo Bonnard

Jo watched her monitor. Moto 2 had left the chase group and halted at the roadside until the Martens group finally came up. In the commentary boxes, voices were going out to France, to Italy, to Spain, to Germany…and many of the commentators were former riders who had been in Marc's situation. Jo reckoned she wasn't the only one to make a remark about the cruelty of the close-up shots of Marc Martens, but this was drama—the Yellow Jersey suffering like a dog just to stay in the race.

Marc Martens

Marc came to a halt, put one foot on the ground and leaned over the handlebars, his body wracked as he stood there, vomiting convulsively.

Seamus stopped with him. Wordlessly he handed a water bottle to Marc, who drank from it and immediately vomited again. Marc took another sip, rinsed his mouth and spat. He drank again, thirstily, and threw up. The third time he tried it, the water stayed down. He took several deep, shuddering breaths and then said, 'Christ almighty! That was bad.'

'You feel better now?'

Marc nodded. 'Thanks,' he said, just as the team car came back alongside with de Groot shouting questions. In reply, Marc said, 'God knows. Maybe something I ate'

It had started with a feeling like biting ants crawling all over his skin, then a burning sensation followed by intense cold and a cramping pain in his stomach, hurting when every breath stretched his diaphragm. He stood for a few seconds, breathing deeply, relieved to find the pain was fading. 'I feel okay now…Let's go.'

Per jumped out to give both riders a starting push on the gradi-

46

ent. Marc found the right gear and got going. He wasn't exactly okay but he did feel better. Whatever the hell it had been, he'd got rid of it. After a kilometre, he started riding strongly and had soon left Seamus behind.

George Ferrer

One hundred kilometres into the stage and farther up the climb, George Ferrer shivered convulsively. His clothes felt like a sodden poultice. Moisture clung to the stubble on his chin. Rain ran from his helmet and trickled under his collar until his jacket felt as wet inside as out. He was tempted to discard it, but he'd need it as a windbreak on the downhill run. He could do nothing about his legs. The embrocating oil shed some of the water but it was no protection from the cold. He had stopped thinking about his feet.

The gradient became steeper. He and the leading riders were now well above the tree line and exposed to the full force of the storm. Trois Têtes was a horrible winding climb made worse by the lashing rain that bounced off the road. The downhill run would be horrendous; the road like a sluice.

Behind him the peloton had stretched into a long line of riders following the wheels in front of them as they trailed up the climb. They all feared being 'distanced.' Loss of contact with the man ahead would make it twice as hard to keep going. It was psychological as much as physical. It destroyed your morale to see the others pull ahead. Every one of them was gritting his teeth to hang on.

Somewhere ahead of George was his team-mate Jacky Bernard, sent out in front to provide a leading wheel later on. With Bernard was Intapost's Danny Breton. Somewhere ahead of *them* were Nardini, Ribero and—for godsake!—Harry Vallon. The stupid bastard had gone off with the two best climbers, looking as though he belonged in their company. Let him go. Vallon was no climber. A month ago, George had taken a practice run over the next climb, a mountain pass called El Puño. It was a stinker. Vallon wouldn't last the pace.

George Ferrer shook water from his face. He could force no more power into his legs but he'd catch up, he hoped, on the downhill run.

Harry Vallon

So this, thought Harry Vallon, was the dreaded climb of Trois Têtes. What about it? It was no big deal.

He knew that *Trois Têtes* meant Three Heads. And so there were! His own, Dino's and Ribero's. Three heads at the head of the race up Three Heads. Hey! That was seriously funny! He laughed out loud.

Dino Nardini's wheel was in front of him, at eye level. That proved the hill was steep, the gradient about twelve percent, or one in eight, so Dino maybe wasn't all that far ahead. In front of Dino was the little Spanish guy Ribero. And Harry had been with them all the way since they'd taken off, halfway up the climb. Ribero had a shock coming. Same for Dino.

Two more climbs? So what? Today nothing could stop Harry Vallon from winning the stage. And the Yellow Jersey? He felt great, so why not?

De-caff wasn't supposed to give you a lift. Must have been the warmth of it that really hit the spot. He'd never in his life felt so strong, so power-filled.

Harry Vallon was flying.

Marc Martens

Six riders behind Ferrer, Marc had caught up with Bob Rothman and was following him up the narrow strip of road between spectators who crowded in from both sides, shouting and yelling. It was like riding through a tunnel of noise.

The awful pain in his stomach had subsided to a mild ache, and he'd continued to sip water. Max had handed him a *bidon* of tea with honey, and he'd begun to feel better by the minute. Now the pain had gone like it had never existed and the only problems were the bloody awful weather and the howling fans.

Head down, pedalling automatically, he still had to be alert for the attention-seekers in fancy dress, or an over-excited child leaping into his path. A teenager pranced dangerously close to him, waving to the motocamera and calling *Hello, Mum*.

Asshole!

At last Marc saw the white line across the summit, and Rothman shouted, 'Follow me. Take my line.' Marc didn't argue. On this wet road, he'd be glad to follow the experienced wheels. The Old Man was a good descender who knew how to judge the corners.

George Ferrer

In the valley, George had caught up with Bernard and Breton, but Vallon was somehow sticking with the two climbers, several minutes ahead.

Grinning cheerfully, Danny Breton said, 'Anybody feel like trying to catch those three in front?'

Jacky Bernard threw a questioning look at his captain and reminded him: 'We pick up food and drinks in the next village.'

'Oh, yes, so we do,' said Ferrer. 'Well, let's replace some energy. Don't try anything daft, boys.'

Danny took it in his usual carefree style. 'Okay. Only joking.'

George Ferrer shook his head. Danny made him feel old. Okay, so Danny *was* just a boy, still had freckles across his nose, but he acted like it was some kind of game they were playing. And yet he was a damn good rider, for a youngster. The youngest in The Tour, in fact, and some day he might turn out great. Of course he was Paul Breton's son, so it figured. Not that Danny ever took advantage of being the son of a cycling legend. In fact, the boy often seemed embarrassed or made jokes when people mentioned his famous father. Not a bad lad at all. But so young.

Jo Bonnard

As the leading trio approached the provisioning zone outside the village of Font Val, Jo explained what was happening. 'Those people standing along the roadside are *soigneurs*. They are the masseurs, medics and other staff, wearing their teams' colours so the riders can pick them out instantly. The *soigneurs* hold out those bright orange bags, which they've filled with the little snacks and drinks that are the cyclists' lunch. It's Meals on Wheels with a difference. Watch this. It takes practice and skill.'

In one fluid movement and without slackening his speed, Dino Nardini snatched a bag and slipped its long drawstring cord over his head. He opened the bag and took out a couple of items. He tucked one into the front of his rain jacket. The other item was an energy bar that he held up to the camera with an exaggerated show of delight.

'Ah, he likes that,' Jo remarked, not voicing her thought that Dino was forever acting and showing off for the benefit of the cameras.

Now Dino reached under his jacket and took a yellow carton from the back pocket of his jersey. He looked at the label and pulled a disgusted face.

'But he doesn't like that.' Jo realised he must have had it with him since the start. How daft to carry a drink he disliked.

Dino offered the carton to Ribero who was riding alongside him. Ribero said something and shook his head.

Amused, Jo asked her viewers, 'Are you enjoying the mime show? Ribero doesn't like it either.'

Nardini then rode closer to Harry Vallon, asked him a question and held out the carton. Vallon scrabbled in his bag and brought out a pink carton. Nardini reached for it and thrust the yellow one into Vallon's hand. He watched Vallon drink it down, and then he opened the pink carton, tipped his head back, swallowed the contents at a gulp and smiled at the camera.

Both riders then shoved the cartons into the empty bags and tossed the bags towards the verge, where some boys pounced on them. A teenager and a little one in a vivid red cagoule both grabbed for Vallon's bag. There was a tugging match, won by the smaller boy who shoved the bag under his waterproof and ran off to stand beside a group of adults further along the road.

Jo laughed aloud this time. 'Well done, the little red boy! He's making sure he keeps that bag. Kids always wait just beyond the food zones, hoping to collect souvenirs of their heroes. In weather like this, I'd call that truly dedicated devotion.'

The three leaders had left the food zone and the picture switched to a new one from Moto 2. It was a fuzzy picture, overlaid with a diagram showing the time gaps between the two groups of riders and the peloton.

Jo explained it. 'This shows that the leading threesome, Nardini, Ribero and Vallon, are four minutes ahead of the chase group composed of Ferrer, Bernard and Breton; and those three are six minutes ahead of the main pack. Sorry, but the picture's breaking up here in the valley,' she added. 'And when they climb El Puño, I'm afraid they'll be in dense mist.'

Tony, the producer, must have been listening and spoke in her earphone. 'Pictures are lousy. Switching to computerised graphics map. Five seconds...four...'

Jo found herself marvelling at a virtual aerial view of the mountain range with the road picked out in yellow. A flashing arrow showed the position of the peloton, travelling up a valley towards the French-Spanish border. In a few kilometres they would cross into Spain before swinging northward again to start the climb of the mountain pass called El Puño—that brutal twenty kilometres of new road she'd driven over. El Puño ran in a zigzag, like a bootlace criss-crossing the face of the mountain.

A dotted red line marked the frontier, right at the top of El Puño. From there the road zigzagged back down to the French town of La Portette where it crossed a river and continued up the last short, steep climb to Les Chalets.

Jo was glad she'd driven the route and could describe it—at least, the sections she'd been able to see through the mist.

The Moto 2 picture came back, flickering badly. 'Just look at that rain!' she exclaimed. 'It's hammering on the backs of this chase group. The two AFA riders are Ferrer and Bernard, with Intapost's Danny Breton. He's the son of the great Paul Breton who won just about everything except the Tour de France. Paul should have won it, because he was wearing the Yellow Jersey when he crashed, just one stage short of Paris. His injuries meant he could never ride again, but his son Danny seems to be having one of his days of greatness.'

She stopped short of saying 'I wish him luck.' Commentators should not be biased, but she'd known Danny since he was a toddler. On her visits to Paul's family, she'd watched Danny grow up. If she had ever had a son, she thought, she would have hoped for a boy like Danny with his smiling brown eyes and generous nature.

Danny was almost twenty-two. Therefore it must be twenty-four years—that long ago!—since she'd planned to spend that weekend in Paris with Paul. What if Paul hadn't crashed? What if he hadn't spent so long in hospital and met a very pretty nurse? What if...

Jo told herself not to be a sentimental ass. There'd been nothing serious in her relationship with Paul, had there? Anyway, Paul had married Nurse Leontine, a warm-hearted, lovely girl who, until her death four years ago, had remained Jo's friend. And Paul was still a friend, although she hadn't seen him for ages—four years, in fact. They just kept in touch by occasional e-mails or phone calls...

Jo's nostalgic moment was ended by Tony's voice saying, 'We've lost all pictures. Switching to the virtual map.' She'd known it was going to be one of those days. She explained the problem to the viewers, listened to the news from her Race Radio earphone, and relayed it as best she could.

'The three leading climbers have started the climb of El Puño. One of them is the current King of the Mountains, Dino Nardini of Chiali. The second is Paco Ribero of Intapost, first to reach the top of the Alpe D'Huez this year, and only five points behind Nardini. The third man is Harry Vallon of AFA, who's a possible contender for the Yellow Jersey, but not usually so good on climbs. He's putting in a remarkable performance today. The chase group of Ferrer, Bernard and Breton is still four minutes back from them, and the peloton's at six—correction, five and a half minutes. The leaders of the peloton must be catching up.'

At last came a picture from Moto 3 at the front of the peloton where the bikes were throwing out jets of spray. The surface of the road resembled a river.

'We can see how the peloton has split into several groups. The first group of six men includes the Yellow Jersey Marc Martens and his team captain, the American Bob Rothman. Marc was in terrible trouble earlier in the stage, violently sick, but he seems to be fully recovered now. He and Rothman are noted for their endurance, so I wouldn't be surprised if they make up more time before the El Puño climb. Fifty metres back is another group including, I think, Leon Jonkers whose overall time this morning was only four seconds—yes, four *seconds*—behind Martens. It's hard to pick out individuals at that distance and with the picture going crazy. Don't try to adjust your TV set. Everyone's getting these broken pictures because of the weather.'

Tony must still have been listening to her. He spoke in her other earphone, saying he would insert short commercial breaks if things got any worse. Meanwhile he switched to a slightly better picture, captioned 'Moto 4. Back of the race.'

'Those are the tail-enders,' said Jo. 'They're trailing up this climb, shattered and demoralised. You may recognise some of them as the sprinters who were well to the fore on the flat stages. This is not their scene, so they form a sort of support group, variously called the *grupetto,* "the bus" or "the laughing group"—the last being ironic because they are *not* laughing. They're cold and wet, their leg muscles are in agony, and so are their minds as they find themselves being dropped farther and farther behind.'

Tony said 'Commercial break of thirty' and Jo watched the grupetto in silence. Leading them was Jan Claes the Flanders Flyer, not flying today. In the Prologue Time-trial, he'd gone like a rocket. Now, he must feel as though he was going backwards. Behind him, Salvatore was levering his tall and hefty body up the one-in-eight gradient, making a gut-busting effort but getting slower and weaker.

The thirty seconds expired and Jo talked over the rain-shattered picture. 'These riders knew they'd have a day like this but they keep going, determined to get to the top, and the next top, and the end of the stage. Some won't make it. They'll get off their bikes and climb into their team cars. There's also a minibus called the Broom Wagon that comes along at the back of the race, sweeping up those who literally fall by the wayside.

'I feel sorry for those who'll make it all the way, only to find they're outside the time limit. It seems unfair that they're eliminated after all that effort, but there has to be a limit, otherwise they might nip into a café for hot drinks. That's what they used to do a hundred years ago when there was almost no traffic. Nowadays, all traffic is held up when roads are closed for the race. Road closures can last for several hours, and so there must be a time limit. It's a percentage of the time taken by the winner, and the percentage varies with the difficulty of the stage.'

The picture wavered ominously, but Jo kept talking. Actually, it was easier to talk about the stragglers. Anyone who had ever ridden a bike would understand what these riders were suffering.

'Most of the mountain specialists are small and lightly built, but they have great power-to-weight ratio, if you know what I mean. Contrast them with the big Viking on your screen—Nilsson, the former Swedish champion, almost two metres tall. Still, Nilsson looks determined. Let's send these riders some up-think as we deal with our picture problems and go to another commercial break.'

Jo sat back and eased her shoulders. She'd been subconsciously copying the posture of the struggling riders. Claes and Nilsson looked shattered. She'd watched them in close-up on the first day Prologue and had thought how young they looked. How young they'd *all* looked at the start! Now every one of them seemed years older. What kind of dedication drove a boy to inflict such punishment on his body? Money, maybe, but the also-rans didn't earn big money. They loved riding bikes, they said when she asked them, and so they did it for a living. We're lucky, they said, having a job we enjoy. While it lasted.

At this level of competition, a rider's career was short. Most of them were burned out by the time they reached their mid-thirties. Then what? Only the top handful earned valuable cash prizes and became sufficiently famous to feature in adverts. Compared with golfers, football players, or tennis pros, most cyclists earned very little. The World Champion cyclist's prize was about nine thousand euros, whereas the World Match-play Champion golfer won two hundred times that amount. Grand champions of cycling might be able to live on invested winnings, but how did the rank-and-file riders save for their inevitable retirement, thirty years before pension age? Jo thought she might research this. It could make an interesting article.

Harry Vallon

Moisture collected on Harry's face again and he brushed the back of a glove across his eyes.

This was the climb up El Puño, whatever that meant, and he was feeling stronger than ever. But Dino's back wheel was still there, level with his gaze. How many metres ahead? One way to find out. Catch up with those wheels that were throwing out jets of spray in sparkling arches. They looked like two wings of water—pretty to watch. Riding on wings.

Harry Vallon was riding on wings today.

No sweat, no pain, no weakness. Legs still strong. A mountain was just a road that went up. A matter of the right gear and the rhythm in the legs. A matter of not being afraid, not dreading the climbs the way he used to do. All in the mind. And today his mind was crystal clear. He was riding on wings.

Dino's wheel disappeared.

It was a tight right-hander, a real whiplash of a bend, and he hadn't seen it! Stand on those pedals and...there was that wheel again, those wings of spray. Mustn't lose sight of those wings.

Someone was shouting his name, screaming in his ear *Harry! Harry!* He turned his head. A girl, wet blonde hair, wet blue jacket, running alongside him, waving a flag. *Harreee!*

Spectators, dozens of them, hundreds of them, all bending forward and punching the air, gesturing and yelling *Paco...Dino... Harry...*Must be near the top. A narrow corridor of people crowding in from the sides of the road. Soon be room for only one bike, and the other two were ahead of him. Pass them now! Must be first over the top, riding on wings. Stand on the pedals. Head down.

Under his nose the mini computer on the handlebars was blinking. His heart-rate monitor, reading two hundred and *what?* The numbers flashing *red?* Aw, come on! That couldn't be right. Bloody thing must be faulty. Rain likely got into it. He felt fine. Never felt so good.

More pressure on the pedals, and he was closer to Dino's bright green pants. Then Dino was beside him...behind him; and there was Ribero's red and white arse rocking from side to side as he swung on the bars, tiring, fading, his legs failing him, not even turning his head as the great climber Harry Vallon surged past and launched himself at the summit.

The girl with the flag was long gone. Other yelling faces, other bodies pressed forward and vanished in a blur behind him.

The summit line flashed under his wheels.

A motorbike engine revved. Must be one of the motocameras filming his triumph.

And now to descend the other side of the mountain. He would fly on these winning wings!

Jo Bonnard

The picture came from the fixed camera at the top of El Puño. Forcing a passage through the crowd was a police motorcycle followed by the vivid orange leading car with its headlights blazing. As the vehicles crossed the frontier at the summit, the Spanish Guardia Civil outriders pulled over to the side while their French counterparts wheeled out their gleaming machines, taking over as race escorts.

Jo switched on the microphone again. 'We're looking through mist at the last hundred metres of the climb. Amid the mass of spectators we can just see the three leading riders coming towards us. In the front is...Harry Vallon! Would you believe it? Vallon's romping up, almost sprinting ahead of Ribero! And Ribero is tired, fighting for every metre, with Nardini behind him, looking much the stronger.

'But look at Vallon! What an amazing performance from this man! He's going like a rocket and he's first over the line. Spanish spectators are out in force, going crazy as Ribero tries for second place. It's hard to tell from this head-on view, but I think Nardini shaved over, just ahead of the little Spaniard. The camera has swung round to see those three, vanishing into the mist of the descent.'

Harry Vallon

Harry was flying.

He would show them something on this descent. Give the couch potatoes something to make them gasp in front of their TV screens. Give the press a story to tell.

He would fly through the cloud on his wings. Swoop down the mountain, lean into the bends like this, with his knee almost brushing the road. Speedway riding! He would race the motorbikes. Give them all something to talk about, something to write about—and not just his good looks.

Eight out of every ten readers of *Go-Girl* had voted him the sexiest man in sport. They'd called him 'Drop-dead-gorgeous Harry' and 'The young Paul Newman look-alike.'

Except, Paul Newman couldn't ride a bike. How often had he watched that old movie, *Butch Cassidy and the Sundance Kid?*

Newman wobbling all over the place, whistling *Raindrops Keep Falling On My Head.*

Raindrops Keep Falling On My...Hey! That was funny! *Verree* appropriate! Harry laughed aloud and whistled a few bars of the tune.

Still whistling, Paul Newman look-alike, he gave the handlebars an experimental wobble.

He felt the back wheel start to skid.

The steel barrier rushed towards him.

Jo Bonnard

'Here come the chasers!' Jo didn't try to keep the excitement out of her voice. 'Danny Breton of Intapost and someone from the AFA team...It's Jacky Bernard. Just those two. Ferrer's not with them. I told you this was a tough climb. The former ace is nowhere in sight as Breton crosses the line a metre ahead of Bernard. And here comes another group. Crikey, they've been shifting! They've caught up five minutes on the chasers. They've really been motoring up that climb!

'Marc Martens is in front. Glued to his back wheel is the American Bob Rothman. Now it's his turn to keep up with his young protégé. Behind them are two Intapost riders—their French climber David Vauban, followed by Chico Montes driving the crowd wild. Someone's waving that gigantic Spanish flag. Well, we're still in Spain—just. Over the white summit line is France.

'Still no sign of Ferrer, unless he's among this next group. Yes, he is! That's Ferrer in the dark blue jacket.' She found herself stupidly pointing to him on her screen—as if the viewers could see her! 'He must have suffered on that lung-busting climb of El Puño, but he's an expert descender so he'll probably get back to Bernard on the downhill run. The Martens group has crossed the summit. There they go, down into the mist and...

'Someone has fallen! It's just coming over Race Radio. Someone has fallen on the descent. I don't know who it is. Reception's bad... One rider. Not a pile-up...It's a dangerous, twisting descent. Some of them go down like kamikaze pilots, but when you can't see farther than a few metres, it's no day for flying eyeballs-out, down a mountainside. Let me listen for a moment...'

Jo clamped her hand over her earphone, straining to hear through the crackle. 'Whoever it is, he fell at kilometre ten. Ten kilometres down the hill already! He must be one of the first five, and he must have been going like a bullet! Still no word. .. I'll tell you as soon as I hear who it is.'

Jo closed her eyes and uttered a silent 'Please God, not Danny.'

Race Radio emitted more static. On her monitor screen, another group was nearing the summit and behind them she made out flashing lights.

'Looks like the ambulance has been called up....Yes, Race Radio's warning team cars to let it pass. A motocamera is following the ambulance as it goes down the mountain to assist the fallen rider. The ambulance siren will blast a warning to the cyclists.'

The radio hissed again and Jo held her breath as she listened. The fallen rider (thank God, not Danny) was number thirty-two... Harry Vallon.

'It's Harry Vallon of AFA who has gone down. What a shame! He was doing so amazingly well. Let's hope the ambulance is a standard precaution and that he's not seriously hurt. He may be concussed or have broken his collarbone, the cyclists' most common injury. We just don't know.'

Tony's voice spoke urgently in her left ear: 'I'm patching in some other pictures. Concentrate on the race, Jo. Ignore those ghouls.'

Dr Vernon

Siren wailing and roof light revolving, Luc, the paramedic driver, edged the Tour's ambulance past three small groups of riders until, ten kilometres down the hill, the police escort signalled and pulled in. Luc stopped behind him, tight against the crash barrier. The headlight of the big motorcycle shone on the twisted wheels of a bike that lay on the roadside, half under the barrier. The police officer was already speaking into his radio as Luc squeezed out, grabbed the hazard beacon from its rack and ran back uphill to position it. Dr Vernon and Joseph, the other paramedic, jumped out and ran towards the bicycle, but there was no sign of the crash victim. They leaned over the barrier and shouted, but there was no answering call.

Vernon was about to climb over the barrier, when the policeman's hand shot out and grabbed his arm. 'Wait. You can't go down there.'

Vernon struggled. 'I'm a doctor!' The black gauntlet gripped like a vice round his biceps. 'There's an injured man...' Then he looked over the barrier. Dropping sheer into the dense mist, slabs of grey rock glistened in the wet.

The officer said, 'It's like that all the way down to the river. I've called for the Mountain Rescue Unit in La Portette.'

'But they can't come up this road for an hour or more!' Vernon protested. 'Not until all the riders have gone down.'

To underline his point, a group of riders materialised from the fog, took the bend cautiously, and were gone. The motocamera abandoned the ambulance and set off after them.

'There's a track on the other side of the gorge,' the officer said. 'The Rescue Unit will come up that way, and it's easier to get down to the river from that side.'

Luc rejoined them, and they stood frustrated until, from across the gorge, there came the muffled sound of engines that the officer identified as the all-terrain quad bikes of the first unit of Mountain Rescue. The engines stopped and a voice shouted through a megaphone: 'Road Patrol? Give us a marker. Use your headlight.... Thanks. We'll rope down now.'

The doctor peered uselessly over the barrier, listening to the clinks, scrapes and occasional shouts of the men climbing down into the gorge. After a while, they heard another engine.

'Second unit. Four-wheel-drive vehicle,' said the officer. 'Equipped with radio communication, a winch and slots for stretchers. It doubles as an ambulance. One of the team is a surgeon from La Portette Hospital.'

From somewhere below them came a shout. 'We're across the river, but we can't see your headlight from here. Can you give us another marker?'

The officer took a heavy torch from a pannier of his motorcycle. Leaning out over the barrier he shone it downward, but the men below were unable to see it. Joseph ran to the ambulance and came back with a roll of bandage He tied it to the torch with a quick, expert knot and hung the torch over the barrier, unrolling bandage as it went down. Its light became a halo in the mist, and then was swallowed in grey vapour. The bandage unrolled steadily, encountering no snags. Only then did Vernon appreciate that this was indeed a perpendicular cliff.

'Ten metres,' Joseph said quietly. 'Bring us another roll, Luc.' He knotted the ends together and continued unrolling.

Behind them, a group of riders appeared, shouting warnings; then an AFA car halted and its driver jumped out, saying he was Jones, the fallen rider's team manager. He listened to the officer's explanation and then, highly agitated, he said he'd have to get out of the way; there were quite a number of riders still on the climb, but the second team car was behind the peloton. He would call it, and tell it to stop when it got here. Jones scuttled for his car and drove off.

From below, a voice called, 'Got it! We can see the torch. We'll have to make our way towards you along the rock-face. The river's too high.' There came the sound of hammering as the rescue team drove pitons into the rock. After what seemed an endless wait, the voice floated up again. 'Can you lower the torch some more?...Good! Hold it there! We're right below you; going to look at a ledge about two metres above us.' There was renewed hammering and an exchange of shouts, and then suddenly a piercing blast on a whistle.

'They've found him.' The officer unclipped a communications set from his motorbike and listened. Eventually he turned to Vernon, telling him the rescuers had got the injured man on to a stretcher but they'd have to rig a pulley line back along the rock-face to the place where they could cross the river. Then they would winch the stretcher up. The second unit was lowering equipment to them now. 'It's going to be a hell of a job.' He broke off to listen again. After a moment, his face grim, he said, 'He's dead. The surgeon's down there; just confirmed it with the support vehicle.'

Dr Vernon slumped dejectedly against the barrier. 'Where will they take him?'

'The hospital at La Portette. Police HQ will relay the call from the Rescue unit to the Tour Director.'

'Oh.' Vernon ran a hand through his hair and was surprised to find it soaking wet. He realised he had been semi-oblivious to what had been happening on the road behind him. He'd been vaguely aware of shouts and hissing wheels, and of car headlights illuminating the fog as they wound round the corner. 'I'd better ask for instructions.' He went over to the ambulance. After a couple of minutes he rejoined them. 'We have to go on. There's been a minor accident near the bridge at La Portette.'

Joseph tied his end of the bandage to the Armco barrier. It was all that he could do. They shook hands with the police officer and left.

Jo Bonnard

A flickering Moto 2 picture came back, showing George Ferrer catching up again with Danny Breton and Jacky Bernard but, although the trio rode strongly, they were still some distance back from the Martens-Rothman group as the leading riders hit the lower slopes of the final climb to Les Chalets.

The rain was finally easing off, and a new picture came from the static camera at the finish. Mounted on a "cherry picker," it was giving a clear image, at last.

'That fantastic zoom lens is focused on a point about six hundred metres below us, but the distance by road from there to here is almost eight kilometres. There's a succession of zigzag bends, right up to the finish. As the riders come round those bends, they'll be able to look down and see the riders who are one level below them. But, of course, those on the lower levels will be looking up...and up...and wondering if the stage is ever going to end. It's a horrible climb at the end of a gruelling day.'

She leaned forward, anxious to see how Marc Martens was faring against the two specialist climbers, Nardini and Ribero. 'I can see the motorbikes of the outriders followed by the leading car. Any moment now we'll see the riders. Here they come. Can we make out who's in this *very* small first group? The front-runner is Dino Nardini, easily distinguished by the Polkadot Jersey under his transparent rain jacket. Luckily, most riders wear these so that everyone can see their team colours. A few metres back is. ... I'm fairly sure it's the small figure of Paco Ribero...Yes, it is. And if he looks over the side, he'll see the Yellow Jersey of Marc Martens, just one bend below him. Farther back is another red-and-white Intapost jersey…Chico Montes, the Galician rider, but he's losing ground. And that's it! That's group one. No sign of Bob Rothman or David Vauban or the Ferrer trio.

'Nardini takes another bend on the inside, where it's steeper—a sure sign his legs are still good. Ribero seems to be slowing. Either that or Martens has accelerated because, as they hit the straight section here, you can see there's less distance between them. Ribero is fighting hard but it looks like the little Spaniard is running out of fuel.'

The leaders rounded another bend where an outcrop of rock hid them from the camera, but another little group had appeared on the first ramp.

Jo peered intently at her screen. 'The tall figure is Bob Rothman. The dark blue AFA jacket belongs to either Bernard or Ferrer… Ferrer it is! And here's Bernard, his young team-mate, not far behind, along with Intapost's Danny Breton.'

Good for you, Danny! Jo thought as she punched the air, grinning widely. Just as well her producer couldn't see her! Eltsport, as she kept reminding herself, didn't approve of personal remarks by commentators. 'The two young riders have kept up extremely well. Now here come Jonkers and Charreau who've just about caught up to the Ferrer trio.' The camera focussed again on last three hairpins of the day. 'Here we go! The last thousand metres, with Dino Nardini still in the lead. But Marc Martens has passed Ribero and is really piling on the power, going like a train. This is going to be a close finish.'

An overlay appeared on the corner of the screen—digital numbers constantly changing. 'We can see the gap between Nardini and Martens is twenty seconds…sixteen…fifteen, and two more bends to go. Dino still looks strong, going for the inside of that bend while Marc takes it a little wider. A seventeen-second gap.' Jo's fists were clenched. So was her jaw. She took a couple of calming breaths. 'Now they climb the straight section, and there are only twelve seconds between them. Dino gains a couple of seconds on the steep bends, but Marc is clawing back time on the straights. We're watching a mighty contest here—Marc's strength versus Dino's uphill acceleration.

'One last bend, and Dino Nardini is still maintaining his fast tempo…Almost at the line…and Nardini gets the stage! Watch the count-down…eight…nine…*ten* seconds ahead of Martens who powered, machine-like, up those final metres, thus increasing his overall lead.' Jo sagged back in her chair. Marc's hold on the Yellow Jersey looked a little more secure, but the way Nardini was riding, Marc couldn't afford to relax.

By the time the bulk of the peloton laboured over the finishing line, Dino, wearing Chiali green, had received his stage winner's prize, and then he'd returned to the podium for the Polkadot Jersey.

Marc Martens was on the podium, going through the protocol of donning the Yellow Jersey again, when the sprinters and stragglers began crossing the line at widely spaced intervals. Jo had plenty of time to recite their names and to listen to Race Radio's roll call of the approaching grupetto. It included a few who had fallen but picked themselves up without serious injuries. Astoundingly, only one rider had been eliminated from the race today, having broken his wrist in a fall.

Another casualty of the day, said Race Radio, was one of the Chiali vehicles that had gone into a ditch at the foot of El Puño and was being repaired in a Spanish garage.

Of Harry Vallon, there had been no more information regarding his crash—absolutely nothing.

STAGE 15

Evening

Jo Bonnard

The rain-clouds cleared as the official vehicles made their way from the muddy grass of the parking area. From Les Chalets, the long convoy crawled down the mountainside. Jo had time to appreciate the spectacular view of mountains that appeared to be gently steaming in the early evening sun. Looking down into the valley, she caught a glimpse of an impressive, star-shaped building. That must be the place they were all bound for—Hotel Starlight III.

In her room she found a glossy brochure explaining that the hotel had been built to accommodate skiers in winter, and thousands of year-round visitors who enjoyed the great variety of outdoor activities in the area. Each point of the star was a self-contained unit with conference suites, bedrooms, its own restaurant, lounge and bar.

Inside the brochure, a well-produced insertion welcomed The Tour in seven languages and listed the allocation of rooms. In this block were most of the media people and the Intapost team. On the back page of the insertion, the Starlight Group looked forward to welcoming The Tour again in a few days' time, at Starlight II, Colmar.

The Tour's normal requirement was a large number of hotels, often widely scattered. Frequently, Jo's allocated hotel would be an hour's drive from the start or finish of her day's work. But the Starlight complex was large enough to accommodate all the teams, their personnel, the organisers and the media.

Jo mouthed 'Wow!' at the mirror, then grimaced at her bedraggled appearance. Her hair resembled an old mop. It had been soaked twice today. Her jeans were still damp from her trudge across the wet grass of the mountaintop carpark. She peeled them off and headed for the shower.

On the back of the door was a laundry bag. An attached notice, again in seven languages, said: *Overnight laundry. Telephone 504 (housekeeping) before 21.00 hrs. Your laundry will be collected and returned by 09.00 hrs tomorrow.*

Jo said 'Wow!' out loud this time. Her norm was washing garments in hand-basins and dripping them dry, but here for once she could have her clothes properly laundered.

Thus she found the scrap of paper in the pocket of yesterday's shirt. *Did Harry Vallon crash...?*

Ten minutes after she had gone off air this afternoon, the announcement had been made: Harry Vallon was dead.

She never *had* got around to asking him about his cut eye.

She sighed, crumpled the note and dropped it in the pedal bin. Then, after a moment's thought, she picked it out again, smoothed it and slipped it into her folder of notes.

Danny Breton

Danny pressed 1 on the Directory of his mobile phone.

Almost at once, his father answered: 'Hello, Danny. Great ride today. Well done.'

'Thanks, Dad. I enjoyed it.' Danny's voice bubbled with enthusiasm. 'Guy said I could have a crack at Trois Têtes, and I latched on to the AFA pair. It was a good threesome, so we kept going. George Ferrer was really friendly, and Jacky Bernard's a nice guy. He's very religious, did you know? Gives a lot of money to a church orphanage.' Laughing, he added, 'And he doesn't approve of swearing.'

'Good for him. He must be unique in the peloton,' came the sardonic response. 'You feel okay? You weren't cold?'

'No. It wasn't bad, except on the highest sections. But sometimes the rain actually hurt, it was so heavy.'

'Heavy doesn't describe it. It broke up the TV pictures.'

'Which channel?'

'Eltsport.'

Danny gave a knowing chuckle. 'With English audio, eh? Does Jo know you've become her fan?'

'Become? I'll have you know she was one of the best journalists when she was in her teens.'

Danny thought maybe he should quit teasing his father. There was clearly some significance in that old and yellowing newspaper clipping that had appeared one day, framed, in Dad's office: *Paul Breton, the Modest Maestro* with the by-line *Jo Bonnard*.

His father said, 'Tell her from me: she did a great job today, talking us through the climbs when we could see damn all.'

'Will do, if I get a chance. She's not likely to seek an interview with a little *domestique* like me.'

'Don't be so sure. She's known for off-beat interviews.'

'Gee, thanks, Dad,' Danny laughed again. 'I thought you were going to say she can suss out budding talent.' He became serious. 'You heard about Vallon?'

'Yes, but it was just a brief statement on the evening news. It's horrible when something like that happens. Anything more known about it?'

'Precious little, but the chatter says that Vallon was doing about sixty.'

'On that descent? Idiotic! What speed did *you* go down?'

'Slow, Dad, really slow. My fingers cramped up, squeezing the brakes all the time. I do listen to your advice, believe it or not.'

'What about tomorrow's stage?'

'We're not sure, but Guy reckons it'll be neutralised. Koch's going to announce something tonight, so you'll see it on the late news.'

'By which time you'll be asleep, I hope.'

'Oh, Dad! You think I'm six years old?' he protested. 'I assure you I'll be asleep within minutes of switching off this phone.'

'Smart thinking, son. You do that. My turn to phone tomorrow. Around this time?'

'Perfect. Goodnight, Dad. Take care.'

'You too. Goodnight, son.'

Danny switched off, smiling. When it came to training, his father could be a strict coach. That was okay. But, sometimes, Dad talked to him like he was still a kid. That was okay too. It was kind of nice to have a caring father.

What's it like, being Paul Breton's son? Danny had talked to his father about the frequently asked question, and his father had been surprised that the young generation had even heard of him. Danny lay back on the pillow, glad that his dad wasn't overly concerned with fame. Danny loved cycling, but he did it for fun.

Guy Lacrosse

Guy Lacrosse, manager and *directeur sportif* of the Intapost team, had checked that all his lads were fed, massaged and relaxing. Just as he was about to go in to the restaurant for a solitary meal, he saw Jo Bonnard walking across the foyer. He looked admiringly at her elegant silky trouser-suit the same grey-green as her eyes. Jo's sense of style, though not her forthright manner, had changed since she'd been the gawky girl reporter that Paul Breton had liked so much. Jo smiled hello and came towards him. Guy had known her since the time he had ridden in the same team as Paul, but although he and Jo went around on the same tours, they seldom had time for more than a snatch of talk. He suggested they should have supper together.

In the restaurant, Jo made her choice from the menu and then said, 'Danny's doing terrifically well in his first big tour.'

'He's young, and I wondered about his stamina, but I think he might turn out to be a great rider.'

'Inherited his dad's talent,' Jo smiled, 'and his looks. He's the image of Paul!' She gave a small involuntary sigh. 'Every time I look at Danny I'm time-warped back twenty-odd years.'

A waiter approached and Guy gave their order, getting into a discussion on wine and giving Jo time to feel foolish about her sentimental outburst.

Paul had been just twenty-nine when he'd been crippled in that accident. The loss of his left foot had ended his legendary cycling career but, since a couple of years after his enforced retirement, he'd been running an increasingly successful car dealership that was now one of the largest in Paris.

The waiter left and Guy returned his attention to Jo. 'Back then, I thought you and Paul were...um...what's now called 'an item."

'Great friends, that's all,' she said; but because that had sounded brusque and was, besides, not entirely true, she added, 'Of course I thought Paul was terrific. I still do. But, romance? No. Not in this male-dominated world of cycling. One whiff of romance would have reduced my credibility to zilch. I'd have been classified as a husband-hunter and wouldn't have lasted five minutes. The level playing field *still* doesn't exist. In my job, it isn't enough to be as good as the men. I have to be better.'

'Times have changed, Jo,' he soothed. 'The Danish team even has those dolly masseuses.'

'Dolly masseuses!' she repeated scornfully. 'Listen to you! Don't tell me times have changed.'

Guy was saved by the arrival of their mountain ham and green figs. They ate, chatting about the race and avoiding the topic of the fatal accident. They had almost finished their main course of Pyrenean trout when Guy eventually said, 'You're going to the media conference tonight?'

'Naturally, but it's not a conference, surely? Walter Koch will simply make a statement. There have been precedents, sad to say, so he'll probably make tomorrow's stage non-competitive.'

'That was certainly his intention when he talked to all the managers earlier this evening. Tomorrow the teams will just ride the route; no points, no winners.'

'Problems for me,' said Jo. 'I hope my producer doesn't want me to commentate on a non-event. I'll never forget the time the riders held that sit-down protest. The trouble was, the teams couldn't agree, but when I aired their differing opinions and tended to side with the Spanish teams, the company gave me a very sharp reprimand. Reminded me I'm a cycling commentator, not Christiane Amanpour.'

'Who?'

'CNN's top foreign correspondent—a politically clued-up lady. Anyway, my bosses said that personal opinions are a no-no. I don't want to go through something like that again.' After a while, she asked, 'What happened at the managers' meeting? Did they all agree to a neutral stage?'

'There was one grumbler.'

'I bet it was Enrico Fiarelli.'

Guy looked surprised. 'How did you guess?'

She rubbed a thumb and forefinger together. 'Money. There were mountain points—for which, read Money—on tomorrow's stage, and Dino Nardini would probably have won a number of them. Also, losing even one day's TV exposure is loss of advertising. It wouldn't surprise me if Fiarelli offers cash to the cameramen to focus on his boys. I shouldn't say that, but I've never liked him.'

'You should have heard him when Dash was disqualified.'

'That was a shameless performance. Did you hear what Fiarelli said?'

Guy grinned. 'Let's just say he was displeased. Dash is a phenomenal sprinter, but a liability. Last year I wanted to sign him up. Now I'm glad I couldn't afford his asking price. Chiali must have thought he was worth it—at the time. I'm not so sure now.'

They discussed contracts, and Jo mentioned her idea to research the current occupations of former cyclists.

'Hmm. Interesting,' said Guy. 'Think of our old Fontaine team. Paul has a car dealership. I'm a team manager. Xavier Dufaux is one of your colleagues. Martinez runs a pizza place in Benidorm, I believe. The others...' He frowned. 'I don't know what became of them, except for Recamier. Remember him?'

'He was one of the *domestiques*. What's he doing now?'

'Driving a forklift truck in a warehouse.'

'That's *exactly* the sort of thing I want to know!'

'There's more money now than there was in my day,' said Guy feelingly.

'For the stars. Not for the majority.' Jo took a final sip of wine and glanced at her watch. 'About time for the meeting.' She sounded suddenly depressed.

'A bad day, Jo, but we'll be back to normal after tomorrow.'

She sat for a moment looking thoughtful, but all she said was: 'I hope you're right.'

Dr. Vernon

In order to complete his notes for the day, Dr Vernon sent for Marc Martens. The boy breezed in, insisting that he felt completely well, that he'd been fine after he'd thrown up his breakfast, and it must have been something he ate that made him sick.

The lab had given Vernon a copy of Marc's end-of-stage test analyses. The doctor studied the printout. No trace of pathogens, and so he could rule out bacterial poisoning. No toxins…Could the vomiting have been caused by an allergy? He lifted Marc's medical dossier from the table, read it and then looked up at the boy. 'You have only one known allergy—sulphates. Nobody gave you any kind of medical product? You didn't take anything yourself? No pills? Did you use any cream or salve?'

'No, of course not. Nothing whatever. I'm fine.'

'What did you eat for breakfast?' Marc recited a list in which Vernon could hear nothing obviously harmful. 'Did you drink anything out of the ordinary?'

Marc gave a mighty shrug and said, 'One extra cup of coffee—black. Dino Nardini brought it over to me, to say congratulations. I don't much like black coffee, but it would have been rude to refuse it.'

Vernon nodded agreement. Then he examined the boy, found nothing wrong, and sent him off with instructions to report any recurrence immediately, drink plenty of water, and get a good night's sleep. He finished his notes with a memo to Marc's doctor, suggesting allergy tests at some future time.

Walter Koch

Walter Koch, recently appointed Director of the Tour de France Organisation, was a former amateur cycling champion. Now an entrepreneur, he had the huge task of organising a world-famous event, always ensuring that those towns clamouring for inclusion had the infrastructure necessary for the thousands of personnel involved. He had secured a number of new sponsors, convincing them of the benefits of international exposure.

Immediately he heard of the fatality, Koch had first telephoned the headquarters of the International Federation of Professional Cycling Organisations and spoken to Herr Doktor Rolf Niemann, proposing that tomorrow's stage be neutralised as a mark of respect. Niemann had agreed to that, and Koch then sent off a batch of e-mails informing the sponsors and requesting immediate replies.

The Tour would continue the following day. The rider's death was a shocking tragedy, but not even a fatal accident could halt The Tour. Commercial TV companies had bought broadcasting rights and sold advertising time on the strength of huge viewing figures. The staging towns spent a great deal of ratepayers' money on hospitality. Hotels took on extra staff and would sue for cancelled bookings. Local sponsors of prize money and goods would sue. Breaking contracts was not an option.

Koch had arranged to speak to the team managers and hoped to have replies to his e-mails before he talked to the media. The Village had already been set up for tomorrow's departure, and he would discuss that with the local mayor. He would also telephone the Mayor of Bellerive where tomorrow's stage was due to finish.

His P.A. Hans Luber came back from arranging a suitable venue in the hotel. 'The staff are very efficient,' he said. 'They even came up with this. It was taken for a tourism promotion last year, just after the El Puño road was opened.' He handed Koch a large glossy poster—an aerial view of a fast-flowing river running through a gorge. On one side of the gorge, a track wound amongst sparse conifers. On the other side was the new road, looking like a wedge chiselled out of the sheer grey rock. Luber pointed to the outside of its most acutely angled bend. 'The accident occurred exactly there.'

Koch shook his head sorrowfully. And the rescue team's task must be immensely difficult. 'Any word from Mountain Rescue?'

'No. It must be getting dark down there. Do you suppose they'll leave the…er…body until morning?'

'I don't imagine so, but I don't intend to press them. They know what they're doing.'

Luber sighed. 'By the way, Mr Jones is here. Do you want to speak to him before the other managers arrive?'

Alex Hubbard

Harvey Jones had rushed off anxiously to his meeting, leaving his assistant Alex Hubbard in charge.

Hubbard had been an amateur cyclist and had once taught physical education in a tough inner-city school—an experience he called upon now as he sensed the jittery atmosphere in the team. 'In a crisis, keep them occupied' had been a staff maxim. At the moment, the riders were occupied with showers and massages. Then they would eat. And then they would have time to talk and to analyse the accident, to no avail.

He knew that Vallon wasn't...he corrected that...*had not been* liked by the rest of the team, and not only on account of banging Paula Ferrer. And that summed up Vallon's interest in her. Vallon clearly regarded Paula much as he regarded the teenage tour-groupies and the girls who sent him their photographs, some nude, and their scented proposals in all shades from sweetly innocent to obscene. Vallon passed them around, laughing, and the lads would smile dutifully; but you could see in their eyes, they thought Vallon was a creep. Hubbard stopped this train of thought. The lad was dead.

∾

Hubbard had been in the second team car, following the last of the riders down the mountainside. He had stopped where the police officer stood speaking into his radio.

'I'm in touch with the rescue unit in the gorge,' the officer told him. 'They're roped to pitons on sheer rock above white water. Getting the body across the river will be a difficult and dangerous job. We'll notify the Tour Director immediately they get the body to the hospital morgue.'

Silently Hubbard thought about the enormous task. 'Please thank the rescue team. They'll hear from us officially, of course, but...' At a loss for adequate words of thanks, he asked, 'What about the bicycle? Can I take it?'

'I don't see why not. Better check, though.' The officer spoke into his radio and, after a short conversation, confirmed, 'You can take it. It's not as though we need it for evidence. It's perfectly obvious what happened. I'm surprised not to have heard of more accidents.'

'Oh, there were accidents but, incredibly, they were all slight. Skids, falls, one broken wrist, I heard.' He could do no good, standing here. He called to his driver, 'Let's get this bike onto the roof-rack.'

∾

73

The mechanics' big van, a mobile workshop, was in the huge car park behind the hotel. Beside the van, the mechanics were standing around the mangled remains of Vallon's bicycle.

'Head-on into the barrier.' Mackay, their burly chief, was growling in his Glasgow accent. 'Look at that down-tube. Bent to near breakin' point! He must've been goin' like the hammers o' hell. Bloody idiot!'

Steve, one of the younger ones, asked, 'Who saw the crash?'

'The officials' car,' said Mackay. 'Well, they didna actually *see* it, but Vallon was behind them when they took the bend. When they looked back, he wasna there. We heard the call on the radio.'

'Did you stop?'

'Just a few seconds. Riders were comin' down behind us.' Mackay looked up and saw Hubbard. 'I was just sayin'...'

'I heard it all. Very sensational. More to the point—did you have the stop-watch running?'

'Aye, of course. I started it when Vallon crossed the summit line. Nardini and Ribero were four seconds behind him, two chasers thirty seconds back, then a bunch at one minute five.'

'Did you keep the watch running?' Mackay nodded and Hubbard looked at him doubtfully. 'I don't suppose you checked it when you heard he'd crashed.'

Mackay, offended, stuck his chin out. 'As a matter of fact, I did. They said on the radio: 'Kilometre ten. Nardini's passed us but no sign of Vallon' and I looked at the watch. It was nine and a half minutes exactly.'

Hubbard frowned. 'Suppose the gap back to Nardini was constant. Allow some seconds for the lead car to react.' He paused, calculating. 'That means Vallon went down ten kilometres in under ten minutes. He must have been doing about sixty kilometres an hour!'

'Nearly forty *miles* an hour! Jee-zuss!'

The mechanics, drivers and Hubbard stared at one another, stunned.

'Blind.' Mackay whispered in awe. 'Ridin' blind on a wet road. All these bends...Even with fog lights you couldna see through the mist, it was that thick. He must've been off his head. I mean, Nardini was dropping fast, but he's a fearless descender; not like Vallon. *He* usually wears out his brake blocks.' He made a screwing motion with a finger against his head. 'He must've gone round the twist!'

Hubbard remembered why he had come out here. 'Listen, lads. I'm going to send the riders round to work with you on their bikes.'

'Why?' Mackay sounded belligerent.

'If they've got work to do, they won't have time to...' He bit back the word 'gossip.' '...to brood about what happened today. I know Vallon wasn't popular, but he was one of them and it's bound to affect them. I want them all to be so tired they'll sleep without holding discussions, which is what we seem to be doing. So, down tools. Go and eat, then everybody gets to work.'

'Fair enough,' Mackay conceded. 'Every bike has to be stripped down, washed and greased, anyway.'

~

Hubbard's idea worked—up to a point. Up to the point when Nat Arnold, hunkered morosely over the wreckage of Vallon's bike, suddenly said, 'The front brake unit's come off.'

Mackay joined him. 'Aye. So it would. The speed he hit the barrier...You've just got to look at how the wheel's buckled. How could it *not* come off?'

'Oh? Is that it?'

'Of course. What are you gettin' at?'

'Maybe it was loose.'

'Loose? Are you daft?' Mackay tapped himself on the chest. 'I checked that bike. Personally.'

'Brakes included?'

Mackay grabbed Arnold and hoisted him to his feet. 'Aye, brakes included. Are you callin' me a liar?'

Arnold stepped back from Mackay's fury. 'Oh, I'm not blaming *you* for it.'

Hubbard stepped between them. 'I'm very glad to hear that,' he said sarcastically. 'I'm sure we're all glad to hear you trust our mechanics.'

In every group of boys, he thought, there's always a troublemaker and Arnold was a typical example. Look at him now, standing with his long nose sniffing for trouble, justifying his grudge against the world.

Arnold glowered at him. 'So why are *we* working on the bikes? It's not our job.'

'In order to keep yourselves busy,' said Hubbard, 'instead of standing around playing Sherlock Holmes.'

A ripple of amusement infuriated Arnold, but what more he might have said was forestalled by Harvey Jones who walked slowly into their midst, saying: 'So that's why you're all here.'

Everyone turned in surprise. Hubbard said, 'I didn't know you were back.'

'Oh? I've been here for a minute or so,' Jones said. He sounded tired. 'Tomorrow's stage is neutralised. Koch will tell the media tonight. They've just recovered the body and Koch has phoned Vallon's wife. She's on her way to...'

'His *wife?*' George Ferrer went rigid, his voice cracking. 'Harry Vallon has a *wife?*'

Jones sat wearily on the bumper of the big van. 'Yes. He married her a year ago. There's a six-months-old baby. He wanted it kept secret.'

There was a stunned silence, and then Ferrer made a choking sound.

Jacky Bernard looked shocked. 'It's nothing to laugh about.'

Ferrer blinked. 'I wasn't laughing. It's just that *my* wife had the idea that...' He stopped and looked at them dazedly. '...that Vallon would...She says it's...It's certainly not mine.' He whirled and ran for the hotel, leaving behind him a twanging silence.

Nat Arnold

'It's about Vallon's bike.' Nat Arnold spoke quietly into his mobile phone. 'In my personal opinion, I think somebody got at the brakes. I don't really know for sure who,' Arnold hesitated, 'but Vallon was having it off with...er...'

'A married woman, shall we say? I know about that.' The man's accent was funny: *ve* and *zat.*

'Yeah, well, her husband's in a right old state.'

'I see. Enough said. Is that all you have to tell me?'

'No. Wait !' Arnold was enthusiastic. Sure about this next titbit, he'd start with a big amount. The man always beat him down over payments. 'This is worth a thousand euros.'

'Five hundred, if it's good…and can be confirmed.'

It had been a nice try. 'Okay, five hundred. Harry Vallon was married.'

'Interesting. What's the wife's name?'

Arnold didn't know, and was offered two hundred euros. About to protest about the price, he found he was holding a dead phone.

Jo Bonnard

Jo and Guy took seats near the back of a large room with a low platform at the far end.

Exactly at 10.30, Walter Koch stepped onto the platform and began without preamble, repeating what everyone already knew— a tragic accident had resulted in the death of Harry Vallon of the AFA team. 'You will,' he went on, 'share my relief in learning that his body was recovered a short time ago. I have expressed thanks on behalf of all concerned to the Police and Mountain Rescue teams.' He paused. 'As a mark of respect for the deceased rider, tomorrow's stage will be annulled. This has the full agreement of the International Federation of Professional Cycling Organisations, of all our sponsors and, I am sure, of everyone on this Tour.' His eyes scanned the audience for a few seconds before he concluded briskly, 'From Bellerive, the Tour will resume normally the day after tomorrow.'

He stepped back while his P.A., Hans Luber, announced that, in fulfilment of protocol, tomorrow's non-competitive stage would be followed by podium presentations to the current holders of the various Jerseys. He then said that the Director would answer relevant questions for ten minutes.

Someone called out: 'What was the exact cause of death?'

'I cannot say, at this time. The cause will be established by the official inquest.' Koch moved to an easel where the tourist poster had been pinned. 'However, may I draw your attention to this photograph?' He used a pointer to indicate the hairpin bend. 'The accident occurred exactly here, in weather conditions of which you are all aware.' He moved the pointer. 'The body was recovered from a ledge down here.'

There were horrified murmurs. Koch gave them time to subside and then went on to say, almost superfluously, that a surgeon on the rescue team had suggested that death was likely to have been instantaneous.

Another voice asked: 'Can we have a copy of that photograph?'

'Not at present, but we hope to obtain permission from the owner of the copyright.'

'Is there truth in the rumour that Vallon's brakes were faulty?'

Heads swung round, and Jo looked along the row of seats to identify the questioner.

It was Henri Ettier His column's by-line was *H. Ett,* pronounced in French 'Hachette,' which was appropriate for the notorious hatchet-man reporter of *Aujourd'quoi.* His hair was sparse at the front and over-long at the back. With his round-shouldered, head-poked-forward stance, he reminded Jo of a vulture.

Koch appeared taken aback by the question. He made a gesture of appeal to Harvey Jones, Vallon's team manager, sitting in the front row.

Jones sprang to his feet and turned to face Hachette. 'Where did you get that idea?'

'I never reveal my sources.' The standard response.

'It's absolute nonsense,' Jones said. 'I heard that suggestion myself, and it's not true. The idea that anyone on a team would interfere with another's bicycle is...It's preposterous.' He sat down abruptly.

Jo murmured 'Oh my God' to Guy Lacrosse.

Hachette was still on his feet. 'I believe I mentioned a fault. Not interference. Thank you, Mr Jones.' His lips drew back in a hyena smile, then he walked swiftly from the room.

Guy looked shocked. He whispered, 'What the hell was Jones saying?'

'Far too much.' Jo clutched his arm. 'When we get out of here, there's something I want to show you. It's in my room.'

~

Ten minutes later Guy was reading the creased note that Jo had retrieved from her shirt pocket.

'Do you know?' she asked him. 'Did Vallon fall, or collide with anyone?'

'He didn't fall at any time—until today.'

Jo took the note back and stared at it. 'Then where did he get the cut under his eye? He was creating trouble in the team, never mind what their press release says.'

Guy sank onto one of the blue-cushioned chairs. 'Serious enough for someone to tamper with his brakes? I can't believe it.'

Jo sat down and laid the note on the small table between them. 'Would anyone have an opportunity to do such a thing?'

'Not on *my* team. Our bikes are locked in the van every night, for security reasons. AFA must do the same. We all do it.'

Jo bit her lip. 'Hachette's 'source' whispered a rumour and Jones knew about it. Now Hachette will write *Harvey Jones denied the rumour that...*and nobody will look at the word *denied*. They'll all fix on the rumour. I don't know how Hachette gets away with it.'

Guy smiled. 'I believe the paper employs a lawyer to edit his copy so that it's not actionable.'

Jo scoffed. 'Make a statement into a question and nobody can sue you, I know. I still think it stinks, the way he slips in the buzzwords. If he wrote *Guy Lacrosse, high on adrenalin (what else?) came in ahead of...*Wouldn't you sue him?'

'It's not libel.'

Jo banged a fist on the arm of her chair. 'Hachette puts thoughts into people's heads, and some of his pieces would choke you with acid fumes coming off the page. But there must have been something or somebody behind his question.' She picked up her crumpled note again. 'I saw Vallon's cut face and my instant thought was that someone had socked him in the eye, and I know that...'

'Someone like George Ferrer?' Guy interrupted.

Jo didn't ask why he'd mentioned George. The Tour was a village on the move, and no village is without gossip. The boys' crude remarks were just another form of gossip.

Guy was looking horrified. 'Surely you don't think Ferrer would sabotage Vallon's bike?'

'No, not Ferrer! We don't *know* if George clouted him, although he had good reason to do so. A couple of times *I've* felt like smacking the arrogant young twerp, but George wouldn't go farther than that, because, as you've just proved, he'd be the obvious suspect. Even good-natured George might lash out in the heat of the moment, but sabotage is cold-blooded.' She leaned forward, emphasising her next words. 'Sabotage would need careful planning and George Ferrer is *not* the planning type. I wouldn't say he's feckless, but he's a scatterbrain. Do you know why he missed last year's World Championships? He forgot the date! And just think how he's squandered everything he's ever earned.' Guy nodded agreement with that, and she went on, 'Let's suppose Vallon's crash wasn't an accident. Somebody whispers 'Sabotage' in Hachette's pointed ears. At once everyone thinks of George Ferrer, and nobody wonders who was the real culprit.'

Guy puffed out a long breath. 'Josephine, you frighten me. You really think Vallon's death was planned?'

'I hope I'm completely wrong but, between them, Hachette and Harvey Jones have made me suspicious.'

Guy said, 'Did you know he was married?'

'Who? *Vallon?* Good God! I didn't know.'

'It's been a well kept secret, but now it has come out. There's a six-month-old baby.'

Jo was aghast. 'His poor wife! This is tragic. When did you learn this?'

'After the managers' meeting. Koch had phoned her to break the sad news.'

'Poor girl,' Jo repeated. 'Do you know anything about her?'

'Chatter spreads like an oil slick. Some of my boys had heard about an Italian girl—Dino Nardini's cousin, apparently. They say Vallon and Nardini were great pals at the time, and Vallon met her when he spent a holiday at the Nardini family's seaside villa.'

'I hope Hachette won't find out about that,' said Jo. 'Muckraking is his mission in life. Nevertheless, the way Jones reacted to his question...Something's going on, and my reporter's nose is twitching. I intend to do some heavy thinking.'

She was already wondering who else had a grudge against Vallon. The common motives for murder, she'd read, were money, revenge, concealing a crime, sex...and she knew which of those seemed the most likely in Vallon's case. Paula Ferrer was one name on a long list.

Then she thought of a phrase she'd seen in a John Grisham book: *Cui bono?* Who stands to gain?

STAGE 16

(Non-competitive)

Jo Bonnard

Jo was awakened at 7.30 by the ringing of the bedside phone. Lifting the receiver she heard 'Ah, good morning, Jo. How are you? This is Harvey.'

'Who?'

'Harvey Jones…Anglo-French Airtrain.'

Since when had she been on first name terms with Jones? She said a cautious 'Good morning.'

'My dear Jo…'

This was getting worse. Smarmy little man; he was after something. 'What do you want?'

'A favour, Jo. You see, it's Claudia, Harry Vallon's wife. I mean widow. She's here and wants to speak to you.'

'To me? Why me?'

'She won't say why. Perhaps she knows you speak Italian, and she's in need of someone who speaks her own language.'

'She's more likely in need of sleep. Tell the doctor to give her a sedative.'

'She won't hear of it. She insists on speaking to you.'

'Oh, all right,' said Jo resignedly, thinking the poor girl might want a woman's sympathy.

'She's upset about Harry's accident, but the silly girl has asked for a complete post mortem.'

Jo's interest-level increased, but she hid the fact under a sigh. 'Well, give me twenty minutes. I'll meet her in the cafeteria—the one in this block.'

'Thanks, Jo. You're a trouper.'

Jo winced. 'What does she look like?'

'Long black hair. Very Italian. She's wearing a black dress.'

Jo groaned inwardly.

∼

Twenty minutes later, she was studying the girl across a table. Claudia had dark eyes in a fine-boned face, but her mouth was already bracketed with defined lines. The result of a year's marriage to Harry Vallon?

Her dress was black, true enough, but low-necked, sleeveless and chic. It was certainly not widow's weeds, and Claudia showed no sign of anguish.

The girl returned her appraisal and said with a slight smile, 'I am not as you expected?'

'Frankly, no.' Jo admitted. 'I thought I'd be facing a girl with a broken heart.'

Claudia's smile widened. 'I knew, from listening to your commentaries, that I would like you.' She gave a tiny shrug. 'It must be obvious that I...was briefly infatuated with Harry. I married him because I was pregnant, and my parents insisted their grandchild must not be born a bastard. My marriage was a big mistake.'

'Why keep it a secret, though?'

'It suited Harry's sex-symbol image. And I...I am a Sacchi, you understand.' Seeing Jo's lack of reaction, she explained: 'We are...a big business family. My mother was a Nardini, but she regards Dino as the family's black sheep. Another cyclist was scarcely acceptable as a son-in-law, so it suited the family to keep very quiet about it.'

Jo nodded noncommittally. None of that was as snobbish as some might think. Twenty years ago, her own father—a bus driver, not a business tycoon—had quarrelled with her, on account of her being 'far too friendly with that cyclist,' meaning Paul, and also because of her passion for this sport. Aloud, she said, 'What is it that people have against cycling?'

Claudia sighed. 'It's the doping scandals, stories of corruption, the input from the betting cartels. It's no worse than many other pro sports, but it gets the worst publicity because it has less money available to...ahm...keep its indiscretions out of the media.'

Jo could still love the athletic spectacle and the excitement although she knew about cycling's murky underside. Nobody, however, had ever tried to muzzle *her*. And yet...and yet...there had been mentions of football teams implicated in a doping scandal—stories that had never got off the ground. One sports paper's front page had carried a rather tentative paragraph on a Monday. On the Tuesday had come five lines of denial from the three football club managers. And that was the last that was heard of doping and football although, a couple of weeks later, cycling had earned two full pages of adverse publicity on account of an obscure *domestique* suspected of blood-doping.

She looked at Claudia with new respect. Of course, the girl's business background explained her awareness of the money involved. 'I heard you are Dino Nardini's cousin,' she said. 'Have you spoken to him?'

Angrily, Claudia tossed her long hair. 'He does not speak to me. It was Dino who introduced me to his friend Harry; but Dino stopped being friendly after my baby was born. He came to see me, merely glanced at the baby and stalked out. I don't understand him at all.'

A few days ago, Jo would have thought Dino's behaviour strange, but she had since glimpsed his dark side. 'That seems...unkind.'

Claudia uttered an expression that Jo had heard—but not from a nicely brought up young lady.

Heads were turning. Jo put her hand over Claudia's and beckoned to a waiter, asking for rolls and coffee to be sent up to her room. 'Come on. Let's talk where there's no audience.'

∼

In her room, Jo poured coffee while Claudia told her she'd gone to the hospital in La Portette where a police officer had shown her a photograph of the spot where Harry crashed.

'I hear you've asked for a post mortem,' said Jo. 'You don't believe he died of a broken neck?'

'Of course he died of a broken neck!' Claudia said explosively.

'But I want to know *why!*' She picked up a bread roll and began crumbling it. 'Mad!' she said. 'Mad, the way he went over that summit! I was watching him on TV and I could scarcely believe it when I saw Harry ahead of Dino. On a climb like that?' She shook her head, the long hair swinging round her face. 'It didn't make sense. Harry always rode with the peloton on mountain stages. He wasn't a great climber. He knew it. Everyone knew it. You certainly knew it.'

Jo hesitated only slightly before asking, 'What do you think the post mortem might show?'

Claudia gave her a cynical stare. 'The same as you think. Performance boosters.'

'The same as *I* think? How could you know what I think?'

'Harry asked me to record all his races—with English audio. So I use your channel, with your commentary. I knew you were surprised by his performance yesterday. Disbelieving, perhaps?'

Jo leaned back, sipping her coffee. This girl was nobody's fool.

Claudia produced a DVD box from the depth of her expensive-looking shoulder bag. 'This is what I want to discuss with you. It's my recording of yesterday's stage. I hoped we could listen to it together, but I see the room has only a TV. Could the hotel lend us a DVD player?'

Jo had a feeling that it was she who was being taken in charge. 'I'll ask. Meanwhile you should eat instead of creating crumbs. Or get some rest. Did you travel all night?'

'No; I was at our holiday flat at Port Bacarès. There's a branch of Sacchi in Perpignan. I phoned for one of the company cars to drive me to La Portette, and then to this hotel.'

Big business indeed, thought Jo as she made for the reception area to ask for a DVD player. Then an idea made her return to the cafeteria where she found her co-commentators. Dufaux waved an invitation to join them. Listening to their conversation, inevitably about the fatality, she realised they were unaware that Claudia had turned up. Jo decided to keep that information to herself. She waited for a chance to ask if any of them had a recording of yesterday's broadcast.

Round a mouthful of toast, Dufaux suggested she try Willem de Groot. The Belgian Fries had someone who recorded every stage for them. Jo thanked him and went out to consult the notice board in the foyer for the location of the Mr Chip team. She made her way across the central area to the identical café of Block 2 where she spotted Willem alone at a table and went to talk to him. By the time she got back to her room, the DVD player had been installed.

Claudia looked relieved to see her. 'Where have you been?'

Jo held up the borrowed disc. 'I got a loan of the French version. It'll be interesting to compare commentaries. Do you understand French?'

'Of course. But we will look at mine first.'

Jo disliked hearing replays of her own commentaries. In retrospect, they seemed to contain too much inane waffle, but she would try to eliminate the cringe factor and to listen objectively. According to Claudia, she had been "disbelieving" of Harry Vallon's triumph.

Claudia skipped the film forward until it showed the first climb. She pressed Play, and there was Jo's voice saying: '...*and only five points behind Nardini. The third man is Harry Vallon of AFA who's a possible contender for the Yellow Jersey, but not usually so good on climbs. He's putting in a remarkable performance today.*'

Claudia pressed the Pause button. 'There! Those are your first remarks. Shall I play that again?'

'Let me get my notebook. I'm so old-fashioned,' Jo smiled, 'I can actually take this down in shorthand. No need to faff about with recorders, and it'll save all the stopping and starting of the disc.'

They watched the recording, Jo's pencil scurrying across the pages, until Claudia pressed the Stop button and asked her to read her notes.

Keeping her voice flat, Jo read the relevant passages. '*In the front is Harry Vallon. Would you believe it? Vallon's romping up, almost sprinting ahead of Ribero...But look at Vallon. What an amazing performance from this man. He's going like a rocket. He's first over the line and...*'

'Harry couldn't accelerate uphill,' Claudia interrupted. 'You knew it. That's why you said it was amazing. Go on, Jo. I think there's one more remark.'

Jo found it. '*It's Harry Vallon of AFA who's gone down. What a shame. He was doing so amazingly well.*'

'Amazingly,' Claudia echoed. 'There were doubts in your mind.'

'It sounds as though there were,' Jo admitted. She stared at Claudia. What were they thinking of? Stage-winners, and ten others picked at random from the top twenty, had to give blood and urine samples for sophisticated new analyses. These were done in the mobile laboratory—three large vehicles that parked near every stage finish. This had foiled the dopers, or so it was said. At least, the rapid delivery of test results had radically increased the likelihood of their being detected. Aloud, she said: 'It would be like *asking* to be found out. Really stupid to take performance boosters.'

'Harry wouldn't do that.' Claudia's statement was definite.

Jo was at a loss. 'In that case, why ask for this post mortem?'

'I think he was given something without his knowledge. Harry would not, knowingly, have taken drugs.'

'Can you be so sure?'

'Yes. He was totally in love with himself and with his own body. He never touched wine or coffee or tea. He said they contained substances that damage the body. He wouldn't go near to where people were smoking. He fussed about the chemicals in shampoos and detergents. He was obsessed about what he called "contamination." I could even say paranoid.' The girl's voice became bitter. 'He would stand under the shower for ten minutes after making love to me. Nothing would have induced him to abuse his precious body with drugs. Nothing!'

Hearing the bitterness, Jo was fairly convinced. She knew that Harry Vallon had fancied himself, but not that he'd been so obsessive. 'What about money?'

Claudia scoffed. 'He was not short of money. By our marriage he had a right to mine.'

Jo now had to believe Claudia. *Had* Harry been given something? An image flashed across her memory. Claudia was looking at her expectantly, but she decided to let her thought simmer for a while. 'Shall we listen to Xavier Dufaux's commentary?'

They changed the discs, and again Jo took shorthand notes of

Dufaux's remarks. They were remarkably similar to her own. She read the relevant quotes.

'*Here come the three leaders, Ribero, Nardini and...It's Vallon! Incredible!...He surges ahead and is first over the summit. An incredible ride! And here comes Danny Breton, the son of Paul Breton who wore the Yellow Jersey in...*' Jo flipped to the next page. '*There's been a fall!...Number thirty-two...Harry Vallon. He crashed at kilometre ten of the descent. Already? An incredible speed...*'

Jo looked up at Claudia. 'Incredible. *Incroyable.* He used the word three times. Then he said: *Il a dû descendre comme un fou.*— He must have descended like a madman.'

'Which supports my belief,' said Claudia. 'Something made him mad. He hated to fall. A little graze on his perfect body would upset him for days. Harry did *not* take stupid risks. The post mortem may tell if he was given something.'

'Given something. You've said that twice.' Jo ejected the disc and replaced it in its box.

'What, when, how, and by whom?' Claudia gave an elaborate shrug. 'I have no idea. I think EPO is injected, but are there pills? Liquids? Something that could be added to food or drink?'

Again that image flickered in Jo's mind. She was wondering if she should mention it, but at that moment the phone rang. It was Harvey Jones.

'Hello again, Mr Jones,' Jo said clearly, giving Claudia a quick lift of the eyebrows as she listened.

Claudia rolled her eyes and shook her head vehemently, so Jo lied glibly that Claudia was there, but asleep. Jones spoke again and Jo winced as she replaced the phone. 'First he called me a trouper. Now I'm a brick. The man's a prat.'

'Prat? The man's a former masseur with no managerial skills,' Claudia said disdainfully. 'I looked into his c.v. before Harry signed his contract with AFA.'

There spoke the big business background, thought Jo.

'Harry had an offer from Chiali,' Claudia went on, 'on his friend Dino's suggestion, I believe. I advised Harry it was a better offer, but he chose AFA because Jones would take care of his precious body. Well, Jones may be a good masseur but he's an incompetent manager.'

'And what do you think of Enrico Fiarelli?'

'As a manager? He's smart. For years he's been working for Publichiali, Chiali's marketing company, so he has a keen nose for advertising opportunities. The team makes a lot of additional money, thanks to him.'

'And as a man?'

'He's a shit.'

Jo threw her head back and laughed. She liked Claudia and was beginning to regard her as a friend. She had no hesitation now in saying, 'When you suggested Harry had been given something, it triggered my memory. I want to look at your DVD again.'

As Claudia retrieved the box, her bag fell open on the table. For the first time, Jo noticed the designer label. Claudia must be one of *those* Sacchis! Seriously big business.

Slotting the disc into the player, Jo found the section she wanted, played it without sound, and then turned to see Claudia's reaction.

The girl's eyes were stretched wide. 'Could that have been it? But why would Dino do that? Because he doesn't like *me?*'

'I doubt that it had anything to do with you. Watch again, and pay attention to Dino's actions.' Jo re-played the short section. 'Well?'

'He took it from his pocket, but he didn't like it.'

'Precisely. If he didn't like it, why did he carry it in his pocket?' Jo ejected the disc and held it in her hand. 'Can I keep this for a while?'

'If you wish.'

'We're making guesses, so don't go around telling people about this. How much did you say to the AFA people?'

'I spoke only to Jones who said no-one had witnessed the accident. When I told him I'd asked for an autopsy, he said Harry had been one of those randomly blood-tested at seven that morning, his haematocrit level was normal, and I was therefore being 'silly.' At that, I realised there was no point discussing it with a man so dim. Eight hours later, that blood test proved *nothing!*'

Jo agreed with that. A lot can happen in eight hours.

Claudia checked her watch and stood to leave. 'I have to go to meet my father. He's flying in to Perpignan to make funeral arrangements, since Harry had no family. May I phone you when I know the result of the autopsy? I'm sure you'll want to hear it.'

88

'Damned right I do!'

They exchanged phone numbers and parted with sincere hopes to meet again

~

Eltsport had decided not to cover the annulled stage, but Jo kept to her schedule. At midday she drove to Bellerive where she took the opportunity to have her punctured tyre repaired. The *garagiste* told her he was busy, but he'd try to get around to the job in an hour or so. Jo sighed impatiently; but it was a sparkling day, and so she decided to walk beside the river that hurried busily through the town. Once free of the houses, the river soon lost its sense of urgency and slid, quietly shining, between grassy banks studded with yellow and pink wildflowers. Of course, Bellerive meant beautiful riverbank! Smiling and relaxed, Jo strolled back to collect the car and the tyre.

STAGE 17

Jo Bonnard

Next morning, Jo was preparing to leave her hotel when Claudia phoned from La Portette.

'I've just been to the hospital laboratory,' she said. 'They found dexamphetamine sulphate.'

Jo sank onto a chair. This was an amphetamine pep-up drug. She knew that the human body could naturally produce some of the hormone-based substances, but not amphetamines, which are therefore easy to detect. Why give him something so obvious? Yesterday's questions flooded her mind again. She recalled her own remark *asking to be found out*—and there was the answer. Amphetamines would make sure he'd fail the end-of-stage dope test. 'How many milligrams?' she asked Claudia.

'They only let me glance at report, with no time to note details; but they told me it was, quote, *a non-lethal quantity*. I guess they were talking in strictly medical terms.'

'I dare say,' said Jo dryly, thinking it had been a callous statement, given the circumstances.

Sounding worried, Claudia went on to say that the laboratory had informed the police who, in turn, had told her that possession of "prohibited substances" is a serious crime in France.

Claudia then said, 'The police inspector asked if I knew where Harry had obtained the drug. I told him exactly the same as I told you. Harry would never, knowingly, take amphetamines. I think the inspector believed me but he said he would have to investigate the matter, as supplying them is also a serious crime.' She paused. 'But it's the reporters I'm worried about.'

'What reporters?' Jo was alarmed.

'Only one, so far. Do you know Hachette?'

'My God! Is *he* there? I wonder who told *him* about the post mortem?'

'I saw him outside, talking to a man in a white coat—a laboratory technician, I guess.'

'Oh, ssshitt!' The implications flooded Jo's mind. She needed time to think. 'What do you intend to do now?'

'Go back to Port Bacarès, collect the baby and his nanny, and fly home to Milano. Why?'

'I'm glad to hear you're getting away from all this. Whatever you do, don't speak to Hachette. I'll be in touch.'

On her way out of the hotel, Jo found that the early editions of several newspapers had arrived in the foyer. Most carried reports of the fatality. *The Whistleblower,* a London tabloid that never reported cycling unless there was a "doping scandal," had conjured up an unlikely photograph of three girls huddled under an umbrella painted *We love Harry*. Never had Jo seen girls wearing sleeveless tops on a cold, wet mountainside. The caption was: *Girl fans wept tonight over the death of sex symbol Harry Vallon*. Under it was the text:

> *Manchester born Harry (29), the son of an English mother and French father, was the spirit as well as the star of the Anglo-French Airtrain cycling team. He made a name for himself here in amateur races before turning professional and going to live in France. Harry died yesterday when he crashed on a dangerous French road. His team manager Harvey Jones pooh-poohed the suggestion that Harry's bike had been tampered with. The tragedy underlines the organisers' lack of common sense in routing the race over minor roads where safety standards don't match those of the UK...*

Smiling faintly at the xenophobia, Jo closed the page and picked up

Aujourd'quoi, almost dreading what she might read in Hachette's column. Written after Koch's media conference, it lived up to her worst predictions.

> *Why did Harry Vallon's bicycle go out of control during to-day's stage? His team's manager Harvey Jones denied rumours that someone had tampered with it. 'The idea is preposter-ous,' Jones spluttered. 'No team member would interfere with another's bike.'*
>
> *Team captain George Ferrer was not available for a state-ment tonight. Neither was Ferrer's wife, model Paula di Luca, a close friend of Vallon.*

Jo shuddered. Word for word, it wasn't actionable; but the insinuations were all there.

Jo tossed both papers into a nearby bin and set off to drive the day's route. Her eyes registered undulating fields of vines, but her thoughts were not on the race. What would happen when word of the post mortem result got around? For sure, that vulture Hachette would dip his pen in a new pot of poison.

Who could have warned him about it? Claudia had talked only to Jones, who had been caught on the hop by that question about Vallon's bicycle, and thus couldn't be Hachette's informant. However, he might have made some unguarded remark to someone in the team—someone who might be Hachette's original 'source.'

Jo searched an imaginary card index of the AFA team.

Alex Hubbard—a decent man who'd be a better manager than Jones. Jacky Bernard—deeply religious and contentedly working his way up the ranks. Vauvier, Thierry, Duval, Johnson, Sims—good *domestiques,* unassuming boys. Nat Arnold—a disgruntled *domestique* who must realise he'd never be anything else. Might he bear an envious grudge of Vallon's fame? Jo put a mental question mark after his name.

And George Ferrer—bound to have been jealous of Vallon. Possibly gave him a smack in the eye, but surely didn't interfere with his bike. Even had he done so, he certainly wouldn't have men-tioned it to Hachette.

Owing to Hachette's insinuations, George Ferrer had been suspected of sabotage and might well have been suspended from The Tour. The post mortem had, in fact, cleared George's name. The sabotage rumour was rubbish. Vallon had crashed because he was hyped on amphetamines.

～

That afternoon Jo, her mind not wholly on the race, explained team tactics to her viewers.

Charreau made the first attack. He sped away from the front of the peloton, pedalling hard and fast with four of his team around him. If Charreau could gain a one-minute lead it would be enough to make him the virtual race leader.

A motocamera went alongside the Mr Chip team car where Willem de Groot was listening to Race Radio, holding a microphone and shouting instructions into the team's earphones. It wasn't hard to imagine the instructions. *Chase! Chase! Get after them!* Clustered round Martens, his team caught up to Charreau.

Then Jonkers and his La Carte team tried the same tactic. After that, Nardini and the Chialis mounted *their* attack. They were all trying to wear down the man in the Yellow Jersey, forcing him to chase after every breakaway group. If the three teams had worked together, Jo thought briefly, they'd have had a better chance of success. But of course they hadn't cooperated. Each of them had a potential victor, and so there had been no combined effort.

The Yellow Jersey was under constant pressure, both mental and physical. Jo had phoned Mr Chip's Public Relations man, asking about Marc's bout of stomach trouble. The doctor's reckoning, said the PR man, was that Marc was allergic to something he had eaten.

There were ten kilometres to go when the slight accident occurred. In the centre of the tightly packed peloton, wheels or handlebars touched and two riders fell. A dozen others piled on top of them, and for a couple of minutes the road was a chaotic tangle of bikes and riders. Moto 2 halted to film the scene as riders picked themselves up. The luckier ones rode off again with nothing worse than bleeding knees and elbows. Some damaged bikes were rapidly exchanged for those atop the team cars. But, entangled with their bikes in the heart of the confusion, four riders lay on the road—Jan

Claes, Chico Montes, Danny Breton and Tom Dash whose crash helmet had come off.

Chico got up, checked his bike and sped away. The camera zoomed in on Danny, laughing as he helped Claes to his feet and picked up Dash's helmet. As Claes rode off he gave Danny a friendly pat on the back, but Dash, his ginger hair in spikes, muttered something over his shoulder and shot away in apparent fury. Danny stood with a surprised look on his face, shrugged and set off again with Dash's helmet tucked into his jersey.

Jo commented that Dash would surely be penalised for riding without a crash helmet. 'But quite frankly,' she added, 'if I were Danny Breton, I wouldn't bother.'

She had trouble keeping satisfaction out of her voice when Claes out-sprinted Dash to the finishing line.

She was less satisfied when she discovered that her allocated hotel was an hour's drive farther on. She set off through crawling traffic, and had barely checked in when Guy Lacrosse rang her mobile phone, sounding worried and asking if she'd seen the TV news.

'No. I just got here. Why? What's the matter?'

'Big trouble. Vallon was on amphetamines.'

'He was *not*. I know about the autopsy and the result, but…'

Guy interrupted. 'How do you know?'

'From Vallon's wife, Claudia. She convinced me he wasn't "on" anything.'

'And you believe her?'

'Yes, absolutely. What's more, I'm damned sure Hachette's responsible for the media getting on to this so quickly.'

'Hachette!' Guy sounded considerably startled. 'In that case, he…I don't suppose you've seen the evening paper?'

'No. Nor am I likely to. I'm in a rather grotty *Pension*, not really a hotel. I doubt if any papers will be delivered here.'

'I'll read this to you, then. Front page, by the way. *Today the Minister of Sport, backed by the International Federation of Professional Cycling Organisations, ordered an urgent police investigation into drug taking, the probable cause of the fatality in the current Tour. Dr Rolf Niemann, spokesman for the IFPCO, said: 'We are extremely disappointed. A problem we thought resolved, has arisen again. We must take a firm stand. All riders will undergo blood tests before the race may proceed.' The Minister has also asked police to initiate a search for drugs on the Tour....A* shocker, isn't it?'

'Indeed it is.' Jo's depression had increased with every word. Now the rumour machine would go into full production. 'What's the reaction from the teams?'

'Fairly rebellious. I can't blame them. But some hotheads are talking about a strike and Koch's trying to defuse things. There's a meeting in half an hour.'

'Well, thanks for the info,' she said. 'There will be more in the morning papers, no doubt. Will there be a chance to see you tomorrow?'

'I guess not. Soon as this stage is over, we travel by train to Colmar and Hotel Starlight II. We arrive in the small hours, so we'll have a day and a night's luxury before the Time Trial. After that, we all move on to other hotels near the Stage Twenty start. Are you driving up to Colmar?'

'Unfortunately, yes,' she sighed. 'But I'll see you there, all being well.'

STAGE 17

Evening

Danny Breton

In the milling around at the end of the stage, Danny Breton had been unable to find Tom Dash. He handed his bike over to the mechanics and located the Intapost bus that would take the team to the Hotel President. By that time, the Chiali bus had gone—also to the Hotel President, he was told.

In the hotel, he went through the routine of shower, massage and supper, and then returned to his room. Tom's green helmet lay on the bureau next to his own. Helmets were costly items. Better take it to him right away. Hopefully he'd got over his burst of petulance by now. Danny couldn't understand Dash's attitude. Minor crashes happened all the time. In fact, Tom Dash had caused many of them; but when it happened to *him,* he threw a tantrum. Of course, Dash was fiercely competitive and this was the world's top cycle race but, all the same, why make such a dramatic fuss over a little crash?

The Chiali team had rooms one floor down. Danny ran down the flight of stairs and consulted a rooming list pinned on the wall. Dash was in a single, number 207. Danny found the room, rapped on the door and walked in.

Tom Dash

Tom Dash shook the translucent cylinder that had once contained a roll of photographic film. He'd thought eight capsules would fill it, but there was only about a centimetre of powder in the bottom of it. He slid the other sheet of bubble-foil from the box, popped the capsules and laid them on the window ledge. They were two-part gels and this was the tricky bit. He had to hold them over the film container, slide the green part free of the white, and let the powder fall into the little cylinder.

That done, he held it up to the light. There still wasn't much in it but he'd used up all the capsules, which was the main thing.

He scooped the thirty-two gel halves into his hand and carried them to the bathroom, intending to flush them down the lavatory. Just in time, he realised they would float. How to get rid of them?

He thought it out. The capsules were meant to be swallowed whole, and the gels would melt inside the body. So, melt them, then. Where? In the hand basin, dummy!

He ran the hot tap, filled the basin, watched the rigid gelatine dissolve, then pulled out the plug. Easy! Now, what about the empty foil packs? Better put them back in the box and tell the *soigneur* to get rid of it; burn it or something.

His case lay open on the bed. He was replacing the empty foils in the box when there was a brief knock on the door and Danny Breton strolled in. Dash slammed the case shut, but not quickly enough. Danny's face told him he'd seen the brand-named box.

But Danny just said, 'I brought your helmet,' speaking in English with a la-di-dah accent he must have learned in some school for rich brats.

Dash grabbed the helmet from his hand. 'Thanks for nothing! What's a goddamn helmet to anybody? Tell me what the hell you're really here for.' He was suddenly suspicious. 'Somebody told ya?'

'I came to return your helmet.'

'Yeah? And now what? You're gonna run blabbing to the Director?'

Danny made an exasperated sound. 'We all know the regulations. We all signed the rulebook. If I don't report this I'll be in trouble, too. But I don't want to get you expelled from the Tour, so I'll give you a chance to get rid of that stuff.'

Dash backed slowly to the window ledge and felt around behind him. His hand closed over the little cylinder of powder. Casually, he put his closed fist in his pocket. But not casually enough. Danny fucking Breton had seen the move.

Danny shook his head sadly, like he'd caught a kid stealing candies or something. 'Get rid of that too,' he said, 'and I won't say anything.'

Dash sneered, hating the sound of Danny's fancy accent, hating himself for drawing attention to what was in his pocket, hating himself for forgetting to lock the fucking door!

'Huh! Think I'm gonna trust ya?'

'I'll give you my word,' said Danny, 'if you give me yours.'

'Eh'll give you may waahd,' Dash drawled, mimicking the upper-crust accent. 'I say, old chap, Boy Scouts honour and all that.'

Danny nodded, staying cool. 'Something like that. You know what you're risking. You know you've got to throw that stuff away.'

'And suppose I don't?'

'Then you'd be a fool. Tell me this time tomorrow that you've destroyed it.'

'Like a good chap, what?' He was laughing at Breton, and the stupid sonofabitch didn't even know it.

'Yes. Will you do that? Okay?'

Like hell he would!

Careful not to smile, Dash said, 'Okay. I'll see ya tomorrow.'

And that soft bastard Danny Breton had better watch out.

STAGE 18

Jo Bonnard

In the morning Jo read the sports pages of several papers. Most column space was devoted to The Tour. *Dope* and *Scandal* figured largely, and all had a distinct whiff of Hachette.

Guy Lacrosse had sent a text message: *Vampires arrived 05.30. Test all riders. Police search luggage. AFA 1ˢᵗ. Nobody leaves til all bags OKd. Warn you delayed start. Guy.*

She set off and, as always, mentally cycled today's route. It was new to The Tour. A succession of rolling hills and S-bends would mean constant changes of pace. The cyclists would call it a 'leg-breaker.'

She was taken almost unawares when the terrain changed. A gentle gradient reached a crest, and then the road dropped abruptly. A series of swooping bends led down to a river spanned by a stone bridge with huge boat-shaped piers. She recalled from her pre-Tour research that this was a famous Roman bridge, built just wide enough for four horsemen to ride abreast. It certainly had no manoeuvring space for a densely packed peloton of cyclists.

Braking cautiously out of the last curve, she drove under a sprint banner. These banners warned that an Intermediate Sprint finish came one thousand metres from this spot. This was today's last sprint and Jo thought its location was extremely dangerous. Unless they got away on the downhill run, the sprinters wouldn't have much chance to get to the front of the pack, because the bridge was only about eight hundred metres beyond the banner. The last two hundred metres of every sprint were ridden at dangerously high speed and, today, those two hundred metres would include that narrow bridge!

At the moment the bridge was thronged with pedestrians. Her speed reduced to a crawl, Jo took a quick glance over the alarmingly low parapet. Over the course of almost two thousand years, men had laid new surfaces one atop the other, thus raising the road level. But they hadn't raised the height of the parapet, and so the ancient stone wall was only thigh-high to the photo freaks leaning over it, clicking away with their high-tech phones and mini-cams, taking shots of the fast flowing river.

A hundred metres beyond the bridge was the sprint finish line and, almost immediately, Jo's car was bumping over cobblestones on a sharp climb. This was the nasty final ascent, and it would torture aching legs. It wound between the houses, spiralling up three kilometres to a town square, a medieval church and all the end-of-stage trappings.

What a stinker of a finish! The climbers would have to stay close behind the sprinters; otherwise they'd have no chance to cut through a tightly packed bunch of riders. In the narrow streets of bone-jarring cobbles, it would be no place for the faint-hearted.

She was told where to park and then found the press tent. It was swarming like a disturbed hive. Many of the reporters sat at computer terminals, clicking through The Tour's website. A dozen people were speaking urgently into mobile phones. On a table a number of newspapers lay scattered. Jo pushed through the mob to look at the headlines.

Dopage: Encore des Scandales was one of the less sensational. *The Whistleblower* had: *Harry Vallon—Drugs Death.*

'So-called investigative journalism,' said Xavier Dufaux's voice behind her.

'Muck-stirring. How are we going to handle this, assuming the stage eventually goes ahead?'

'I don't see how we can dodge it, but I'm not going to talk about rumours. Only facts, provided we can get them. Not a chirrup out of Race Radio yet.'

'Let's take a look at the website,' she suggested.

They went to stand in front of a screen. Evidently the Director was still making his appeal to reason. The latest update read:

> *Walter Koch warned of possible lawsuits should the threatened strike go ahead. He told assembled riders: 'If we have nothing to hide, we have nothing to fear. The police have a job to do and I cannot, nor do I wish to, interfere with the law.' He assured the teams of his entire sympathy with their frustration and said he would do all in his power to minimise the disruption.*

Jo phoned Tony to ask for contingency plans.

Bob Rothman

Bob Rothman got to his feet as Willem de Groot came in to the hotel room followed by two policemen. Bob's room-mate, Marc Martens, kept his head bent over his motor sport magazine.

Bob addressed Willem. 'They've sure taken their time. We've been waiting for this damn-fool inspection since before breakfast.'

'I know. Let them get on with it now,' said Willem, tight lipped.

The policemen frowned, not understanding the exchange. 'Do you speak French?' the older one asked.

'*Oui.* A little.' Bob held a thumb and finger millimetres apart, then he waved his hand in a be-my-guest gesture over the neatly folded contents of the bag that lay open on the bed.

The officer wriggled his fingers into fine rubber gloves and emptied the bag item by item before turning his attention to the zipped side compartment. Bob watched impassively as the man flipped open his toilet bag, took out his razor, toothbrush and comb, and laid them on the bed. A small cylindrical container rolled out of the bag. Lifting it by its lid and base, the officer held it up to the light and shook it. Everyone could see it held some kind of powder.

'*Qu'est-ce que c'est?*'

Bob frowned, reached for the container and examined it. 'Damned if I know,' he said mystified, and then remembered to speak French. '*Je ne sais pas.*' There was no label, nothing to indicate its contents. 'I've never seen it until this moment.'

Marc tapped him on the arm and said in English, 'You shouldn't have touched that. Your fingerprints are on it now.'

The senior man regarded Marc with narrowed eyes and asked him to repeat that, but in French.

Marc, typically belligerent, switched to French and said accusingly to the policeman, 'You let him handle that. His fingerprints weren't on it before, but they're on it now.'

'How can you know he didn't handle it earlier?'

'He says he's never seen it, so he's never seen it. He's been my team captain for two years. I know him. He's not a liar.'

Bob got the gist and murmured, 'Thanks, Marc.' He turned back to the officer. 'Look, this isn't...Sorry. *Pardon.*' He struggled to explain, in halting, American-accented French, that it was not his. He had no idea it was there. It was not there this morning when he...ah...made?...his bag.

The officers held a murmured exchange, and then the senior one asked Bob if he had left the bag unattended at any time.

Marc translated, and Bob said he had—but only while they went for breakfast.

Had he left the room open?

Bob nodded, then he appealed in English to Marc. 'How do you say *lock?*'

Marc helped him out, saying in French: 'We never lock our room. We might not come back at the same time.'

The officer addressed Marc, the French-speaker. 'Today, which of you was the first to return?'

'We came back together.'

The officer laid down the cylinder before moving to the other bed where he systematically emptied Marc's case but found nothing out of the ordinary.

Picking up the little container again, he placed it carefully in a brown envelope produced by his assistant. He closed the envelope, wrote the date, place and time on it, then both officers signed across the self-seal flap.

'I'm taking this substance for analysis.' The older man beckoned to Rothman. 'You come with us to await results.'

Marc translated, and Bob turned to de Groot. 'That could take hours! I've never seen the damn thing in my life. I don't know what the hell's in it and I didn't...' He stopped abruptly, looking thunderstruck. 'Holy shit! Do you suppose somebody planted it while we were down at breakfast?'

'That idea did strike me. I think maybe it struck the police officer, too,' said de Groot. 'Obviously I believe you, Bob; but you've really no choice at the moment. Go with them and wait while they analyse whatever it is. Meanwhile I'll talk to Koch. I'll come to the police HQ as soon as I can. Marc, you stay here. Don't leave this room until I send for you.'

Still protesting, Bob Rothman left between the two policemen.

Exiting from the hotel, they walked into a dazzle of photographic flashes. The police vehicles had attracted a swarm of pressmen.

～

It was some time before Willem de Groot returned to Marc with bad news. 'They're holding Bob. We can't do a thing about it. Take the bags to the minibus. Sign on in The Village and get your bike.'

'We're starting?' Marc was aghast. 'Without The Old Man? We can't do that!'

'You're starting and you're riding. That's what you're here for.' Willem was in no mood for one of Marc's arguments. 'The decision was made at this morning's meeting. Whatever the delay, The Tour continues. Move yourself. The others are waiting for you.'

As the Mr Chip team walked down the hotel steps, a mob of reporters shouted questions and brandished microphones on long stalks.

Pushing through them, Marc found Jan Claes beside him muttering: 'What the hell's happened?'

'They're questioning The Old Man. They found something in his bag.'

'Christ! What? You don't believe...?'

'Of course not, you asshole! But he was dumb enough to handle it, so his fingerprints are on it.'

Behind them, de Groot snapped, 'Get on the bus, boys, and *shut up!* These pressmen have long ears.'

The stage had eventually started, two hours behind scheduled time. Tony Johnas had called back with Eltsport's decision to record only the last 25 kilometres for a programme that would be broadcast late in the evening. Jo and her Eltsport colleagues had gone off for a quick lunch, and were now back in the press tent, listening to Race Radio.

'*Riders were subjected to a compulsory blood test early this morning,*' said the impersonal voice. '*Three riders are not starting today. Numbers sixty-six and one hundred and thirty-seven were found to have haematocrit levels above the limit. The third non-starter is number fifty-one. He is assisting the police, pending analysis of a substance found in his luggage.*'

Jo gasped as though she had been slapped. Number fifty-one was Bob Rothman! She didn't want to believe this. Rothman was, and had always been, one of the most respected riders.

Dufaux was equally disbelieving. 'Bob Rothman found with a *substance?* This is like...like being told your mother's a hooker!' Then, after a moment's thought: 'What kind of substance? They haven't done the analysis yet. It could be aspirins, for all anyone knows.'

Jo sighed with a feeling of helplessness. 'Hachette's going to love this. But what are *we* going to say about it?'

'We explain that "high haematocrit level" means the red blood-cell count is above fifty percent, making intense physical effort a danger to health. We can also explain that the cause may be simple dehydration and nothing sinister need be read into the exclusions.'

Biagi said with mild sarcasm: 'Thank you, Doctor Dufaux. And what do you suggest we say about Rothman's arrest?'

'Don't use that word. Simply quote Race Radio.'

'And for heavens sake put a lid on the shock-horror-scandal stuff,' Jo added. 'We may get some more information in the next few hours.'

It was, however, only one hour before the information came through. The substance found in Rothman's possession was dex-amphetamine sulphate. Rothman had strongly protested his innocence, but was still "assisting the police with their enquiries." The Eltsport group exchanged horrified looks.

A hush had fallen on the press tent. Looking around, Jo caught sight of an old colleague, David Duffield, guest commentator for a rival channel. He was leaning back in his chair, looking dejected. He must have felt her gaze, because he looked up at her and shook his head slowly and sadly.

Then Biagi, their bald and overweight Italian colleague, growled, in a voice that carried: 'If Rothman's guilty, I'm a podium girl.'

Nobody felt like laughing, although some smiles eased the tension. But Biagi had struck a chord. There were nods and murmurs of agreement.

Tony Johnas

In the studio in Luxembourg, Tony Johnas watched the bank of screens. Top left was the input from the static camera at the stage finish. A pretty town square, bright with flowers and fluttering bunting, was otherwise a scene of bored inactivity. Policemen strolled across the shot, marshals stood around idly, spectators leaned on the barriers.

Tony flipped a switch. 'Jo, stand by. I'll start recording in sixty seconds as of...now.' And above the screens, the light started flashing.

He selected the Moto 2 picture and waited. The light blinked off at the instant Jo began her commentary, apologies and reasons nicely prepared.

The riders were in a compact bunch, from which Tony judged that they were simply slogging along, with nobody prepared to start racing yet. At a guess, they were fed up because of the delayed start. He was fairly sure the route-planners had expected them to be strung out in small groups by this time. The Route Book specifically mentioned a dangerous winding descent to a narrow bridge. Nobody had foreseen a peloton of a hundred and fifty-odd riders crossing it *en masse*. Having lost just over thirty since the start, this Tour had a high survival rate.

Tony was quite startled when Jo's commentary repeated his thought about survivors.

'...a hundred and fifty-five left in the race. The Tour always takes its toll with crashes, and even ultra-fit men like these can get sick, just like normal mortals. In fact, they suffer worse than we do. One year, a rider got a wasp sting that closed his right eye. To reduce the swelling he needed cortisone, which is a prohibited substance, so he had to give up all his chances and go home.'

Tony noticed that, this time, Jo didn't voice her opinion on the ruling.

He changed to a helicopter shot—a moving mosaic of colours crossing the landscape.

Jo sounded worried. 'No team seems to have got itself organised. The team colours are scattered haphazardly, as you can see. If I were a *directeur sportif*, I'd be into my team's earphones loud and strong, telling them to get their act together. In just a few more kilometres, they'll come to a descent with a number of tight bends. It'll be chaos if they go down in a bunch.

'Aha! Somebody must have read my thoughts. On the right-hand side of the pack, three of the bright greens of Chiali are weaving their way through to the front, along with two Intapost riders in the red-and-white jerseys—Chico Montes, I think, judging by his style of riding, with David Vauban. It's not easy to spot individuals from this height.'

Just then, the helicopter descended and hovered above the group.

'I'm sure he can't hear me,' Jo laughed, 'but thank you, pilot! I can now identify Chiali's group as their sprinters—Bruno, Salvatore and, of course, Dash. But they're bunched, rather than in their famous green line. And with them are three more Intapost riders—Gregory, the American, followed by the Viking sprinter Nilsson, and Danny Breton.

'Nilsson's the only true sprinter of the Intapost team. I guess that David, Chico and Danny, good climbers, have been sent ahead with Gregory to give Nilsson more protection. Also, the three of them may fancy their chances on the final climb.

'Now, on the extreme left of your picture you can see that the road seems to vanish. That's where it makes a dramatic plunge down to the valley and across a river.'

The chopper swung round to film a heat-hazed view of a medieval hill-town, its stubby church tower thrusting up from amongst the clay-tiled roofs of the houses.

'That's where they're making for. Once across the river, the road winds up and around that hill, like a snail shell. Cobblestones all the way. It's a narrow, steep, three-kilometre climb—a nasty finish.'

Tony fed in a commercial break and, while the adverts were running, Jo informed him of the instructions from Race Radio: 'Moto 1 is to go ahead. No motocameras alongside the riders from now on. Team cars already ahead, stay ahead. All other cars remain behind the last riders.'

Tony would have only three pictures to juggle with—Moto 1, the chopper, and the static camera on the finish line. 'Thanks, Jo. Ending commercials in five seconds.'

The helicopter had a good shot of the peloton streaming down the bends towards the river.

Jo's commentary continued: 'To add to the thrill, the organisers decided to put a sprint very close to the finish, and that sprint includes a narrow bridge. Marc Martens plus three of his Mr Chip team are trying to get to the front. Chiali and Intapost are also making a determined effort to be first at the bridge. It's essential for the big hitters to get away from the pack here.

'This shot is from Moto 1, crossing the river ahead of the riders. You can see for yourselves that there simply isn't room on that bridge for more than four or five riders elbow to elbow. A crowd has gathered at the banner marking the end of the sprint. No room for spectators on the bridge itself, of course.'

Tony switched again to the shot from the helicopter. It was flying low, camera on full zoom. A fabulous picture!

Jo's voice said: 'Here come the leading riders, jostling for position. In the front line are Gregory and Nilsson of Intapost, Bruno of Chiali in the centre, then Intapost's David Vauban, and Jan Claes of Mr Chip.

'Right behind them are Danny Breton, nearest the upstream parapet, with Chiali's Tom Dash alongside him. Next to Dash is his team-mate Salvatore. Chico Montes and Cedric Charreau have also squeezed into that second line.

'They're on the bridge now. Dash tries to jink, but can't get around Nilsson. Now Dash shoves his elbow into Danny Breton! And now he's leaning on him...Oh, *no!*'

Tony winced as Jo's voice rose to a near scream.

'Oh my God! Did you see that? He forced Danny over the wall!'

Tony experienced a producer's nightmare. Stay with the drama of the figure plummeting off the bridge, or...? The race comes first. Tony switched to the Moto 1 shot of Dash crossing the sprint line just ahead of Nilsson; but Jo's voice continued, high pitched in outrage.

'That was deliberate! Danny Breton was scraping the wall and Dash just shouldered him over.'

Tony broke in. 'Cool it, Jo. The race. We'll replay the incident later.'

'We'll replay the incident later,' she repeated tonelessly. Then, in fury, 'Incident? That amounted to assault! Dash the Crash has overdone it this time. I've never seen such a blatant...'

'Jo!' Tony's voice was peremptory. 'The race!'

Jo's angry expulsion of breath was audible. 'They've started on the final hill. Climbers are trying to make their way between the sprint specialists. Ribero's made it to the front. The former mountain bike champion is used to the rough and tumble. And talking about tumble, Danny Breton took a twelve-metre drop into the river. I just hope that...'

'Jo!'

'Now Nardini's making his way up, standing on the pedals but at least not using his elbows, like his team-mate Dash. Behind Nardini is Martens, pushing a bigger gear, relying on the strength of his legs.

'One kilometre to go and Ribero's still in front, but Nardini's closing on him. Come on, Ribero! Don't look back!...The gap's narrowing. Five hundred metres and there are just those three, dripping sweat and fighting for the stage victory.

'Neck and neck now. Two hundred metres...And Ribero's fuse has blown. All the power just went from his legs...And so Nardini takes the stage, Martens second. Ribero crosses the line now, rocking on the handlebars.'

Tony said, 'Feeding-in the helicopter shots.' His voice clipped, he added, 'And cool the emotion, Jo.'

He fed in the stored film in slow motion. His mouth tightened in anger as he listened to Jo Bonnard. Making no attempt to disguise her feelings, she talked through the tense episode.

'This is where Dash tries to pass Nilsson, but they're all too tightly packed. He won't shove his team-mate Salvatore aside, so he uses his elbow, pushing Breton against the wall. Danny Breton takes his foot off the pedal, trying to regain his balance. Now Dash leans on him. It's deliberate! Just look at the angle of his bike! That wall's only thigh high, and Danny goes over.

'There's the splash as he hits the water...His head breaks the surface, but the current sweeps him under the bridge. Oh, there's a safety boat! Thank God for that! Did someone foresee a possible accident? *Accident?* That was no accident!

'We can see the boat crew leaning over. Looks like two divers in the water...lifting Danny aboard...speeding the few metres to the shore. Pray to God he's not seriously injured. I've seen some foul riding in my time, but that was the most bloody-minded action I've ever...'

Damn the woman! Tony decided he'd have to scrub the commentary and do a voice-over for the evening broadcast. He killed Jo's microphone switch and plugged-in to the commentaries going out live to France and Italy.

'...very dangerous,' Dufaux was saying. 'I'm astonished there weren't safety nets rigged along that bridge.'

Biagi's excited Italian had a bias towards the Chiali rider. 'Dash clearly had the speed to go ahead, but was boxed-in. There wasn't enough space on the bridge.'

Tony switched over to the static camera that had swung round to film the rostrum. Nardini held his stage-winner's bouquet aloft before tossing it into the crowd, where it was caught by one of the *I Love Dino* girls, wearing a very tight version of the T-shirt and an ecstatic expression.

Martens came up for the Yellow Jersey, his face inscrutable.

Then the results board displayed a score table, showing that Dash had won maximum points for all three sprints of the day. The board flickered, went blank, then lit again. Nilsson had been awarded the third sprint. Opposite Dash's name was DQ: *Disqualified*. Jo was unaware that her bitter satisfaction was not being recorded.

The commentators closed the systems and Tony, coldly angry, got back to Jo on her mobile phone. 'That was not good. I can't use it. You overstepped the company policy on biased, personal opinions.'

'I told the truth!' she all but yelled at him. 'I'm damned if I'll pussy-foot around that hooligan Dash. Danny Breton may be seriously injured, and you *saw* that dangerous little bastard push him deliberately. Are you going to fire me for saying so?'

Tony took it seriously. 'That decision isn't up to me; but...'

'Tony, I'm fed up with political correctness.' She clicked off the connection.

STAGE 18

Evening

Jo Bonnard

Race Radio had gone off air. Jo removed her earphones and sat back feeling drained. No news about Danny, but she wouldn't phone Guy Lacrosse. He'd have more than enough to contend with.

She went back to her car, manoeuvred through a congested mass of vehicles, and drove to her next hotel, some distance away. As soon as she reached her room, she activated her laptop and got onto The Tour's website. Nothing on Danny yet, but its last page had an update on Rothman.

> *A police spokesman said there was some doubt about how the drug came to be in Rothman's luggage. Fingerprint examination showed that the container had been handled by the police officer wearing rubber gloves, and by Rothman; but that there were underlying prints belonging to a third person yet to be identified.*

Jo was prepared to bet the amphetamine had been planted by the "third person." Not likely, however, that they'd fingerprint everybody on The Tour, unless Rothman had a hotshot lawyer. But what was going on? The post mortem showed that Vallon had taken amphetamine, but Claudia insisted that Harry wouldn't touch drugs.

Therefore someone had fed them to him. Jo had her suspicions about who had fed them, and how it had been done. Now it seemed probable that somebody had slipped the same drug into Bob Rothman's luggage. The same person? If not, who? And furthermore, why?

Her mobile phone rang. It was Guy Lacrosse. 'Thought I should tell you, Jo. Danny's okay.'

'Oh, thank God.' To her astonishment she burst into tears.

'I knew you'd be worried. They helicoptered him to the University Hospital in Toulouse. He has a broken tibia—shinbone. He hit underwater rocks. If he'd gone in head first, I hate to think of what might have happened.'

'I know. My God, I can't get that picture out of my mind. Had it not been for the safety boat...' She got her tears under control. 'You know that Dash deliberately pushed him?'

'Are you sure? It happened very quickly.'

'Very sure. I saw the chopper shot in slow motion. You should make an official complaint because the *Commissaire* saw it and disqualified Dash from that sprint.'

'Did he indeed? In that case I'll get onto it. Danny was my priority, so I let the *soigneurs* deal with the stage finish. Now listen, Jo; I phoned Paul from the hospital. He's flying in from Paris tonight.'

'I'll meet him,' she said at once.

'The flight gets in to Toulouse at eleven-thirty.'

'That's no problem. Will the hospital let us in if we go straight there?'

'No. I checked. Nine in the morning's the earliest.'

'Still no problem. I'll bring Paul back here. This hotel's not far from the airport.'

'Thanks, Jo. I'm at the station, about to board the train. Hell! The train's leaving! *Au revoir!*'

～

Eltsport's edited coverage of the stage went out at ten in the evening and Jo moodily watched it in her hotel room. True to his word, Tony had wiped her commentary and replaced it with a bland voice-over, talking about the "unfortunate accident." '*With all the jostling, Breton couldn't keep his balance*' he'd said while running the shot from the helicopter. It was not, however, the slow motion version, and everything happened too quickly for the casual viewer to appreciate that the "jostling" was deliberate. At least the *Commissaire's* vehicle had been close enough to see it.

Worried about Danny, Jo found the hospital's phone number, only to be told that information on patients was given only to spouses, adult children or parents. Damn it! So much for her claim to be his Aunt Josephine. It was scarcely a lie. After all, that was what Danny had called her in his childhood.

It was only a quarter to eleven but she found herself pacing the room and decided to drive out to the airport. She needed time to find a parking space and locate the arrivals gate, didn't she?

It took her all of fifteen minutes to accomplish that. She was thirty minutes early, and when she checked the arrivals board she saw that the Paris plane was not now due until 23.35. Damn! Thirty-*five* minutes to wait. She should have brought something to read. The news-stand had no evening papers

Why was she fretting over a five-minute delay? Paul didn't even know she was meeting him.

She sat thinking about Danny and willing the clock forward until, at last, the board flickered. *Paris—Landed.* Now the luggage would be unloaded and driven to the conveyor. The passengers would have to wait at the carousel for ten minutes or more, but nevertheless she walked over to join the dozen meeters-and-greeters at the gate. They were all doing the same as she was—standing on tiptoe, craning their necks. Maybe all airports were infected with some kind of anxiety virus.

Finally, here was Paul. He was carrying a small attaché case and his old sports bag was slung over his shoulder, the way he'd always carried it. In jeans and a pale blue polo shirt, he looked fit, tanned and lean; no visible grey in the dark hair that still fell over his forehead in that unruly wave. Was it her imagination, or had his limp improved? It was much less noticeable than she remembered.

He'd seen her. A look of surprise crossed his face, followed by a frown.

Oh, hell! He must think she was here with bad news!

He was scarcely out of the gate before she ran to throw her arms round him, babbling: 'Danny's okay. He's going to be fine. He's all right.'

'Hey, take it easy.' Paul put his luggage down, freeing both arms to hold her, patting her gently on her back, as though *she* were the one needing comfort. And no wonder! She was crying all over his shirt. Above her head, she heard him ask: 'What are you doing here?'

'I came to meet you. I knew you'd be worried and I came to reassure you...'

'You came to meet me, so late at night? *Ma chère Jo.*' He hugged her again.

'It's the very least I could do. I thought of you worrying all the way from Paris. I thought you'd need someone...someone to talk to.' Sniffing, she let go of him and took a step back. 'Oh, Paul, what a welcome! Dripping tears all over you. I'm sorry. It's just been such a *hell* of a day. When Danny went over that bridge...God! I thought he was...I keep seeing it over and over, like a video loop. Did you see it?'

'Yes, on France 2, on a set in the office. I got a fright. Then Guy phoned to say Danny wasn't so badly hurt as had been feared, thank God; then he phoned again from the hospital. What's the latest?'

'All I know is what Guy told me. Danny *is* going to be fine, but I've got the phone number of the hospital. They'll talk to *you*, his parent. They wouldn't give information to his *Tante Joséphine.*'

Paul was uncomprehending for only a moment. 'You tried already?'

She nodded. 'Also, you can see him at nine o'clock tomorrow morning. I've booked you into my hotel. It's only a few minutes away.'

'*Ma chère Jo,* you're a marvel! Thank you.' He pulled her close and kissed her, much to her confusion.

Don't read too much into this, she warned herself. He'd always called her *Ma chère Jo.* Yes, but he hadn't kissed her like that since...

She resorted to practicalities. 'My car's in the short-term parking. Come on.'

But when he took her hand as they walked toward the exit Jo, rationalising like mad, decided they were both overwrought, and it was her fault. Or maybe emotion was another airport virus.

They didn't speak again until they were sitting in Paul's room, from where he had phoned the hospital and heard reassuring news. The hotel room was a replica of hers at the far end of the corridor—standard chain-hotel beige and brown. The furniture consisted of twin beds, a small Formica table and two brown-upholstered chairs with wooden arms. Jo found it unspeakably dreary, but at least there was a minibar, from which Paul extracted glasses and miniature bottles. He poured the drinks and sat smiling at her across the table.

Jo took a grateful swig of brandy. 'What a helluva day!' she said. 'You heard about Bob Rothman? Then all the hanging about, wondering if the stage would start at all, and then Danny...I really thought he...And Tony semi-threatened to fire me.'

'Tony Johnas? What for?'

'My commentary....Oh, you don't want to hear about it.'

'Yes, I do. What about your commentary?'

'I expressed a personal opinion.'

'What exactly did you say?'

'Exactly? I don't remember. I guess I was distraught, watching Danny go over the...Anyway, I was absolutely furious, and apparently my personal opinion of Dash was a bit too strong for...Look, it's not important. You don't need to hear *my* worries when you've worries of your own.'

'And I told you, I do. You're in a real state of nerves, and you need to talk about this. So, come on—tell me.'

'Well, all right.' Jo took another fortifying gulp of her drink. 'Tony stored the shot from the helicopter. Tonight, damn him, he ran it at normal speed; but this afternoon he replayed it in slow motion, and it was very clear what happened. I said that Tom Dash deliberately pushed Danny over that wall, which he *did,* believe me.' After a pause, she said, 'You know, Danny should take out a civil action against Dash. It was an assault.'

'Hm, maybe.' Paul scratched his jaw thoughtfully. 'Right now, I'll let Guy deal with things. I got him on his mobile while I was waiting at Orly airport. He said he was on the train, but he'd already made an official statement to Walter Koch, who would e-mail the statement to the Federation.' A quick grin lit his face. 'Despite what I used to tell him, Guy is actually quite bright.'

'We had supper together, the evening after Vallon...' Jo stopped talking, thought for a few moments, and then said, 'Paul? How do you rate this Tour?'

'Fast, hot apart from that rainstorm, tightly contested...That's not what you're asking, is it?'

'Incidents.'

'Ah! Vallon.'

'And Bob Rothman with dope, and George Ferrer all but accused of sabotage, and now Danny...'She shook her head slowly. 'Maybe I'm seeing things out of proportion, but Danny's like my own...my own family. Heavens, I've known him since he was a toddler! He was a super little boy. He's still great—generous, funny, good-natured...Oh, Paul! He could have been...'

Paul came quickly over, sat on the arm of her chair and gave her a hug. 'But he wasn't. You're upset because you're tired. You really should get some sleep.'

Jo leaned gratefully against him. 'I'll try,' she said, ashamed to find herself sniffling again. 'I'm afraid I'll keep seeing that video loop in my nightmares.'

'Would another brandy help? Or...there are two beds here, if you want to...'

'No! No, I'll be all right.' Jo got up and made hurriedly for the door. 'You must be tired as well. I'm sorry.' She had done little but apologise all night. She'd meant to be so reassuring and helpful. Instead, she'd poured out her own troubles, literally cried on Paul's shoulder. And he...had been giving her some mixed messages. So, what kind of signals had *she* been sending?

She stuck a smile on her face. 'Things will look better in the morning,' she said tritely; and got out of there, fast.

Transit / Rest Day

Toulouse

Jo Bonnard

Jo reached for Paul's hand as they looked at his son lying in the hospital bed. The boy's dark, wavy hair was tousled on the pillow. His eyes were closed, and the long lashes lay like two dark fans on his face. Even in sleep there was a humorous tilt to his mouth...*He looks so like Paul!*

Jo closed her eyes briefly on the imprinted memory of another hospital bed all those years ago, and repeated her mantra: 'He's going to be all right.'

'Sure I am.' Danny's sleepy voice startled them. Without opening his eyes he said, 'Jo? Is that you? What are you doing here?'

She took a deep breath of relief. 'I'm holding your father's hand.'

'Dad?' Danny's eyes were still closed. He squeezed them more tightly, and then opened them, blinking and unfocussed.

Paul leaned over him. 'Hello, son. Of course I'm here. You think I'd be calmly selling cars in Paris? Guy phoned me, so I got on a plane.'

'Guy...the race...the bridge...' Recollection enlivened Danny's face. 'What's happened? Where...?'

'Take it easy.' Paul laid a hand on the boy's arm. 'You're safe in a hospital in Toulouse. Guy and the team are in Colmar.' At that Danny stirred feebly, so Paul added, 'Transit day, aka rest day. You can rest.'

Paul's attempted joke elicited a smile. 'Guess I won't be riding tomorrow.'

'You guess correctly,' said a brisk voice.

Jo and Paul turned to see a white-coated, competent-looking woman with dark hair coiled on the back of her head. The woman introduced herself as Dr Arlons, Senior Traumatologist, and then she took a folder of notes and x-ray plates from the nurse trotting in her wake. Consulting these, Dr Arlons gave a satisfied nod and smiled at Danny. 'You'll be riding again soon, knowing how determined you cyclists are.' Suddenly her smile dazzled. 'I had Laurent Jalabert as a patient, some years ago. Superbly fit! He healed in no time. So will you,' she assured Danny. 'It's a nice clean break. We had only to pin it.' She turned to Paul. 'I'm sorry I don't remember you, but one of my colleagues told me about you. Fourteen bones in your foot were crushed, he says. What an awful thing to happen! Nowadays, we might do some bionic surgery in a case like that. However,' her voice became cheerful again, 'your son won't need anything except time. He can get out of here in a couple of days. Leg still in plaster, of course. You'll make sure he has physiotherapy?'

'Of course.'

'Splendid.' A brisk nod and, with a whisk of her white coat, she strode off.

'Dad?' Danny stirred again. 'Did you watch the stage on TV? You saw what happened?'

Paul nodded. It was Jo who said, 'Dash the Crash ought to be sued. Deliberate dirty riding.'

'A bit more to it than that...Dad? I don't want to make trouble over this. I'd better tell you about it.'

Hearing the repeated appeal of 'Dad?' Jo asked, 'Is this between you two? I'll go for a coffee if you like.'

Danny bit his lip, considered, and finally nodded. 'Dad will tell you later, if he thinks he should.'

As Jo left the room she heard Danny say: 'I've got absolutely no proof, but...'

She softly closed the door and took the lift down to the cafeteria.

A newspaper stand caught her eye. She chose *L'Equipe,* the Spanish sports paper *Marca,* the Italian sports gazette and Hachette's rag,

Aujourd'quoi. She joined the queue, bought coffee and carried it to a table where she could study the papers.

The French report was strictly factual. She looked next at *Marca's* version of the incident on the bridge:

> *Competitive—of course; frustrated—obviously; the fastest—without a doubt. But Tom Dash went over the limit today, and Danny Breton went over the wall and into the river. Breton got off lightly with a broken leg. Dash got off lightly too. Only a disqualification from that last sprint. No fine. No suspension. Nevertheless, it was a crazy place for a sprint. A low wall, and a boat was the only safety measure. At least there was that. But come on, you Federation bosses! Have you nothing to say about dangerous routes or dangerous riding?*

The Italian version was:

> *Chiali's Tom Dash, the fastest sprinter in the world, found himself boxed in by Breton. The French rider, not renowned for bursts of speed, had ridden into a dangerous situation. With the line in sight, nothing stops Tom Dash, and Breton was in his way. If Breton had done the intelligent thing and dropped his speed on the approach to the bridge, he wouldn't be where he is today—in hospital, lucky to have nothing worse than a broken leg.*

Jo sipped her coffee and acknowledged that the Italian columnist's comment wasn't unreasonable. Was it only her affection for Danny that made her see Dash's action as more than mere competitive zeal? Putting her personal bias aside, she was still convinced it had been a deliberate assault.

On the Rothman story, reports in all three papers were even-handed. The police had released him pending further investigations. Everyone seemed to be giving him the benefit of the doubt. He was, however, out of the Tour. If this had been someone's intention, it had succeeded.

What was Hachette saying about it? With something like reluctance, she opened *Aujourd'quoi.*

Can of Worms headlined the column that was peppered, as always, with those libel-proof question marks.

> *Two riders with high haematocrit levels! Well, well! Surprise blood tests bring nasty surprises. Or is it such a surprise? Do we really believe EPO doping has been stamped out? Do we believe TV commentator Dufaux's insipid lecture on dehydration? Or do many of us take the cynical view that plenty of riders still have their own winning ways?*
>
> *If not EPO, what about amphetamines? First Vallon and now Rothman. Makes one wonder, doesn't it, who else might have a stock of pep pills up their sleeves or wherever they hide the stuff?*
>
> *'I'm completely innocent,' bleated an ashen-faced Rothman emerging from his sojourn in police custody. 'That stuff must have been planted.'*
>
> *So who planted it? Far be it from me to point a finger (however tentatively) at a rising young star who, from his temporary elevation, sneeringly refers to Rothman as 'the old man' and who seems to have more than passing knowledge about fingerprints as evidence. Not altogether surprising knowledge for a former juvenile delinquent with at least one court appearance to his name. Makes one wonder all over again, doesn't it, about this new can of worms?*

Jo felt sick. How could Hachette get away with this? His "rising young star" clearly referred to Marc Martens. Of course Marc called Rothman "The Old Man," but so did everyone on the team. It was an affectionate nickname; no trace of a sneer.

Hachette insinuated that Martens had planted the stuff. The team's press handout stated that the two riders were always roommates on the tours. Marc Martens might thus have had the opportunity, yet Jo would bet several years' salary that Marc would never do such a thing. But what about his being a juvenile delinquent? What muckheap had Hachette raked to get that? The paper's legal watchdog hadn't blue-pencilled it. *Was* there truth in it?

The thick book called The Tour Guide was in her luggage. It contained a brief c.v. of every rider. She knew that Marc had previously been with a second-level team in Belgium, but before that...Jo wasn't sure. She would look it up.

Hachette seemed intent on spreading discredit. He'd pointed the finger first at AFA's Ferrer, then Rothman from Mr Chip; and now Martens was in the line of fire. Then came his snide remarks about the high haematocrit of the riders from the Kurit and Rotoral teams. And from Intapost, Danny was out of the race.

It struck Jo that Hachette had targeted nobody from Chiali. He had made no mention of the bridge incident, or of Dash's disqualification. It was Hachette's kind of thing, so perhaps he had simply missed the early edition of the paper. Perhaps.

She looked up to see Paul coming towards her. He shook his head at her offer of coffee, saying, 'Let's go back to the hotel. I want to tell you what Danny said.'

'You're sure? Danny seemed to want it kept private.'

'He's got himself in a quandary. But if I can't tell *you*, Jo, who the hell *can* I talk to?'

~

Half an hour later, Jo understood Danny's quandary. They had looked up the relevant regulation in the rulebook, which had to be signed, *'having read and understood the rules,'* by every member of every team—riders, mechanics, medics, *soigneurs*, the lot.

The precise wording of the paragraph began: *Any person withholding information concerning the use or possession of any prohibited substance will be deemed to be an accessory...*

'Damn!' said Jo. 'We can't go to Walter Koch without implicating Danny.'

'That boy's got a lot to learn,' said Paul, exasperated. 'Giving Dash a sporting chance!'

'He would. That's typical of Danny. He's a kind-hearted boy.'

'Soft-headed, more like.'

'I wonder,' said Jo, 'if Dash *did* get rid of it.'

'Danny has no idea. Dash came alongside him on the bridge, and muttered: 'I'll teach you to keep your fucking nose out of my business, you bastard.' And the next thing Danny knew, he was in free-fall, as he put it.'

'The Mr Chip and Chiali teams were in the same hotel,' said Jo, 'so Dash could have planted the stuff on Rothman. But is Dash using amphetamines? He's never tested positive for dope.'

'Mm.' Paul sounded doubtful. 'Don't forget that Chiali emerged clean from that drugs raid. Where on earth could they hide the dope while the police were searching?'

'I don't know,' said Jo. 'Or...Wait! Maybe I do. One of the Chiali vehicles went into a ditch in Spain. Only a bent front wing, I heard, but it just got back yesterday. Don't you think a simple repair took an *extraordinarily* long time? I wonder if it had a supply of drugs aboard, and stayed on the other side of the border until the searches were over.'

Paul smiled broadly. 'Now *that* bit of reasoning is worthy of Miss Marple. But...' he became serious, 'you could be right. Strange things happen. Yet I can't see why anyone would plant the stuff on Rothman, of all people. The Federation will listen seriously to his protest of innocence. He's highly respected; known to be honest.'

'Perhaps for that very reason—to make things all the worse.' Jo took the folded newspaper from her bag. 'You haven't read Hachette's latest masterpiece. Un-edify your mind with this.'

Paul read it. 'Marc Martens?' he said, horrified.

'Vicious, isn't it? You know, the evening after Vallon's crash, Hachette made sure everyone was suspicious of Ferrer. If Ferrer had been suspended, there would have been *two* good AFA riders gone. Now Rothman's suspended and Hachette's making insinuations about Martens. Trying for another double whammy against Mr Chip?'

Paul studied the column again. 'This stuff about Martens's delinquent past...'

'It's appalling. His whole career could be blighted by that trash-merchant Hachette. I can't believe it's true, and I meant to look up Marc's c.v. in the Tour Guide'

'I've got a copy of the Guide right here.' Paul got up to take it from his bag.

Jo found the page. They read it, Paul leaning over her shoulder. 'It doesn't go back far enough,' she said. 'Is there someone who might know more about Marc's background; his early years?'

'Per Cornelius,' Paul replied instantly. 'He retired two years ago but he knows Belgian cycling inside out. If he can't tell me, he'll know who can. I'll phone him right now.'

He made the call. Jo heard him say: 'Oh…Right…Will do.' Then he laid down the phone saying, 'He's not there. He's expected back in an hour or so. I'll call again later.'

Jo looked at her watch. 'Then I'll have to leave it with you. Will you call my mobile if you learn something?'

'Why? What do you mean?'

'I have to get moving, Paul. I was supposed to spend today driving to Colmar. These damned transfers are hell. I wish the stages went from A to B, B to C, and so on, but we'd never tour France like that.' She shrugged a gesture of apology. 'I'm sorry, but I really must leave.'

Paul was aghast. 'You're going to set out *now*? To drive for what's left of today and most of the night? I hadn't realised…You stayed here for Danny's sake?'

'Mainly for *your* sake. You'd had a fright. You needed somebody. I mean, somebody to meet you, somebody to talk to—not that I made a very good job of it. As a friend and comforter, I was a dead loss.'

He shook his head at her. 'Driving in the dark, across the Massif, and up the…It's not on, Jo! Especially since we sat talking until after one in the morning. Did you sleep at all?'

'Not much, to be honest. I dozed a bit, but I kept seeing Danny…'

Paul put his hands on her shoulders and steered her towards the door. 'You're going to catch a couple of hours' sleep, right now. Go on. It's time you had someone taking care of you.'

'I've got to get to Colmar,' she protested, but he continued walking her doorwards.

'*Ma chère Jo,* will you stop being so independent? Please, do what I ask. And trust me. I'll see to it, that you get to Colmar.'

Dirk Leyden

In the police station in Liege, Captain Dirk Leyden picked up the phone, wondering who was making a personal call. 'Leyden here.'

'Good afternoon. My name's Paul Breton. I don't suppose you'll have heard of me, but I used to ride for the Fontaine cycling team.'

'*Paul Breton?*' Dirk gasped. Everyone interested in cycling had heard of Paul Breton! Then immediately Dirk felt foolish. This must be Ricky Berger playing one of his jokes. 'Oh yeah?' he laughed. 'Nice try, Ricky. And I'm James Bond.'

But a few sentences later, Dirk realised this was no leg-pull. It was indeed Paul Breton, saying: 'Eddy suggested I should phone you.'

Eddy? There was only one Eddy. Dirk Leyden was astonished again. 'What about? '

'I'm hoping you can tell me about. ..' Breton paused. 'Do you read Hachette's column in *Aujourd'quoi?*'

'As seldom as possible. Why?'

'Let me read you today's gem.'

Dirk listened with growing disgust. At the end, he said, 'Good God! I get the inference: Marc Martens.'

'Everyone's drawing the same conclusion. Can you tell me if there's any truth in it?'

Dirk grunted. 'Huh! A tiny scrap of truth, enlarged completely out of proportion. For example *at least one court appearance* implies there were several; but it was one. Just one. '

'Was he a delinquent?'

'Depends how you define 'delinquent.' He borrowed a bike without the owner's consent and nicked a packet of cigarettes. His one court appearance was in connection with that. It was nine years ago. He was given a telling-off.'

'So the whole thing is...'

'Grossly exaggerated. Absurd.'

'I'm very glad to hear that. According to Eddy, you launched Marc Martens on his career. What can you tell me about Marc?'

'When Marc was fourteen he joined our youth team and won everything in sight. Turned pro at nineteen and went on winning. He's tough, determined and committed to his training. *You* know what that means—no nights out with your pals, early to bed and out riding in all weathers. He works very hard. I know he's mule-headed stubborn and damned annoying at times, but I assure you, Monsieur Breton, there's nothing wrong with his character.'

'That's what I hoped to hear. But call me Paul, for heavens sake. I'm not that old!' Both men laughed and Paul went on: 'Now I'll ask another favour. Can I pass this information to a journalist?'

'Depends on which journalist.'

'Jo Bonnard.'

'Ah. Yes, that's okay.'

'She'll be as pleased as I am to hear the truth about Marc. Hachette's smears made her furious.'

'Then let her set the record straight. But ask her to refer to me as 'a police officer,' not by name. Right?'

'I'll tell her. Thank you.'

'Happy to have been of help,' said Dirk. 'By the way, how's your boy?'

'He's doing fine, thanks.'

'Good. I've seen Tom Dash in action. A dirty rider, that young man.'

They brought their conversation to a close and Dirk Leyden replaced the phone.

He loathed sensational journalists like Hachette. And if he wanted to pin a 'delinquent' label on anyone, it would be on Tom Dash, not Marc Martens.

Paul Breton

Paul let Jo sleep undisturbed until five in the evening when he knocked gently on the door of her room. He heard her say, 'I'm awake—just about,' so he went in, sat on the edge of the bed and handed her an envelope. Yawning, she sat up and opened it. It took her a few moments to understand that she was looking at a flight ticket—Toulouse to Colmar next morning. A big hug expressed her delighted thanks.

Then her smile faded a bit. 'What can I do about the company's car? '

'I fixed that with Stefan Eltlinger.'

'The owner of Eltsport? You know him?'

'Sure. Who do you think supplies the fleet of cars for you media people?'

Her mouth dropped open. 'You?' She began to laugh helplessly. 'You know, I never really thought about it, but who else could it be?'

Paul gave her a satisfied smile. 'Come on, then. We'll go and see

Danny again, and afterwards we can have a leisurely supper and time to talk.'

'You're terrific! Give me ten minutes to shower and change.'

'Oh, we'll go somewhere simple. No need to wear your ball-gown and tiara,' he joked. 'Besides, I think you look great in these jeans.'

'These jeans I've been sleeping in for five hours? No way! I *do* have a decent outfit for evenings. Don't look so alarmed,' she laughed. 'It's just a trouser-suit.' She swung her feet to the floor and stood facing him across the bed. 'Did you learn anything about Marc Martens?'

'Always the reporter,' he sighed. 'Journalism still comes first?'

'First before what? It's my work. My livelihood.'

Paul decided this was not a good time for a serious talk. Jo was scarcely awake. He'd leave it until later to say what he wanted to say.

Jo Bonnard

With an old-fashioned and politically incorrect wolf-whistle, Paul had expressed his admiration for the pistachio-coloured, silk jersey trouser-suit. Now they were on their way to the hospital, and Paul related what he had learned about Marc Martens.

'Nine years ago!' Jo exclaimed. 'I wonder how long Hachette's been waiting to hatch that rotten egg. I'd like to see it explode in his face.'

'Face? Wrong part of the anatomy for hatching eggs.'

Jo spluttered with laughter. 'You haven't changed!' She became serious again. 'Thanks to you, I'll have time to talk to a few people in Colmar tomorrow. We're only broadcasting the last ninety minutes of the time trial, so I'm not due on air until four-thirty. I'll try to undo Hachette's damage. Set the record straight, as your police officer expressed it.'

They reached the hospital and Jo, thinking that Paul would like some time alone with his son, offered to divert to the kiosk for the evening editions of the newspapers while Paul went directly to Danny's room.

Several papers had latched on to the Martens story with phrases like...*any truth in the rumours?...a shady past?* Those damned question marks and careful wording. Nasty, damaging stuff that would do Marc's morale no good at all.

Jo had no trouble in finding Hachette's column. A headline: *Pride Comes Before A...*was printed above an over-enlarged photograph of a dramatic splash—presumably taken as Danny hit the water. Hachette's text was decidedly anti-Danny. She scanned phrases.

Who does he think he is?...The over-blown ego of a rookie riding on his father's name...thinks he can mix it with the men...a deliberate attempt to hold up the fastest man on wheels?...Maybe a ducking will cool his ambition.

Better not let either Paul or Danny see that.

Jo dropped Hachette's paper into a trash basket and made for the lift. She squeezed in amongst a crowd of evening visitors. Everything Hachette wrote was malicious. Normally xenophobic, he usually found every excuse for the shortcomings of a French rider. But this was atypical. Tom Dash wasn't French and he was, moreover, riding for a team sponsored by an Italian company. Why come down so heavily in his favour?

The lift stopped and Jo was swept out with the crowd of passengers. She found she was on the wrong floor, looking straight at an Addicts Anonymous poster. DRUGS—WHO'S PAYING?

Who's paying? The thought stopped her in her tracks. Who's paying Hachette?

She walked slowly and thoughtfully up the stairs to Danny's room.

Fully alert this evening, Danny pounced on the papers. 'Marc Martens is two minutes ahead of Charreau already, and he should win the time trial tomorrow. I think he'll win The Tour, in fact.'

'Is he generally popular?' Jo asked.

'Sure. He can be abrasive, but he's a straight talker. You always know where you stand with him. And he's a great rider, but no bighead, which is more than I could say about some others.' Danny turned a page. 'Of course, God's Gift still has the mountain points.'

'God's Gift?' Jo laughed. 'First time I've heard him called that. I take it you don't think so much of Dino.'

'A pain in the arse, the way he plays up to the public. And as for that smirk...' He imitated Dino's famous, slow and sexy smile, and sent Jo into hoots of laughter.

Paul moved round to look over his son's shoulder. 'Nardini has moved up to fourth spot—not bad!'

Without a trace of self-pity, Danny said, 'I was in front of him yesterday. Maybe I could have beaten him.'

His father gave him a mock cuff on the shoulder. 'Don't kid yourself. He'd have whipped past you on the final climb.'

'True,' Danny grinned, unoffended. He turned another page. 'The Belgian Fries are doing well. We hoped Intapost might win the team award, but it looks like Mr Chip could take it. Their Jan Claes has taken most points for the...*what?*...'Prince of the Sprints,' it says here. Don't they invent such romantic titles? King of the Mountains, and now Prince of the Sprints. Where's Dash? Yippee! Down to third on the points-table, and our Nilsson is fourth. Ten points back, though.'

'Ten?' Jo queried. 'I made it eight.' She muttered a calculation: 'Six for a win. Take six from Dash's previous total and add six to Nilsson's...The report's wrong. It credits him with four for a second place. Should be six. Just proves you can't believe all you read in the papers.'

The three happily talked shop for half an hour, and then Danny suddenly said, 'Jo? Aren't you supposed to be in Colmar?'

'I'm boarding a plane at ten in the morning, and Eltsport will lay on another car for me at Colmar, thanks to your father.'

Danny apparently heard nothing remarkable in that. He said, 'And you, Dad?'

'I'm taking over Jo's present car, waiting until you're fit to travel, then I'll take you home to Paris if it's okay with Guy.'

Danny looked pleased. 'I can work with you in the gym.' He turned enthusiastically to Jo. 'We've got a complete gym in the house. Dad converted the big kitchen. You must see it. Why not come and visit us again some day? You haven't been back since... Well, a long time.'

Jo, hearing him sidestep a mention of his mother's death, simply said, 'I know.'

Paul said, 'Danny's right. It *has* been a long time.'

Jo avoided both their eyes. These two hadn't planned some father-and-son conspiracy to entice her into a visit, had they?

~

Jo and Paul left the hospital and went in search of a restaurant. Paul spotted a bistro cheerfully decorated in blue and white, with candles on the tables and reproductions of Toulouse Lautrec posters all round the walls. Furthermore, it smelled wonderful, which no doubt accounted for the place being three quarters full; but Paul secured a corner table. A waiter placed a pottery jug of the local red wine on the table and gave them short, hand-written menus. Jo chose *coq au vin,* having recognised the mouth-watering aroma. Paul ordered a steak and salad, but no bread and no potatoes.

As the waiter went off, Jo smiled at Paul, teasing him gently. 'Such a healthy diet and a home gymnasium, eh? No wonder you're in such great shape.'

'Not bad for my age.'

'Don't smirk,' she laughed. 'Danny wouldn't like it.'

'But he *would* like you to come and see us again. So would I. What are you doing at Christmas, for example?'

'I'm planning to write some articles.'

'Where?'

'Oh, I don't know yet,' she shrugged. 'The Algarve, maybe, or the Costa del Sol.'

'Alone in some rent-a-flat,' he said sadly, 'even at Christmas. Why not spend Christmas with us?'

Jo gave him a smile but was unwilling to make a commitment. It wouldn't be the same without Leontine. Her previous visits to the family had been made in the relaxed atmosphere created by Leontine. Once or twice there had been flickers of the old chemistry with Paul, or shared laughter over a joke from before Leontine's time. But Leontine, serene in a secure marriage, had had the wisdom to let it pass. Now there was no Leontine, and Jo was not at all sure how she would cope with such a changed situation.

The waiter, bringing appetisingly arranged plates of food, provided a welcome distraction. Jo tasted the *coq au vin,* said 'Mmm,' echoed by Paul as he cut into his steak, and they both dedicated the next several minutes to the enjoyment of excellent cooking.

When they'd eaten and were savouring their second glasses of wine, Paul looked across the candlelit table and took a deep breath.

'You and I seem to have had too many meetings in hospitals,' he said, turning his wineglass slowly between his fingers. 'After I crashed,' he went on, 'I know you spent a week sitting beside me in the hospital. When my parents got there, they told me you insisted on sleeping in the waiting room. In fact, I'd been conscious enough to be aware of your presence...But you went off to report on the Criterium races, the World Championships, the...'

'Just a minute!' she interrupted. '*But you went off*...You make it sound like I just got up and walked out on you.' Without being aware of it, she leaned forward, the mildly aggressive body language expressing her annoyance. 'Was that how you saw it?'

Was it? She felt shocked. Of course he could have had no idea of the many heart-searching hours she'd spent debating with herself. Could she leave? Yes. Paul was out of danger, in expert care. His parents had arrived. His team and many other cyclists came to see him. Had she *wanted* to leave? No! But she had to keep her job. Her editor had been puzzled, knowing nothing of her blossoming friendship with Paul, but had given her a week off work. How could she have justified a request to extend her absence?

She subsided into her chair and, after a moment, said: 'Sorry for the outburst but, however belatedly, I want you to know I didn't coolly walk away from you. I had a contract, and breaking it wouldn't have helped either of us. I thought I'd explained that to you at the time. You must have been more deeply sedated than I realised.'

'I must have been,' Paul said automatically. Then: 'I'm the one who should apologise...for making assumptions. I reckoned you didn't want to marry a cripple.'

'Marry?' she jerked bolt upright, startled and confused. 'There was never any mention of marrying. Anyway I...'

'You were nineteen and I was ten years older.'

She laid her wineglass firmly on the table. 'Let me finish my own sentence, Paul. I was going to say: I thought we were friends—okay, great friends. Like we still are. Like we've always been. You married Leontine.'

'And never regretted it. She was...'

'Adorable,' Jo supplied. 'Now I'm finishing *your* sentence; but Leontine really was the kindest, most caring person I've ever known. She just radiated warmth. I miss her. I can't imagine how it must be for you.'

Still twisting his glass, he nodded, watching the glow of candle flame through the wine. 'When she died, a friend who'd been in my situation told me: *Coming to terms with it takes as long as it takes.* Of course I miss her. I have lovely memories of her, but I also have to get on with my life; and it's a good life, apart from...having nobody to confide in. That, I *do* miss.'

He sat absorbed in thought for fully a minute until Jo finally reached for his hand. 'It must be awful for you. But you're lucky to have Danny. He's a great boy.'

'He is; but a son is...different.' He took another mighty breath. 'Why did you meet me at the airport?'

Jo floundered a bit at this change of tack. 'Because I...I thought you needed somebody, and I...' About to apologise again, she stopped talking.

'That's it. You thought I needed somebody, and you were right. Everybody needs somebody. Even you, independent Jo.'

'Me?' she said stupidly.

'Yes, you.' He shifted the candle to one side and reached across the table to clasp both of her hands. 'I've not told you, but, over this past year, I've been listening to your commentaries. It's lovely to hear your voice. I was disappointed that you weren't on air yesterday and I had to switch to France2. I think about you so often. Do you ever think about me?'

'Occasionally,' she said lightly. Avoiding eye contact, she found herself gazing at Lautrec's wonderful poster-portrait of Aristide Bruant. Aristide, his red scarf thrown over his shoulder, stared back at her from under his big black hat, arrogantly mocking: *Woman, you're a liar.*

So she looked Paul straight in the face. 'That was a lie. Yes, I think about you...every time I see Danny...and when I...'

'When you're commentating and you mention me in passing?' At last he smiled. 'I've wondered...But last night I knew it. We need each other, Jo.'

Jo stared at him for long moments. 'Do you mean...?'

'Yes, I mean what you think I mean.'

Jo felt as though she'd been sandbagged. She hadn't thought of a step as mighty as this. Eventually she said, 'My contract with Eltsport runs for another two years. That means I have to stay in the cycling world. You know what a nomadic life it is.'

'I know. And come winter, you just rent a flat somewhere. Wouldn't you like to have a haven—a place to call *home?* People who care for you? I'd like you to think about it.'

'Think?' she said. 'You've really floored me. I'm just not sure about it. You'll have to give me time. No, listen,' as he was about to interrupt her. 'I can't cook. I'm not domestic. I've never owned a stick of furniture in my life, and I...'

This time he got his interruption in. 'Exactly! Your entire life is in two suitcases. Your address is care-of-Eltsport, or an e-mail.'

Indignantly she said, 'I've got a whole raft of stocks and shares, and a pension plan. But that's not the point. I'm used to doing my own thing, being independent. Do you think I could just slot myself into a ready-made family?'

'Yes I do, and we wish you would.'

We. So Danny *was* in on this.

Paul held her hands tighter. 'When I think about you, with no home, no family...That's what I want to offer you, *ma chère Jo.* People who love you.'

But before she could say another word, Paul held up his hands in mock surrender. 'All right,' he said lightly, 'you need time to think. But you could still visit us. Christmas dinner?'

'I can't cook.'

'Ah, but I can. You've no idea, the range of my talents. And before you make your next objection: the new kitchen's equipped with a dish-washer.'

Despite herself, Jo started to laugh. 'I can see what makes you such a fabulous car-salesman. Okay, okay,' she capitulated. 'I'll come and spend Christmas.'

'Good! Maybe by that time you'll have...'

A loud buzz came from Jo's bag, which she'd hung on the chair-back. 'Damn! My mobile phone.' She fished for it. 'Oh, good evening, Tony,' she said, followed by: 'Oh?...No...Yes...,' then: 'By plane, tomorrow morning...Easily...Bye.'

She switched off. 'Tony Johnas. He'd phoned Xavier Dufaux, who said there was no sign of me. Did I have some problem with the car?' She smiled. 'A bit transparent, that. He was really angling to know why I'm still in Toulouse.' Her smile faded. 'He'll put two and two together, eventually.'

'Does it matter?'

A small shrug didn't disguise her concern. 'You know I'm not his favourite commentator at the moment. Cycling's still a man's world. I've still got to fight for my career.'

'I know what it means to you,' Paul said. 'Against the odds, you've made a real success of it and I'm not suggesting you should give it up.'

'That's part of the trouble. I don't want to give it up.' She leaned toward him, her expression serious. 'You, of all people, know about my passion for cycling; and mine is one of the most privileged jobs in the business. As a reporter, I rushed about in a car, able to see only the starts and finishes. As a commentator, I get to watch all of the stages *and* get an overall picture of everything. I still rush about in a car, of course,' she admitted with a smile. 'It's not a career that would easily combine with domesticity.'

'Who's talking about domesticity?' Paul spread his hands, smiling, then resumed his earnest tone. 'Our discussion was about having someone who cares for you. Think again about last night at the airport. You can't wrap your arms round a career and cry on its shoulder.'

Transit / Rest Day

Colmar

Nat Arnold

In Hotel Starlight II near Colmar, the lift had gone up and down several times before it emptied of all but two passengers. One of them was Arnold, who could now relate his snatch of information while the lift sank to the basement garage. There the other occupant got out, leaving Arnold to return to level four with a 200-euro note in his pocket.

Not bad, thought Arnold, for a lucky glimpse of Tom Dash leaving Harvey Jones's room and a chance meeting in the lift. It had even saved him price of a phone-call!

His little sideline had started in the Stage 4 *Village Départ*. The man had come and spoken to him, asking for "any little snippet about the team." The no-quibbles payment told Arnold that this must have been an important snippet.

Arnold shrugged. The deal earned him some cash. He needed it. The team was winning bugger-all and the renewal of his miserable *domestique*'s contract was very iffy. He could see himself having to go begging round second-string teams that would pay him peanuts for another year's boring work.

He'd done all right as an amateur in England, and then he'd joined a French pro team where his face didn't fit, or whatever. After a whole year, the damned Frogs hadn't even given him a chance as team leader. They'd said he'd have to work harder, increase his training and learn the bloody Frog language. As if! So he'd quit bothering and done the least work possible. AFA had seemed a better chance, but...same story. And now he was thirty, still amongst the nameless ones, and qualified to do nothing except ride a bike. Every bloody euro he could put in his pocket, he would. No questions asked.

Enrico Fiarelli

An hour later, Enrico Fiarelli stood in another block of the Starlight II complex, his eyes hidden behind mirror shades. He was in a rage. 'Twice!' he shouted. 'Once is bad enough, but twice is too much! What the hell were you doing?'

'Winning the sprint.' Tom Dash thrust out his jaw aggressively. 'Like I'm supposed to do.'

Fiarelli dropped his voice to a whisper, deliberately adopting his movie-*Mafioso* style. 'But you didn't win it. You were disqualified. I didn't give you a contract to make a fool of yourself and the team. It's bad for our image. And I've had an official complaint, too. I am not a happy man.'

'Well, hell, I was trying to win.'

'But you failed.' Fiarelli's head darted forward, snake-like. 'Failed spectacularly. Watched by thousands.'

'So how was I to know? The motocamera was way in front of the race.'

'Hel-i-cop-ters.' Fiarelli pronounced with care, speaking to a moron. 'Zoom lens-es. Never heard of them?'

'How was I to know?'

Fiarelli narrowed his eyes. 'Your year's contract expires in two months. Maybe I won't renew it. Maybe I'll let you go to AFA, eh?' He saw Dash twitch. 'You think I don't know about the secret talk you had with Jones? Were you planning to come and tell me that AFA was interested in you?'

'Well, hell,' the boy blustered, 'this is a business.'

'You're a fool, Dash. You haven't the brains for business. You let yourself be seen leaving Jones's room. You were going to tell me you had another offer, and ask me for a bigger salary. That it, eh?'

Dash, half sulky, half defiant, said, 'Well, Nardini sets out *his* contract terms.'

For the first time, Fiarelli hesitated. 'Nardini has a business background. He's smarter than you.' He chose his next words with care. 'What has he been telling you?'

All defiance this time, Dash said, 'He gave me a slice of the action.'

Fiarelli pulled a thin cheroot from his pocket and took his time over lighting it. Studying the burning tip, he said, 'I'm surprised.'

Indeed he was. It was unlike Nardini to slice any action involving money. The plan—to go for more TV exposure, bigger bonuses and, of course, maximum prize money—was a confidential deal between Nardini and himself. Surely he hadn't told Dash about the little irregularities concerning the Publichiali Company?

Dash had been signed-on as a sure-fire winner of sprints; but if Nardini was cutting him in on the money deal, that was something else. He, Enrico Fiarelli, did not like being sidelined or kept in the dark.

He stuck the cheroot in the corner of his mouth and squinted at Dash through the smoke. 'The team doesn't need dead weight, and right now that's what you are. Dead weight and a liability—ruining the team's image with your disqualifications.'

'Oh, yeah? Compared with what we're doing to the image of the other teams...' Dash abruptly shut his mouth.

Fiarelli blew a cloud of smoke towards him. A liability was the word. The stupid *bastardo* didn't just throw away points with his idiot stunts right under the TV lenses. He couldn't keep his trap shut.

'Get your butt out of here and tell your business associate *Signor* Nardini I want to talk to him.'

Nardini had gone too far. Bad enough making all those payments to that French reporter for the so-called Media Campaign; letting Dash in on the game plan was too much of a risk.

STAGE 19

Time Trial

Jo Bonnard

The Tour de France had started again after the Rest Day—a term not to be taken literally, because the teams had travelled by overnight train from Toulouse to Colmar, and then spent the afternoon practising on today's course. They did not, in fact, have much rest. Their bodies were used to prolonged effort followed by rapid recovery, and they didn't dare break that rhythm. In fact, some riders disliked rest days, claiming it was hard to get going again. In the words of Spanish rider-turned-manager Laguía, 'A cyclist's body is like a sponge. The more you squeeze it, the more it can absorb.'

Jo had explained much of this to the viewers while the earlier part of the time trial was in progress. She had also told neophytes that a time trial is a race against the clock, with the cyclists setting off alone at one-minute intervals, each trying to get round the course in the shortest time.

Commentating on time trials was not easy, as the action was limited to one rider at a time. On her monitor was the lone figure of David Vauban, complete with St Christopher ear-studs. Being a climber, he wasn't expected to gain many advantages today. This was a fairly flat course, with only two small climbs in the second half. It would suit the strong endurance men like Mike Gregory of Intapost, who had achieved the best time so far—one hour, fourteen minutes and twelve seconds.

The commercial break ended, and Jo listened to her countdown. On screen was the view of the finish—double white lines across the road and a large digital time-display on an overhead gantry.

'Finishing now is Seamus Patrick of Mr Chip, with a time of one hour, sixteen minutes and…ten seconds. That puts him just into the top twenty where he'll probably stay until the leading riders have their turn. They go in reverse order, so Marc Martens will be the last away and this course should suit his powerful riding.

'Excitement will build towards the end, but just now I have an opportunity to answer an e-mail from Jeremy, aged twelve, who can't understand how Charreau is in second place without actually winning any stages. You're not alone, Jeremy, so I'll tell you how it's calculated. Every rider is timed every day and his times are added up. The man with the least time is in first place. Got that? Also, every stage is a race within the race, and there are time-deduction bonus points for stage winners. Not just winners get points. Points also go—in decreasing numbers, of course—to the second, third…down to twenty-fifth on flat stages. Another way to win points is to be first, second or third in the intermediate sprints along the way, or to be placed on the climbs. The number of places and points depends on the category of the climb.' Jo hoped the viewers weren't bored rigid by the technicalities but she soldiered on, explaining the importance of time trials. 'Five-times Tour-winners Jacques Anquetil and Miguel Indurain, real maestros, were so good at this, they gained several minutes over their rivals.'

Still nothing very televisual was happening, and it was a relief to hear Tony say: 'Commercial break in ten.'

Dufaux, sitting next to her, switched off his microphone and slid open the partition. 'Heard the latest news? Jan Claes has been made team captain in Rothman's place, rather than Marc Martens. Must be some truth in the rumours about Martens.'

'The rumours are a load of rubbish!' she said angrily. 'And you'd do well to pass that around.'

Dufaux's eyebrows rose. 'Really?'

'Yes, *really*. Take it from me, on impeccable authority, Hachette's completely out of line.'

'Did you learn that in Toulouse? What else were you doing there?'

There was a certain leering innuendo in his tone. 'Learning facts,' Jo snapped. 'And thinking.'

Acting upon her thoughts she had phoned Claudia Vallon, asking for her help. Claudia had said she would look in the Mercantile Register and telephone Jo with the result of her research, whether or not it proved fruitful.

The ad break ended and Jo brought her thoughts back to her work.

'Nobody has beaten Gregory's time, but the top ten have yet to start. *They* go at two-minute intervals to avoid complications. If someone catches up with the rider in front, he must either pass, or ride side by side, and they must maintain a six-metre gap. That rule prevents riding in somebody's slipstream, which would give an unfair advantage.'

She talked about the progress of each lone rider. Eventually Nardini set off, followed by Jonkers and Charreau. Finally, Marc Martens got the countdown and rolled down the starting ramp.

Jo had made notes listing Marc's *palmares*—every stage victory, every event, however minor, that he had won. She recited the lot and added the fact that, from the age of fourteen, Marc had been dedicated to the training and commitment required to achieve such success.

On the screen, captions appeared showing comparative times at the halfway point.

'Here's Marc Martens approaching the halfway mark. Look at the caption...He's fourteen seconds faster than Charreau! He's increased his overall lead.' Moto 1 drew alongside him as, in the background, a horse and rider galloped along a field, parallel to the speeding cyclist. 'Oh, look at that!' Jo exclaimed. 'This is brilliant photography! You often see horsemen racing the cyclists. Watch how that horse is galloping, its mane and tail streaming out. That gives you an idea of Marc's speed. Now the horse is pulling up... and Marc powers on.'

The picture shifted to the finish line again. Rider after rider came in, but none had bettered Gregory's time.

'Nardini's due to finish next,' said Jo, 'and then the last three men will...Here comes Nardini! He must have been flying over the last five kilometres. He's approaching the line at one hour, fourteen...eight, nine...ten! He has beaten Gregory's time by two seconds! Tough luck for Gregory who's been top of the list for a while, and must have been sitting biting his nails; but Nardini did a terrific ride.'

She was glad she had made notes of time trial speed-records to talk about, because there was an interval of more than two minutes before she could say: 'Ah! Here comes Jonkers....Oh! Not a good ride for someone of his ability. It has left him absolutely exhausted,' she added as the camera swung round to see him collapse into the arms of his *soigneurs*. 'He's lost about two and a half minutes, which puts him down one place in the rankings, so Nardini is now third overall. Gregory's fast ride moved *him* from thirteenth up to sixth place. I told you the time trials are important.'

The next shot was from Moto 2 on the circuit. 'This is Charreau,' Jo said. 'Never an elegant rider, he seems to be fighting his bike, stamping down on the pedals and grabbing the bars as though he wants to strangle them. His awkward-looking style is usually effective, but not today. We see him approach the finish line...now. He's lost a lot of time! And he was a few seconds slower than Nardini, so he has also lost his second place. That puts Nardini into second spot and breathing down Marc Martens's neck. The final stages will be vital.'

Now only Marc remained on the course. Moto 1 was still running alongside him.

'I hope,' said Jo, 'there are young cyclists watching Marc and learning how to ride a time trial. Head steady, back flat, elbows in—a narrow, aerodynamic position, and keep your body still. He doesn't stand on the pedals. That makes your bike rock, and every side-to-side movement means less forward movement. Marc is pedal-power personified.'

The picture cut to the camera at the finish. 'If you look at the time-display you'll see the tenths of seconds reeling up. Marc has less than a kilometre to go. Watch that timer! Can he do it? One hour *twelve* minutes...He'll do it!...*Yes!*' She was yelling. 'One hour, twelve minutes and fourteen seconds. Wow! That was an extremely fast ride!'

The final results appeared on the screen, followed by overall rankings. Marc Martens was still top of the list with almost two minutes' advantage over Nardini and Charreau, who were separated by a matter of seconds.

Jo sat back and stopped talking. Had she over-enthused about Marc's victory?

~

She had found him around midday. He was obviously stressed, with bitten fingernails.

'Wearing the Yellow Jersey is hell,' he'd said. 'This shit in the newspapers...One day I'm a national hero, the next I'm a national disgrace. I got fan mail, but now it's hate mail. I ride a bike for a living because I love my job. At least, I used to.'

At that point she had told him: 'I'll do what I can to stop these vile rumours. I know the truth about your teenage years. The information came from a police officer.'

'Dirk! He's the best.' Marc smiled. 'I'll call him, soon as this time trial's over.'

'You should do that. He seems to be a good friend who'll straighten your head out.'

'My *head?* I've got him to thank for my whole *life!*'

And Jo had seen that Marc, the supposed man of iron, had tears in his eyes.

~

As Marc mounted the podium to collect the trophy, Jo decided to set the record a little straighter. 'Marc has come a long way since his potential was spotted by a young police officer who became, and still is, his great friend and admirer. I'm sure that officer is extra proud of Marc today.'

And, she thought, to hell with company policy on personal opinions!

STAGE 19

Evening

Jo Bonnard

Hotel Starlight II, near Colmar, had the same layout as Starlight III where everyone had been lodged on the night they'd learned of Vallon's death.

The central area served as a crossroads, making it a paradise for a reporter who could learn a lot by observing all the comings and goings. In these final days of The Tour, it had the air of a marketplace. Ahead of the official date, contracts were sought or re-negotiated behind doors that opened and closed like some bedroom farce.

That evening, Jo was standing beside the newspaper kiosk in the central area, when she saw Nardini and Dash emerge from a lift and walk towards her. They appeared to be having an argument. She dodged behind a rack of magazines, picked one out at random and held it open in front of her face.

As they walked past her she heard Dino's angry voice. 'How could you be so stupid? Putting it in the wrong bag!' And Dash's sullen retort: 'How in hell was I to know? They're all the same.'

Putting *what* in *which* wrong bag? Jo watched them out of sight and, after a few puzzled moments, she thought she knew what Dino had been talking about

Jo was replacing the unwanted magazine when she caught a

glimpse of Paula Ferrer's face on the cover of the one next to it. Inset on the photo, a text-box asked: *Is Paula Pregnant?* Out of curiosity, Jo bought the magazine.

Then she went to look at the notice board. In the team competition, the top three were Chiali, Mr Chip and Intapost. Tomorrow's stage, especially its hill climbs, would be hard-fought. If Nardini won most of the mountain points, the team prize would go to Chiali although, in view of its financial situation, Intapost was bound to make a colossal effort.

Jo knew the value of the Team Award. The winner would attract additional sponsors whose investment could buy additional, top-ranked riders. Success would breed success. The money won by each team member was no fortune, but his contract-value would increase.

She turned her attention to the list of individual rankings. Would Marc be fit for tomorrow's climbs after his effort in the time trial? Advertisers always sought out the winner. Nobody really cared who came second. This was all about fame, and the spin-offs were substantial.

Figuring in adverts could multiply a rider's salary by ten. Endorsing a product was another earner, as were fees for personal appearances. Of course this had its downside. More than one star had neglected his training to give interviews, open shopping centres, sign autographs, and to be wined and dined to the point where lack of fitness made his next season a catastrophe. Balancing cash against continued success required a level of business sense that few boys possessed.

Nardini seemed to be an exception.

That thought reminded Jo that Claudia had promised to phone around this time. Jo hurried to take the call in the privacy of her room.

∼

'I found a connection,' said Claudia. 'It's a printing company.'

'Printing?' Jo reached for her shorthand pad. 'All right; go on. I'm taking notes.'

'It was a complicated search,' Claudia began. 'Chiali has so many subsidiary companies dealing with various aspects of the business. So I started again at the other end. Instead of trying to discover *if* you were right, I assumed you *were* right, and set out to prove it.' She paused for breath. 'I started with Herc—Dino's company. It manufactures the T-shirts, but the printing of his logo is sub-contracted to a printing company called Primotinto, which prints everything for Chiali. Another subsidiary is Publichiali. You know that it handles all Chiali's publicity and marketing?'

'Yes, I know, because Publichiali is the registered sponsor of the cycling team.'

'Well,' said Claudia, 'about a year ago, Primotinto was merged with Publichiali.'

'In other words,' said Jo, 'Primotinto and Publichiali are operating under their own names, but they're really the same company?'

'Correct. They're both owned by the same shareholders. Now, this is the interesting part. Shortly after the merger, the majority of the shares of the joint company were bought by Herc!'

'Hold on.' Jo had a sense of excitement. 'I must get this straight. Do you mean that Herc actually owns Primotinto *and* Publichiali?'

'That's right. Herc owns fifty-one percent of the shares.'

Jo let out a slow whistle. This was going to be a major scoop. 'Good girl! You've found the answer.'

'I have?' Claudia sounded mystified. 'In what way?'

'Herc—owned by Dino—has controlling shares in Publichiali.'

'Yes. So? Why is it important?'

'In Federation rules, no team member is permitted to be a share-holder, or related to a shareholder, of the sponsoring company.'

'Oh. I see. But why make such a rule? Riders would surely be better motivated if they have a financial stake in the company.'

'Maybe so; but it's a recent rule, intended to prevent favouritism. A rider should be employed on his merits, not because his Daddy's a shareholder...or a shareholder himself, as in Dino's case.'

'But Dino was already on the team at the time of the takeover. Why would he want to buy Publichiali shares?'

'Because,' said Jo, 'as owner of Publichiali, he employs Fiarelli who officially controls the team. But Dino's the one who dictates the team's policy.'

'Can't he do that anyway, as team captain?'

'Officially, he can't. Unofficially, a few star riders may have some influence. But Dino has overstepped the unofficial line by a long way.'

'Dino is not so clever as he imagines. As a would-be entrepreneur, he takes the most stupid risks.'

Jo preferred not comment on that. She said, 'You did a lot of work. I truly appreciate it.'

'It was interesting. I rather enjoyed it. Anything else I can do to help?'

'Well...Yes, there is. Do you happen to remember the name of the Police Inspector at La Portette?'

'Inspector Simenon. I remember, because of Simenon who wrote the Inspector Maigret books. Why? Are you going back to La Portette?'

'Perhaps; depending on how things turn out. I'll have to decide how best to use the information about the companies. I'll let you know what happens.'

They said their goodbyes. Jo switched off her phone and sat looking over her shorthand notes. She'd gone after this as a journalistic scoop, but here was a clear breach of the rules. Should she pass this information to the Federation? In the past, she'd kept quiet about one or two dubious matters. It was not her business to act like a policeman's nark. But this was serious. Nardini was not only breaking the rules, but his control of the Chiali team seemed total. If she was right about that overheard snatch of talk, he had even told Dash to plant dope on Marc Martens.

Assume she was right. Dino's intention was to ensure Marc was thrown out of the race with his reputation in ruins, if not his whole career. The dope had gone into Rothman's bag by mistake, but the consequences for Rothman could have been equally damaging. Fortunately, Rothman had been released, and the police investigators were re-examining the fingerprints. Perhaps Rothman's long-standing repute as an honest man had something to do with that. And then there was another point. If, as she suspected, Nardini had prompted Hachette's question about Vallon's brakes, he had jeopardised Ferrer's career by having him suspected of sabotage.

All of which brought her to the question of Vallon's death. That scene on Claudia's DVD had prompted a theory. If the theory were correct, Vallon's death had not been accidental. Forethought must have gone into it. Manslaughter?

And then Dash, Nardini's henchman, had almost killed Danny Breton.

That was the bottom line.

But, Jo's conscience objected, wasn't that just a flash of bad temper? Scrub that. Dash had told Danny: "I'll teach you to keep your nose out..." It had been an assault.

Jo realised that, for almost the first time in her adult life, she desperately needed somebody to talk this over with. For somebody, read Paul, of course. She wished she could discuss her dilemma with him; not to pass the buck of decision-making, but to hear his opinion. Paul had said he missed having someone to confide in. How well she understood that, now!

She found it easiest to clarify her thoughts at the keyboard. She opened her laptop, clicked Word, and typed for half an hour.

Then, as there was nothing more that she could do at the moment, she poured a drink from the minibar and picked up the magazine she'd bought. It was a gossip glossy, with articles about celebrities, but she was so cocooned in the world of cycling, she'd never heard of any of them—except Paula. She flipped through it until she found: *Pregnant Model Paula di Luca Fights Wine Giant Chiali.*

The heading was followed by short text captions on the full-page photo-spread.

Paula has already starred in two of Chiali's TV commercials—part of a planned series of five. The company sued her for breach of contract when she announced she could not complete the series. Her fans will be disappointed, but she says she is pregnant!

Paula, pictured here attending Saturday's premiere of Total Destruction II, looks as glamorous as ever...but more than a tad over her normal catwalk weight.

Her lawyer stated that the Chiali Company hadn't read the small print in his client's contract.

Seemingly it covers this happy eventuality...although Paula isn't looking too happy about it.

Jo closed the magazine, her mind whirling. This whole business was getting to be like Rubik's Cube. Just as you think you've got it sorted out, another twist upsets your logic.

She eventually got her thoughts into order and went over them point by point.

Paula di Luca, otherwise Paula Ferrer, might well win her court battle with Publichiali, of which company Dino Nardini was the majority shareholder. Court battles come expensive to the losers.

Had George Ferrer been targeted just because he was Paula's husband? Poor, romantic George. Marrying that bimbo had been his biggest error.

Jo had seen the two excellent Chiali commercials on Italian TV. They were like episodes of a serial story with topical jokes and cliffhanging endings. They'd ended with the caption: *To be continued.* The planned continuation was now wrecked. The film production must have cost a great deal. Faced with a big financial loss for Publichiali, Dino would have blamed Harry Vallon, the presumed father of Paula's expected *bambino*, for causing the fiasco.

Jo decided to phone Paul, hoping he'd be back from visiting the hospital.

She was in luck. 'How's Danny?'

'Fine. Getting bored—a sign of recovery. And between visits to Danny, I'm bored, too. I miss you, *ma chère Jo.*'

'And I'm missing *you,* for several reasons. Right now, I need to discuss a problem, but it's not something easily explained over the phone. Can you find a cyber-café?'

'There's an Internet lounge in the hotel.'

'Is there?' Why was she surprised? A hotel near an airport, and not all travellers had laptops. 'That's good. I'll e-mail you, with attachments. I need your opinion on them, if you wouldn't mind.'

'Of course I wouldn't mind. You know something? It's nice to be needed.'

'You mean that? Because there's something else I'd like you to do. Look at the fourth segment of that DVD I asked you to keep for me. A couple of minutes of it might interest Police Inspector Simenon, the officer investigating Vallon's death. I won't say any more now, because I don't want to influence you with my theory.'

'I'm intrigued. I'll do that before I go on the Net. Give me an hour or so and I'll get back to you.'

~

After fifty minutes, Paul called back. 'I printed those attachments so as to read them carefully. There's not much to discuss, is there? I agree with you that Nardini and Dash have gone too far.'

'What about that fourth section of DVD?'

'An interesting bit of film. I understand your theory. You might well be on to something. Put your ideas about in writing, and send me another attachment.'

'Right. And then what?'

'The Federation should be told about Nardini's shareholdings. In fact I know Rolf Niemann pretty well. I could have a word with him, if you like. If I think it's appropriate, I could mention your theory as well.'

'Would you do that for me? I don't know what to say.'

'About what?' Paul was puzzled.

'About your help. Thank you sounds inadequate, but I'm not used to...to someone doing things for me.'

'D'you think you could get used to it?' She could hear the smile in his voice.

STAGE 20

Morning

Paul Breton

Paul had called the Federation's head office in Bern, and had been pleasantly surprised to learn that Herr Doktor Niemann was actually here in Toulouse, staying in one of the plusher hotels. A phone-call to that hotel resulted in an appointment to meet Niemann this morning.

Rolf Niemann, in his youth an Olympic middle-distance runner, had been a pioneering specialist in sports medicine. After working for several years as the Tour's official doctor, he had become the Federation's medical adviser. The Federation had later appointed him to their board, and he was now their chief spokesman.

He came to the door of his suite and shook hands cordially. 'Good to see you, Paul. Come and sit down.' He followed his guest across the room. 'No need to ask how you are. Very fit, I see, and you're walking better than the last time I saw you. Been fitted with a new boot or something?'

Since Paul's foot had been amputated, he had suffered a painful limp caused, more than anything, by the weight of a clumsy boot. He said: 'This is the latest technology, with a normal looking shoe. It's lightweight and remarkably flexible.'

'May I have a look?'

'Of course.' Paul sat and extended the new prosthetic marvel.

Niemann had, after all, been The Tour's doctor who attended Paul at the time of his accident.

~

...A crazy accident. Pouring rain, and the road slick with gale-blown leaves. Paul's wheels suddenly slipped and he went sliding on his side across the asphalt, entangled in the frame of his bike. The race director's car was right behind him. The driver braked and swung the wheel to avoid him.

But the car aquaplaned. Wheels locked, it skidded to a halt with its bonnet crushed against a tree...and Paul Breton's foot crushed under its rear offside wheel...

~

'Bionics. A wonderful advance.' Niemann straightened. 'Now, let's prioritise. How is Danny?'

'Mending fast. He'll be out of hospital in a couple of days. He was lucky.'

'Lucky to have fast reflexes and powerful deltoids. That back flip in mid-air saved his life.'

'Back flip? What back flip?'

Niemann walked over to the TV unit. 'The official helicopter shots were too distant for our purpose, so the Federation contacted the local TV station to ask if they'd filmed the incident.' He held up a DVD. 'This was filmed from the end of the bridge. A hand-held camera with an excellent zoom lens.' He slotted the disc into the player. 'Watch.'

A slow-motion sequence showed Tom Dash ramming his shoulder into Danny. The camera remained on Danny as he tumbled over the parapet of the bridge and began to fall, head-down. Then, like a cliff diver, Danny threw his arms up and back, so that he hit the water feet first.

As Paul watched, he had a sudden recollection of Danny aged ten, refusing to learn to dive. Seemingly Danny had a phobia about hitting his head on the bottom of the pool. Could a phobia possibly be a premonition?

Paul was brought back to the present when Niemann stopped the disc and said: 'A statement will be released later today. The Federation will sanction Dash for his action and will also present the filmed evidence to the police. I assume you're here to discuss charging Dash with assault?'

'No, I'm not,' Paul said, surprised. 'Guy Lacrosse is handling that side of things. I'm here because I wanted to give you some facts about another member of the Chiali team.' He hesitated. 'Also some ideas about the scandal over amphetamines.'

Niemann frowned. 'We're extremely disturbed by that. I'll be glad to hear your ideas, but start with the facts.'

Paul reached into his briefcase for the printouts of Jo's e-mailed attachments. He handed a page to Niemann.

Chiali is a parent company. Subsidiary companies handle various aspects of the business. For example, Publichiali is responsible for all publicity, including sponsorship of the cycling team. Publichiali was merged with Primotinto, the printers. Later, the majority of Primotinto-Publichiali shares were bought by the clothing company called Herc. And Herc is owned by Dino Nardini.

Niemann sank onto the chair opposite Paul. 'Good...heavens!' he said slowly. 'That makes Nardini the major shareholder in the sponsoring company. That is against the regulations. He can't get away with this. Where did this information come from?'

'The Mercantile Registry of Milan.'

'I'll ask our legal department to check this out. That will take time, though, and they'll want to know the basis of my request.'

Hearing the implied question, Paul chose his words with care. 'The investigation was made at the request of a friend of mine. Someone I've known half my life. Her name's Jo Bonnard.'

'The journalist? I read her articles. They're perceptive. What prompted her to investigate?'

'A number of things. I'll come to them shortly. She also sent me her ideas about the amphetamines. They start with the Dex found in Bob Rothman's luggage. How does the Federation view his claim that he knows nothing about it?'

'We're very inclined to believe him. Never in his whole career has he come close to a positive dope test. In fact, there has never been a hint of suspicion about him. He's a serious sort of fellow, quiet and unassuming. The police tend to take his word, too, in view of the underlying fingerprints on the little cylinder of powder.'

They don't yet know whose are the fingerprints, but they're not those of Martens.'

Paul was startled. 'I know a certain journalist hinted at Martens, but...'

'Hachette, yes. We couldn't let the rumour run without taking some action. The French police got Martens's prints from their Belgian counterparts. They didn't match.'

The IFPCO had acted quickly, Paul thought. He handed over another sheet of paper. 'This is Jo's theory.'

Mr Chip and Chiali teams were in the same hotel. Therefore, many people could have planted the Dex. So I asked myself: Cui bono? Who stands to gain? I concluded that Nardini is the most likely candidate. When he bought Publichiali he invested a lot of money and he's trying to protect his investment by discrediting his rivals in various ways.

The drug was probably put into Rothman's bag by mistake. Not by Nardini, but by Dash. I overheard Nardini tell Dash: 'You put it in the wrong bag.' Dash replied: 'They all look the same.' I think he was referring to the team's identical sports bags, and the Dex was meant to go in Martens's bag.

I also have the idea Nardini is paying Hachette, who was supposed to write something along the lines of 'I'm not surprised the dope turned up in Martens's luggage,' but changed it to fit the new circumstances.

Niemann looked up again. 'Hachette again, eh? Because he knew of Martens's delinquent past?'

'Supposedly delinquent,' Paul corrected. 'Let me tell you the truth about Marc Martens.'

Niemann listened, his lips tightening, as Paul related what he'd learned from Dirk Leyden. At the end of it, Niemann said, 'So Hachette, as often, was distorting the facts. The man is a menace.'

'A clever menace. When Dash slipped up, Hachette had to alter his article, but he did it without dropping the rotten insinuations about Martens. May I leave it at that for a moment? I'd like to show you this.' From his attaché case he produced the magazine he'd bought that morning at Jo's request.

Niemann took the magazine, glanced at the cover, and gave Paul a strange look.

Seeing Niemann's expression, Paul laughed. 'It's not my usual reading material. I want you to look at the article on page eight.'

Niemann frowned, turned to the article, read it, and then said, 'I've never heard of Paula di Luca. Apart from her contract with Chiali, I don't see the relevance.'

'The relevance is that Paula de Luca is Paula Ferrer, the wife of George Ferrer. But it's more than likely that Harry Vallon sired her expected child.'

The Doctor sat back, an expression of extreme distaste on his face. 'Must we discuss gossip?'

Paul held up a hand. 'Hear me out, Rolf. The woman's pregnancy has cost Publichiali plenty, and if she wins her court case, Nardini will lose more. Read the rest of Jo's ideas.'

If Hachette is in Nardini's pocket, that would explain why, after Vallon crashed, Hachette made sure that everyone suspected George Ferrer. If Nardini victimised George to get back at Paula, was he, at the same time, diverting attention from his own action against Vallon? Apart from race rivalry, Nardini intended to discredit Vallon, whom he'd blame for wrecking Chiali's advertising campaign.

Niemann was frowning over the page. 'Nardini's action against Vallon? What does she mean by that?'

'Jo strongly suspects that Nardini fed Harry Vallon the amphetamine.'

'Just a moment!' Niemann looked up, shocked. 'Is she suggesting that Dino Nardini deliberately caused Vallon's death?'

'Not at all. Read the next bit.'

Niemann recommenced reading.

By giving him Dex, Nardini hoped that Vallon would win the stage. In which case, Vallon would certainly have registered positive in the dope-test and been expelled from The Tour. Nardini did not intend Vallon's death. According to the post mortem analysis, the quantity of Dex was 'non lethal.'

However, I emphasise that all of this is supposition, based on a few minutes of film. (Segment 4 of the DVD.)

Niemann frowned darkly. 'She thinks Nardini gave Vallon the drug? How?'

'Do you know Frutactiv—a very sweet drink that's supposed to be a rapid energy-booster?'

'I know of it. It's harmless and moderately effective.'

'I believe Dex is soluble and almost tasteless, so Frutactiv would disguise any faint taste. Jo's theory is best explained by this.' He took the DVD box from his case. 'She gave it to me for safe-keeping. Could we watch a two-minute segment?'

As they watched it, Niemann sat rubbing his chin, deep in thought. After a fairly long silence he said, 'You keep mentioning Dex, a brand-name of dexamphetamine sulphate, a so-called 'pep' drug that the medical profession uses mainly in the treatment of narcolepsy. Are you picking that well-known name at random?'

'No. It was Dex. The name's very clearly printed on the packet.' Paul drew a breath and let it out like a sigh. 'This brings us back to my son's fall from the bridge. This morning, he said I could tell you the reason for Dash's action.'

He told Niemann about the minor collision, and about Danny going to return the helmet and seeing Dash's case open on the bed. 'On top of the case, Danny saw an open packet of Dex. He'd heard of it, from chatter in the peloton. He said the brand name was clearly printed in large green letters.' Reluctantly, Paul went on to explain why his son had broken the disclosure rule.

Niemann got up and paced over to the window. Looking down on the busy traffic, he said, 'This is a private conversation. Nevertheless, I cannot be selective over which parts of it I act upon.'

'I realise that. So does Danny. He expects to be sanctioned.'

'He almost paid with his life.' Niemann turned to face him again. 'He *did* intend to report Dash if Dash didn't comply. My strong recommendation to the Board will be a fine for a minor infringement.'

'You're being very generous. Thank you.'

Niemann shook his head. 'Sports today are big business. There's an increasing tendency to law-of-the-jungle tactics. Sportsmanship and gentlemanly conduct are worthwhile values that have all but disappeared. I'll do my best to prevent any sanction more serious than a fine.'

He went over to the DVD player. He pressed the Eject button, and then he stood for a few moments, looking at the disc. Eventually he turned to Paul. 'This is a home recording? Might I borrow it?'

'Hmm...As I told you, it isn't my disc...May I ask why you want it?'

'This hotel has WiFi,' said Niemann. 'I could download the DVD to my laptop and then send it on to the Federation in Bern. We employ a young man who does astonishing things with a computer. I imagine he will be able to make still photographs from it. I could phone him and tell him the precise sections I'm interested in.'

'That seems all right,' Paul was still a little doubtful. 'Provided I can have it back.'

'Of course! Let me make that phone call.'

Paul waited while Niemann spoke to someone in German, then to another person in French.

'...The sections are: the cyclist in the jersey with red spots gives a carton to a rider in dark blue. Got that? Next is...'

He went on to complete his list, and Paul was impressed by Niemann's recall of the action he'd watched only once.

Niemann ended his conversation, turned to Paul and said: 'Could you come back for the disc at six oclock this evening?'

'Yes, that's fine.'

The two men shook hands and Paul left.

STAGE 20

Afternoon

Jo Bonnard

It was extremely hot. The heat wave seemed to have followed The Tour's special train all the way to the Vosges Mountains. Here, in the foothills, trees offered occasional shade along rolling country roads that ran between a patchwork of green and ochre fields.

Jo Bonnard's eyes flicked between her stopwatch and her monitor, on which was the lone figure of Chico Montes. He had shot away from the peloton almost as soon as the stage began, and was now impressively far ahead of the rest. Moto 1 would therefore be with him for some time, and Jo was glad of the lucky chance that had brought him across her path the previous evening. She had stopped to chat to him and could now add a little biographical note to her commentary.

The advert break ended and she took up the commentary again. 'Still out here on his own is Chico Montes, Intapost's fair-haired rider from a small fishing village in Galicia, in the northwest of Spain. He's never called anything else but Chico, although his real name is Baltasar. He got the name Chico—meaning small—because he was the youngest of three children. He's a *domestique*, one of the unsung heroes of the peloton, and he's the mainstay of his family. His father and two older brothers were fishermen who died two years ago in a freak storm. It's good to see Chico getting his chance to shine today.'

Into the shot came the famous yellow motorbike that scooted back and forth. The man on its pillion wrote updates on his chalk-board, so that riders could see the time gaps between the groups. Not every rider had earphones for the team-car-to-cyclist communications. Despite the high-tech, those didn't always work too well. Trees tended to break-up the radio waves, and so the low-tech chalkboard was a reliable way to keep riders informed. The black-board man held the board in a position that allowed Chico to read it. Jo peered at her screen, trying to read the figures. It looked like twelve minutes and something.

There came a change of shot captioned: Moto 2, Chase Group.

'Those are the four chasers, more than twelve minutes behind Chico Montes. My goodness! Look who's in the group—the Yellow Jersey himself, Marc Martens.'

And that was it. The monitor flipped back to Moto 1. Jo was annoyed that she'd had no time to say more. She killed the microphone and spoke to Tony. 'What's up?'

'Problems with all signals, except Moto 1. I'll give you a commercial break in ten seconds.'

'Fair enough.' She clicked the microphone on again. 'Sorry, viewers, but we have a technical problem. We're going to another ad break, but we'll be back with Chico very shortly.'

Jo wondered how long Chico could stay out there, especially in this heat.

⁓

During their chat yesterday evening, Chico had asked for news of Danny. 'You know I was right behind Danny in that pile-up?' he said. Jo nodded, and he went on: 'When Dash brought him down along with Claes, I could have gone around them, but I snagged Dash's wheel instead. I hit the deck myself, of course, but I didn't see why Dash should ride away free after causing so many people to crash, especially when one of them was Danny. He's not just one of my team; he's my room-mate. A good pal.'

'Are you saying Tom Dash deliberately went for Danny and caused that pile-up?'

'It was deliberate, for sure, but his target was Jan Claes—a rival sprinter, you know. Danny was just unlucky, being alongside Claes. But that Dash is a dirty rider. A real son of a...'

Jo grinned. She knew the Spanish expression. 'Say it! I agree with you.'

Chico grinned back. 'Right. You're in touch with Danny, you said? Can you tell him best wishes from the team? I tried to call him on his mobile phone. Then I heard its ring-tone.' He gave a chortle of laughter. 'It was in Danny's case, right beside me! How stupid can I get, eh? Tell him I closed it down and put it in my case. Oh, and the battery charger, too. I'll keep them safe for him.'

She wondered what Chico was thinking about now, as he battled the heat and the loneliness.

Chico Montes

Chico raised his head and brushed sweat from his eyes, trying to read the chalkboard. It read: 12' 36 and the numbers 53, 43, 119, 129.

More than twelve and a half minutes in front of a four-man chase group. No so bad! But Chico knew who was wearing the number 53 on his back—Marc Martens, no less! Who were the others? Chiali was team four, and 43 was Salvatore. And 119 was...? Don't know. And 129?...Zenkov! That was some chase group! Where was the peloton?

The chalkboard man was wiping the board and writing: Pel. 14'00

Chico got his head down. Just keep going as long and as far as he could, and win as many points as possible for the team. At today's start, they were only one point down on Mr Chip, but six points below Chiali. His job was at stake here. So were the contracts of all the Intapost boys.

He'd taken off on that first long drag of a climb and nobody had chased him. Only a Category 4, but worth five points for being first at the top. Then the sprint—another six points. That made eleven. Take away the six points' deficit, giving plus five. Five up! Intapost must be virtual leaders over Chiali.

But wait a minute. Salvatore maybe got some points back there. If he'd been the first chaser over the sprint line, he'd get four points. So maybe Intapost was only one point up, after all.

Well, there was another sprint somewhere along this road. With a twelve-minute margin, he'd win that one, God willing. It would be great to get the team prize and have some worthwhile money to send home to the family. Plus, if the team could get the GSG sponsorship, he'd have a secure job next year.

He reached for his water bottle, swallowed a little and poured the rest over his neck. The sun was behind him, burning. Zenkov, the blond Russian, had the right idea, letting his hair grow long.

Might be a good idea to eat something, keep up the energy level. Guy was forever telling them to eat before they felt hungry and drink whether they were thirsty or not. There were a couple of energy bars in his back pocket. He felt around for one, tore the wrapper with his teeth, crammed the bar into his mouth and chewed. What did it taste of? Nothing in particular. Hazelnuts, maybe.

He'd got used to the swarm of motorbikes—police outriders with blue lights flashing, a TV motocamera, a radio commentator, and a stills photographer who turned around just then. Chico recognised him. It was Graham Watson, taking his photo! Maybe that image would be in *Ciclismo!* Or even on the Graham Watson website...

Chico was on a lone breakaway, and the TV picture would be captioned *Head of the Race!*

He turned his head at the sound of a car coming up beside him. Guy Lacrosse grinned out at him. 'How's it going?'

'Okay. But it's hot.'

Guy passed him two *bidons* from the cool-box. 'The water's cold, so don't gulp it down. Did you eat? Good. The sprint's ten kilometres ahead. You'll make it. The Martens group's still ten minutes behind you.'

'Ten? It was twelve and a half.'

'They're catching up, but you'll take the sprint no problem, and then ease off. When you come to the Col du Sapin climb, drop back into the pack.'

'How many points did Salvatore get?'

'Only two. The Russian beat him. We're three points up. Okay? You're doing brilliantly, Chico.'

The car slowed, leaving Chico to his lonely ride.

≈

At the team meeting that morning, they'd talked about the climbs. They'd all looked at Paco Ribero, but Guy wagged a finger at them. 'Paco's not doing all the work. It's a long stage and I want somebody to go off on the first climb and put a scare into Chiali and Mr Chip. My guess is that Nardini and Martens will chase any breaks, so let's try to tire them out before the third and last climb. That's where the stage will be won or lost, and that's where Paco will attack. Right?'

'Sure, boss.' Paco Ribero grinned. 'I feel good. I can beat Nardini today.'

'Do it,' said Guy. 'Now, the Col du Sapin. That's yours David.'

David Vauban snapped his fingers. 'You bet! I know every metre of that climb. I was *born* on that hill! Well, I mean in the village, you know, in a house, not actually on the...Sorry. Daft remark.' He stopped talking and laughed with the rest of them.

Guy let the laughs subside. 'Fine. So, who's going off on his own? Chico? Think you can stay ahead of a chase?'

~

Chico was five kilometres from the sprint and the chasers were getting closer. God, it was hot! The water must have lost its chill, and now he could drink it. Mustn't dehydrate. Just keep riding. If you can ride in the peloton, you can ride on your own. It's the same number of kilometres, so there's no difference.

Who was he kidding? In the pack there's always a slipstream, a few easier moments. Here on his own, with no one to give him shelter, there was no respite.

He kept his eyes on the road that stretched ahead, dead straight. Was he moving at all, or was the road rolling beneath him while he pedalled, pedalled, legs hurting, but getting no closer to that point where the sides of the road seemed to meet? It was called the vanishing point. He remembered that from school, from that art teacher who was great at drawing. What was her name? Señora Medina. She'd talked about perspective and the vanishing point. Imagine remembering Señora Medina, here on a road in France.

Where was he? No idea. Push on. Turn the pedals. Get to that sprint...

At last, there was the banner. He was aware of houses, of people standing in the shade and clapping. A voice shouted *Bravo!* And then he heard *Chico!* Somebody knew who he was! The shout was taken up: *Chico!* He was across the line. He'd done it! Six more points.

A whistle shrilled. A policeman was holding a yellow flag to warn that the road swung sharply to the right through the village, then up the Col du Sapin—a winding Category 2 climb. The chase group must be closing on him, but he'd keep going. He'd stay in front for as long as his legs held out.

This had been a great day for him. Even in this small French village, people knew he was Chico Montes. And what about the folks back home, far away in Galicia? They'd be watching the TV and cheering even louder. Into his mind came an image of his grandmother. She was wearing her blue flowered pinafore, holding her rosary and praying for him. Was this telepathy? He'd phone home this evening and ask what Grandma was wearing today. She'd given him the little gold cross that hung round his neck. He briefly closed his fingers around it, knowing that Grandma was watching him. Then he gave the motocamera an enormous happy grin, even as the slope began to hammer his thigh muscles.

Jo Bonnard

'Chico made it! Well done!' Tony had recovered the pictures, just in time. 'He's through the village, heading for the climb to the Col du Sapin. That's Pine Tree Pass in English. The chasers must be gaining on him, though. There they are!' she exclaimed as the Moto 2 picture came up, with a caption overlay reading 6' 00.

'Look at that! They've made up more than six minutes. Of course, Chico must be getting tired, but this is a powerful group composed of Martens, Salvatore, Zenkov and Haagens, a first-year professional.

'Chiali has obviously sent Salvatore up the road, as he's their strongman. But again he was third in that sprint, so he has gained only two more points while Chico got another six. If I've calculated correctly, Intapost is now leading the team-points competition, hence the high-speed chase.

'Mr Chip started the day five points behind Chiali, but I'm surprised they've let Marc Martens take up this chase. He didn't contest the sprints, however, letting young Haagens have the points. I guess Marc is saving some energy for the final climb. He looks unperturbed, as usual. The Spanish call him The Machine. The French refer to him as The Man in the Iron Mask.

'This close-up shot explains the names. He hates to let anyone see his fatigue, or his suffering; or even his pleasure. Look at him now. Not a flicker of emotion.'

Why was Marc in this chase? Without his mentor, Rothman, it seemed that Marc was panicking, giving way to the nerves he'd talked about yesterday. He'd removed his earphone, too. Either it wasn't functioning, or he was choosing to disregard advice and do his own thing.

Moto 3 was filming the peloton, now only eight minutes back. Intapost and Chiali riders were surging towards the front of the bunch, both teams hoping to control the speed. They must have realised that the gap was too wide, and they had to get cracking before they hit the climb.

Moto 1 was still with Chico, but the chasers were now visible behind him.

'Here they come,' Jo said. 'The chasers have Chico in sight. He's been on his own for ninety kilometres…Aah, he's been caught but he's wisely not trying to latch on behind them. He'll likely get in amongst his team-mates in the peloton.

'The chasers are working together, taking turns at the front, letting the others ride in the slipstream. It's like a relay. Watch Salvatore in front…He slackens his speed and Zenkov takes his place…Zenkov drops back and Martens takes the lead…Now it's Haagens's turn. Beautiful cooperation. This is super.'

The rhythm of the four-man relay was a joy to watch. Jo was disappointed when the picture changed to a helicopter shot. 'From above, we can see that the shape of the peloton has changed from a bunch to a single long line. That's a sure sign of high speed. They're steaming along, only three minutes behind the chase group, who have reduced their pace. Shortly they'll be on the nasty climb to the Col du Sapin. These are not huge, long climbs like the Alps or the Pyrenees, but they're tough. The Col du Sapin is only twelve kilometres, but it has some steep hairpin bends.'

The road swung to the right and up into the pine forest where there would be welcome patches of shade. Between dark green embankments of trees, the peloton looked like a long, multicoloured ribbon. At the front, in a blur of red and white, the Intapost riders rode in line, setting a cracking pace through the village. As always on the climbs, the spectators had been out with the whitewash, painting the names of their heroes on the asphalt. The camera zoomed in on DINO inside a heart shape. RIBERO was there as well, but—over and over again—was DAVID, DAVID, all the way up the hill.

Jo had done her homework. 'No wonder the name David is decorating the landscape. Intapost's David Vauban has just whisked through the village where he was born twenty-six years ago come November. Maybe his family's waiting to see him in the village. More likely, they'll be among the crowd at the top of the hill.'

David Vauban

They had caught up with Chico. Shouting 'Seven points! Stupendous!' they swarmed past and he drifted into the middle of the pack.

At the front of the line, Paco Ribero yelled, 'David? You going yet?'

David rode up to him. 'Not until we pass the old sawmill. Told you about that ramp this morning. Salvatore and Haagens will think they've hit a wall. So will the Russian.'

'But not Martens.'

'We'll see.'

A minute later, they approached a corner and David muttered: 'See you later.' He sped off, going for the outside of the bend.

Ahead of him, sure enough, Salvatore and Haagens were standing on the pedals, but both were labouring. They'd cracked.

He passed them. A bend to the right, then the next straight. DAVID painted on the road. The family would be waiting by the big pine tree at the top, nothing surer. A tight corner and...Gotcha! The Russian was rocking. Done for. Now, where's Martens?

Steep section. Watch out for the corner and keep tight to the side. A short straight, the false summit and four bends down to the old bridge.

Over the bridge. Count the turns of the pedals—he'd practised this a hundred times—seven, eight, nine, change gear and go!

A big swing right. There's Martens! Got his hands down on the hooks but he's picked the wrong gear. Too big for the next ramp.

Wait for the corner. Last change of gear. Now!

My whole family is up there. Most of the village. My pals...I've got to win this, so go-go-go!

Marc Martens

Marc was on his own and hating it. This evening, de Groot would make the whole team watch the recording. They'd watch him and analyse, searching for any mistake, any bit of bad judgement. Worse than that, the world was watching him because he was the wearing the Yellow Jersey. But if his strength ran out? If he couldn't keep up the pace? The bloody media would tear him to shreds.

The TV cameraman was zooming in on his pedalling rhythm, his gear mechanism, on every blink, every breath and every trickle of sweat. Keep the stone face. Show them nothing.

David Vauban shot past, going like a rocket.

Where the hell had he come from?

Marc flicked the gear-change and went after him. He'd been caught in the wrong gear. This ramp was steeper than it looked, and bloody endless. The guy was flying, pulling away from him. It mustn't happen. He had to stay on Vauban's wheels.

Another hairpin bend. Was this just a Category 2 climb? And a Cat 1 still to come. Oh, shit!

Pain gripped his legs, the muscles hurting from lactic acid. Mustn't get into oxygen debt. Marc opened his mouth wide, sucking in air. Ignore the bloody cameras.

Marc closed his mind to Vauban, to the summit, to the next climb. He focussed his thoughts on breathing, and visualised the oxygen reaching his blood, feeding his leg muscles, fuelling them with the power to push the pedals.

Jo Bonnard

'They're almost at the top, and Vauban can't drop Martens. Half the village seems to be up there with banners and flags and an enormous picnic table. What a crowd, cheering their local boy. And they've got a band! What fun! This is the kind of party atmosphere that makes The Tour special.

'Vauban takes a look over his shoulder, but he has reached the white line. He's done it! David Vauban lifts a hand to wave to his home crowd as he crosses the summit line, just three seconds ahead of Martens. Whew! That was a whale of a race!'

Jo realised she was shouting—had been shouting for several minutes. 'Excuse me while I catch my breath,' she said. 'That was tremendous. It hammered a few riders. We saw Haagens and Salvatore come to a near halt, and then Zenkov was labouring.'

The pictures were constantly changing from one camera to another.

'A new chase group has formed, with Ribero at the front. Three other Intapost riders are with him. Three Chiali riders are coming up to them, with Nardini second in the line. His is the Polkadot Jersey between two bright greens. Look at those faces! Teeth-bared determination on every one of them. Just behind them is Charreau, followed by Ferrer in dark blue, catching up to them.'

Now came a helicopter shot. 'The peloton is still on the climb. From this height it looks like a ribbon chopped into different lengths—the groups that are scattered all the way up the hillside. There's a noticeable gap back to the tail end—the sprinters in their "laughing group," no doubt...and I've just heard on Race Radio that Leon Jonkers is amongst them! He looked really whacked after yesterday's time trial.

'Ah, good! We're back with Moto 2 at the top of Col du Sapin. Ribero and Nardini are out of the saddle, sprinting. It's hard to tell who was first over the line. At a guess, Nardini was a centimetre in front.'

An advert break came up, and Race Radio confirmed her guess about Nardini. Jo drank from her bottle of water. It wasn't often she shouted herself hoarse, but this was one of the most exciting stages of the whole Tour.

It had been Walter Koch's intention to emphasise the team-sport aspect by allocating a larger amount of prize money to the winning team, than to the individual stars. Jo had approved the idea. It meant more money for the "unsung heroes," as she'd called the *domestiques* who were lead-out men, water-carriers and providers of a slipstream for their leaders, but who got little glory and less cash.

But with the Intapost team fighting to stay afloat, Chiali fighting to hold on to their lead, and so few points separating the top three teams, this stage had suddenly changed in quality. Suddenly it was more like a battle than a race.

She drew breath to go on again.

'Moto 1 is following Marc Martens down the other side of the pass. David Vauban is about two bends ahead of him, travelling at speed; but he knows this road. He's been riding on it since he was a child. Marc is going down more cautiously. Whoops! Be careful! That was a wild skid and the road surface looks rough. He took the wrong line on that bend, and he doesn't have time to run out of road at this stage of the race. The chasers are also on the descent. Nardini's known as a 'kamikaze' on these downhill swoops. He's just ahead of Paco Ribero whose teeth are clenched, whether in pain or grinning like a demon, I wouldn't like to say.

'Those motocameras are doing a fantastic job, getting close enough to bring you the pictures, but having to keep out of the riders' way. Watch it, lads!' On the screen, the road surface swung from horizontal to vertical as the motorbike heeled over on a bend. Jo hissed breath through her teeth. 'Anyone who doesn't like roller-coasters, close your eyes until I tell you. These bends are making me giddy. I don't know about you, but I'm leaning over at every bend, along with the motorbike. Hold your breath.'

A wider section of road allowed Moto 2 to draw alongside Ribero. Not content with whizzing down the hill, the little Spaniard dropped down off the saddle, the seat of his pants just above his rear wheel. He hooked his hands under the bars and tucked his head between his outstretched arms.

'*Don't do that!*' Jo exclaimed in horror. 'Anyone who's thinking of trying that...just don't do it! We know he's cutting wind resistance to the minimum, but that is *dangerous*. If he hits a pothole, a stone, whatever, he's got absolutely no control.' She watched, dry-mouthed, for over a minute.

'That's better. He's back on the saddle. A big silly grin on his face because he shot past Nardini; but that was madness!'

Jo revised her opinion about the team prize. She had never seen such cutthroat rivalry.

Paco Ribero

Guy would give him hell for that, but Paco had enjoyed it. It took him back to his BMX days, before mountain biking, when stunts had been part of the scene.

He'd given Nardini the zip treatment. And how about those guys on the motocamera? Change of pants for them.

Off the hill, five kilometres flattish, then they'd hit the big hill. No sign of David yet. He must have gone down like a water-park ride.

The plan was working. Chico, then David, knocking hell out of Martens before the big climb. Then only Nardini to worry about.

The last climb was going to be Ribero versus Nardini. And he, Paco Ribero, had told the boys he'd win.

Paul Breton

'They're all trying to hammer Marc Martens.' Danny Breton hunched forward, intent on the TV screen in his father's hotel room.

The two leading riders had started up the climb to the stage finish. Vauban was still in front, with Martens doggedly adhering to his back wheel, but either they had slowed or Ribero and Nardini had speeded up. The screen captions showed the time gap between the pairs was steadily decreasing.

The helicopter camera was on the peloton. The front-runners were closing on the chasing pair while, a long way back, the tail end was just coming down from the Col. Like beads running off a string, they poured down the bends.

Moto 4 was with them. The beads became recognisable riders and the France2 commentator reeled-off a list of names as riders crossed the screen: '...*Jonkers is struggling, followed by Arnold of AFA, then Nilsson of Intapost...Claes of Mr Chip, Bruno of Chiali...Salvatore, tired after his long chase. The sprinters have been decimated by the Col du Sapin climb. Dash is not amongst them. If you missed the news before this broadcast, Dash was excluded from The Tour on the decision made by the Federation...'*

Danny turned an astonished face to his father. 'They've chucked him out?'

Paul nodded. Rolf Niemann had phoned to inform him that a statement would be released to the media. Dash was on a six-month suspension from professional competition, as from the date of his dangerously aggressive riding on the St Martin Bridge. Danny and Paul Breton were requested to be ready to provide statements, but Paul saw no point in worrying Danny over something that might not happen. He also knew that Federation lawyers would make an investigation of the ownership of Publichiali, but he had assured Niemann he would remain silent about that and about Jo's doping theory.

Danny's attention was back on the screen.

David Vauban had dropped behind Martens and made a brave effort to stay there, but the gap widened between them. Then Ribero and Nardini caught up with him, shot past him and kept going.

Their fast pace took them alongside Martens. Nardini put in a burst of speed. Ribero matched his acceleration and the two climbers overtook the Yellow Jersey. Martens reacted instantly, pouncing after them. He stuck close to Nardini's back wheel.

Moto 1 went alongside the lightweight figure of Ribero, now leading the trio.

As Nardini rode into the shot, Paul wondered fleetingly if the Italian was unknowingly wasting his time. 'Dino Nardini's a damned good climber,' he said. 'At a guess he's riding on ninety-five percent of his ability, holding back a reserve of energy for the last two thousand metres.' The camera swung round on Martens. 'What about this fellow here?'

Danny watched. 'He's going through hell. His legs...' He put his hand down and massaged his own thigh, vicariously suffering the pain.

Paul saw his son's subconscious gesture. Danny had the physical ability to win races, but he was too kind-hearted. It seemed that Danny just didn't have that fighting instinct, that indispensable will to win.

He was emphasising with Marc Martens, too. Apparently his liking for Marc ignored the fact that theirs were rival teams. With mild regret, Paul thought that his son would probably never wear the Yellow Jersey. Then, with no regret at all, he realised he was proud of the boy for reasons more important than cycling.

On the screen, the man in the Yellow Jersey had lost another couple of metres. The two climbing specialists hadn't increased their speed. Marc was slowing.

The picture shifted to George Ferrer, who was riding at his own pace, refusing to panic. His steady rhythm was more effective than bursts of speed that couldn't be maintained. He was gaining on the leading trio as they rode under the two-kilometre banner.

The picture changed again. 'Come on, Marc!' Danny was talking to the man on the screen, living the climb with him. 'Come on! Stay with it. Charreau started the day two minutes down. He's closer now, but he can't catch you in two kilometres; not if you keep going, man! Bloody well keep going!' The anguish in Danny's voice was matched by Marc's expression. A daze of pain had replaced the iron mask.

Some twenty metres ahead of him, Paco Ribero and Dino Nardini were now side by side.

Paul had lived through moments like these. Both riders had saved that five percent, he thought. What mattered now was mental strength. Who would break first? Panic and go now, and you could burn up too soon. Wait, and you could leave it too late. You had to suss out the other. Watch his hand. It would flick the gear and he'd be gone. They were waiting...waiting...

'Nardini's gone!' Danny shouted as Nardini changed gear and shot off, rocketing up the last thousand metres. Ribero went after him. 'Paco hasn't got Nardini's sprinting power.'

'They're not there yet,' said Paul quietly. 'I'd have waited. It's a steep finish. Watch the gap.'

The gap was ten metres...then five...then only two. Nardini was standing on the pedals, but beginning to rock.

From the camera on the finishing line, Ribero was hidden behind the Chiali rider. Impossible to tell if he was still gaining ground.

Then the two bikes were side by side with four hundred metres to go. Was Nardini fading?

At the 150-metre board, Nardini ran out of gas. Ribero romped over the line, grinning like a demon. He sat up, both arms punching the air, performing a victorious boogie-woogie on the saddle.

Nardini laboured on, running on fumes. He crossed the line with his head bowed over the bars and the Chiali *soigneurs* surrounded him. One of them wrapped a big towel round Dino's shoulders and supported his bike as he wheeled him toward the Control Area with its laboratory units.

The seconds ticked away. The camera was aimed at the final curve, waiting for Martens. Or would it be Charreau?

The police outrider appeared...the motocamera...then Martens! Fighting just to get there, Marc crossed the line, and then let his body droop over the handlebars. A pack of reporters rushed at him and were eventually strong-armed off by a contingent of *soigneurs* and marshals, backed up by policemen.

The seconds went on ticking as Charreau approached the line. Danny was counting aloud. 'Three, four, *five* seconds back. Marc gets twelve points for third place. He's still in the lead by seventeen seconds.'

'Think again. Charreau gets ten for fourth place.'

'Oh, hell, so he does. Seven seconds, then.'

'And Nardini's bonus points? Forgotten them?'

'Oh!' Danny used his fingers for a rapid calculation. 'Hell's teeth! He's only fourteen seconds down! But Marc's still the leader.' Danny leaned back in his chair. 'Whew! I don't know how you feel, Dad, but I'm exhausted, just watching that.'

The commentary continued as riders crossed the line. '*Now comes George Ferrer. He has kept up well with the younger men like David Vauban, who crosses the line at the front of a small group...*'

Danny took the remote control and lowered the sound. 'You didn't tell me about Dash this morning.'

'I was busy,' said his father, 'fetching you from the hospital. He's on six months' suspension.'

Danny whistled softly. 'Unless he's got a cast-iron contract, he'll have problems getting into a team next season.'

Paul looked curiously at his son. 'Are you sorry for him?'

'In a way. Isn't it because of what I told you about him?'

'No,' said Paul crisply. 'The decision was made on filmed evidence of his dangerous riding.'

'Oh. What about the box of Dex? I...um...I suppose I'll be sanctioned too.' Unwilling to let his father see his anxiety, Danny carefully shifted his plastered leg while he asked, 'Did Doctor Niemann say anything?'

'He can't make Federation decisions on his own.' Paul put finality into his tone. He was not at liberty to say more.

STAGE 20

Evening

Dino Nardini

Dino lay on the bed, his hands behind his neck, gazing at nothing. Fourteen seconds off the Yellow Jersey...and it didn't matter. Not now.

Tom Dash flung off The Tour. A disaster. He should never have brought Dash into the scheme.

A great scheme, all gone wrong. Martens must have been allergic or something. He just got sick and recovered. And then Harry Vallon broke his damn fool neck. Christ! That had been a hell of a shock. The Dex was supposed to make him win, not turn him into a madman on a blind descent.

I should have stopped at that. Dino twisted on to his stomach and buried his face in the pillow. One big opponent gone, no chance to get at Ribero or Vauban, but he'd thought of another way to get Martens out of the race. And he gave the job to Dash, but the stupid bastard loused it up and planted the stuff in Rothman's bag.

So, Rothman was out, but he'd never been a rival. Then Dash went after Danny Breton because he thought Breton would talk.

Nardini threw himself convulsively round again and pressed his hands over his eyes, as though he could shut out his vision of the future.

Now Dash would talk. The arrival of the police car had been a bloody shock, its revolving lights attracting every pressman in the area. Dash was so stupid, he didn't even think of wiping his finger-prints off the tube of Dex powder. The cops would ask him where the stuff had come from, and Dash would blab that Fiarelli had got hold of it.

Fiarelli had wanted the team to use it. 'Tiny, undetectable quantities,' he'd said. 'Just enough to give us an edge.' But Dino had come up with a brighter idea. *Detectable* quantities fed to his main rivals. Dex would enable them to win stages, only to fail the dope tests and Goodbye. Such a clever plan!

'Stupid. Stupid. Stupid.' Dino groaned aloud. He thought he'd been so smart, getting control of the companies. Chances of any-one learning that he owned Publichiali? Remote. Almost nil. To make big money, you have to invest. His father had refused to help, so he'd tried it on his own. He'd invested a lot of money. So smart! Dino Nardini the big businessman, now in neck-deep shit, his career on the skids, advertising contracts scrapped. What was left? Publichiali fighting that bitch Paula Ferrer in court, and Herc making T-shirts for somebody else. He heard himself sobbing and pulled the pillow over his face.

Seven hundred and fifty thousand U.S. dollars. That's what he needed to pay for the operation in the American clinic; the only place that was pioneering a new procedure; the only chance of giv-ing Gina a normal life. Poor kid. Nobody knew about her, or about Carlotta. He hadn't married her...to maintain his playboy image, he'd explained, and Carlotta had understood, even after Gina was born.

Gina, his daughter...two years old. They'd tried three doctors. The third had diagnosed the baby's problem—a rare heart-abnor-mality that those dollars might cure.

Dino Nardini threw himself face down again, and wept as he had not wept since he was a tiny child.

Jo Bonnard

The hotel called *Le Jardin* was tonight's lodging for the Eltsport crew. Once again, coincidence had allocated the same hotel to the Mr Chip and Chiali teams.

There was no TV set in Jo's room. She went down to the ground floor and opened a door marked *Salon TV*, only to find the Mr Chips watching a DVD with the sound turned off. 'Oh, excuse me. I was going to watch the sports news. I didn't know you were using the room,' she said, backing out.

'No problem, Jo,' Willem de Groot called out. 'Join us. Sit down. Sports news starts in twenty minutes. We're just running through today's recording. You don't mind watching?'

'Not in the least.' On the screen was Paco Ribero, doing his madcap plunge down the hillside. 'What was Dufaux's comment on that?' she asked.

Willem restored the sound, and immediately Dufaux's voice said: *excessivement dangereux.*

Jo joined in the burst of laughter at such perfect timing. Then Willem skipped the film forward and played the final three kilometres of the stage.

As they watched Marc cross the finish line, she applauded. 'Tremendous! You're not just a time trial ace. That hill was brutal, and you stuck with the two best climbers in the business. Congratulations.'

'Thanks, Jo.' Marc gave her a brief smile and went back to glowering at the screen, not at all happy.

'What's annoying you?'

'Look at those idiot reporters! Microphones shoved up my nose before I even got off my bike. And stupid bloody questions. *'How do you feel?'* Assholes! Can't they see? Can't they think?'

'You're dead right.'

In Jo's opinion, *'How do you feel?'* was a pathetic cop-out. A something-to-say noise, made by hacks who hadn't a clue. But the pressure was getting to Marc. The last stage wouldn't be the usual formality and, with only a few seconds' advantage over Nardini and Charreau, something as trivial as a puncture could displace him from the top step of the Paris podium.

Willem extracted the disc and switched over to television just as the sports news began. Jo, the professional broadcaster, admired the presenter's timing as he spoke over film-clips: *'First, The Tour, and a dramatic stage dominated by three Intapost riders. Chico Montes stayed out on his own for over ninety kilometres, winning the prize for the day's most courageous ride. Then their French rid-*

er, David Vauban, demonstrated how to climb the Col du Sapin. Finally the bold effort of Paco Ribero secured his stage victory.'

Once again, Jo found herself giddily watching what was evidently destined to be a famous descent.

The picture cut to the studio background and the presenter saying: *'More cycling news: American rider Bob Rothman has been cleared of all suspicion regarding...'*

The boys leapt to their feet, whooping, cheering and exchanging high-fives.

'Shut up!' Jo yelled, with no affect on the hullabaloo. She moved closer to the set, but could hear only snatches: *'...the fingerprints were... earlier today...'*

The boys quietened down and Jo returned to her chair.

The presenter was reading from a page. *'Dr Niemann, spokesman for the Federation, refused to comment, saying that any statement must await the outcome of legal proceedings.'* He looked up. *'For the latest on tennis...'*

Willem switched off the set and the hubbub broke out again.

'I told you!' Marc crowed triumphantly. 'I knew The Old Man would never touch dope.' He swung round on Willem. 'Did you know about this?'

'Yes, but I was told to say nothing until it was made public.'

'Will he renew his contract for next year?'

'I don't know. He's been talking about retiring.'

'He's still a great rider. Tell him the team needs him.'

'Tell him yourself,' said Willem, adding with gentle sarcasm, 'Tell him you'd miss the arguments.'

'Of course I argue with him. Arguing is the quickest way to learn.'

Listening to the exchange, Jo smiled. The supposed rivalry, the ex-champion versus the new young aspirant, was invented by the uninformed.

Willem got to his feet and invited Jo to join the team's table for supper.

She sat next to Marc. 'I take it you're staying with this team next season?'

'Of course,' he said, 'despite The Godfather waving a chequebook.'

'The who?'

'Fiarelli. Came looking for me. 'Chiali's interested in you,' he says.'

'And you said...?'

'I'm not interested in Chiali...Well, who wants Don Corleone for a manager?' Imitating Marlon Brando's husky voice, Marc added, 'I'm gonna make ya an offer ya can't refuse.'

Jo laughed, but concealed her surprise. She hadn't known that Marc could be funny.

She glanced towards the table at the far end of the room where the Chiali team was eating. Nardini wasn't with them.

He still hadn't appeared when she finished her meal and went outside. It was a beautiful, calm evening and the large garden, which gave the hotel its name, was lamp-lit—a pleasant place for an after-dinner stroll, somewhere she could think in peace.

Paul had phoned her earlier, telling her about his meeting. Dr Niemann, he said, had already collected evidence of Dash's attack on Danny, but Danny's failure to disclose his knowledge of the Dex would likely earn him only a minimal fine. The Federation would also conduct a formal investigation into Publichiali. However, Paul added, this would take some time.

Jo hoped he hadn't sensed her disappointment. This had been her chance for a journalistic scoop. Her report was already in her laptop's memory; ready to send as soon as the official statement came out, and before any of the men—her so-called colleagues—had time to lay a male-chauvinist finger on his keyboard.

About her dope theory, Paul said only that Niemann hoped to have photo-prints made from the DVD.

Dino Nardini

Dino had to get out of his room. He couldn't stand the laughter and noise in the lounge. He didn't want to talk to anybody, didn't want to eat. The garden looked peaceful.

He was walking slowly along a path when he saw someone strolling toward him. The stroller came under one of the lamps and he recognised Jo Bonnard. Damn! The path ran straight, between flowerbeds. No escape. He came to a halt, prepared to turn away, but she came right up to him and said, 'You're in trouble.' It wasn't a question.

He ran his tongue over his teeth. 'Yes.' He didn't look at her.

'Over Dash?'

'Yes, Dash. Everything.' He kicked moodily at a small pebble. 'How can I ride the last stage? Even if I blow my chance of the Yellow Jersey, I'm still King of the Mountains, up on the podium. How can I face my fans?' he said desperately. 'It will make things worse afterwards, when it all comes out.'

'That you own Publichiali,' she said softly.

He couldn't have been more shocked if she had hit him. 'How the *hell* do you know that?'

'I know. And before you ask me, I passed on what I know.'

'You bitch! You've had your knife into me for a long time.' He jabbed an accusing finger towards her. 'You've known since you wrote that article.'

'Wrong! At that time I didn't know, but your reaction to it made me wonder why you were so furious.'

'You bloody journalists!'

'Don't call *me* a *bloody journalist!*' Roused to equal fury, she did her own finger-pointing. 'You, who've been paying Hachette. Haven't you? *You* used Hachette to pin suspicion on George Ferrer because his bitch of a wife let *your* company down.' Her fury went up a notch. 'You didn't care about implicating Bob Rothman in a dope scandal that could have wrecked his reputation. And then you and Hachette thought you could put the blame on Marc Martens, and to hell with his entire future. And because of *you*, Danny Breton damn nearly died!'

'That had nothing to do with me.'

'Don't give me that bullshit!' she raged. 'If not from *you*, where else did Dash get that stuff?'

'Stuff?' Dino decided to act innocent. He would try to bluff this. 'What 'stuff' are you talking about?'

'Dexamphetamine sulphate. Dex. That stuff.'

Oh, Christ! What else did she know? He heard himself stammering: 'That was...It was Fiarelli...We were going to take it in small amounts that wouldn't show on the dope tests. Then I thought we could give amounts that *would* show, to other people like...'

'Like Harry Vallon?' she said. 'A carton of pepped-up fruit juice?'

Dino gasped and took a step backwards. 'It...it all went wrong. It was the strongest taste. Banana flavoured. I meant it for Ribero, but he...He hates the taste of bananas.'

'So you gave it to Harry Vallon. Enough dope to blow his mind.'

'No! No!' Dino was almost screaming. 'There wasn't that much. But on top of the coffee...'

'What coffee?'

'Before the start. He was standing beside me. He had a chance of winning the Yellow Jersey. So had I! So I gave him the coffee.'

'With Dex in it? And the fruit juice was a *second* dose?'

'I'd forgotten about the coffee.' It came out as a wail. 'It's true! I swear it. I didn't mean him to die! Not even though I was jealous of him.' He turned his head away and muttered, 'You see, he...he has a beautiful, healthy baby.'

Jo paid no attention to that and went on relentlessly. 'You *forgot* about the coffee, *forgot* about everything but yourself, your lust for glory, your greed...' Suddenly her rage subsided. Sounding almost weary, she asked, 'Why did you do it?'

'For the money. I need three quarters of a million dollars.'

'*What?*'

'All those investments. Then the tax people caught up with me. Tax evasion. Undeclared earnings. We kept it out of the media.'

'We?'

'Well, Fiarelli really. He knows people...'

'How fortunate,' she said sarcastically. 'So you need money for your tax debt?'

'*No!* Not for that. I owed them plenty, but I paid them. That's why I need the cash.'

'You paid them, but you still need money? Why do you need such an amount?'

'Because I...' To his horror, he began to cry. With tears running down his face, he said, 'I need it for the baby...My little daughter.' Through helpless sobs, he told her about Gina. 'It's the only place that does the operation,' he said at the end.

For some time Jo was too shattered speak. Now she saw the point of Dino's remark about Harry's healthy baby. Claudia's baby. She recalled what Claudia had said about Dino's odd behaviour, how he'd walked out after seeing her baby.

Eventually she asked, 'Wouldn't your father help?'

'No. Because I didn't marry Carlotta.' He made a gesture of appeal. 'Jo, surely *you* understand? You got it so right in that article. The reason I'm famous, the reason the advertisers want me—it's because I'm the playboy with the glamorous girlfriends.' Bitterly he added, 'My image brings in more money than my riding.'

'So you do realise that,' Jo said. 'And your Carlotta goes along with it?'

'Yes. She understands. We're going to be married when my career's over.' He began to sob again. 'It's over now.'

After a moment, Jo said, 'All right; I believe you didn't intend Harry to die. But why did you go on to target Marc Martens?'

'Because he was too strong. I'd already given...' Dino abruptly shut up. He drew a breath and started again. 'We had to get rid of the stuff anyway, because of all the police searches.'

'I assume the second team car—the one that was damaged—was carrying the bulk of the supply, and you told the driver to stay in Spain until the searches were over.'

Dino's mouth dropped open. 'How did you...?'

'Know? I didn't; but it wasn't so hard to guess. Go on.'

'Well...we had sixteen capsules with us. We had to get rid of them.'

'And instead of flushing them down the drain, you told Dash to plant the stuff on Martens, but he put it in Rothman's bag. Yes, I know that, too.' Suddenly worn out by too much emotion, Jo said, 'Dino, let's sit over there.' She led the way to a bench and, after a breathing space, tried to reduce the tension by saying reasonably, 'By riding for a team that you own, you've broken Federation rules. But you haven't broken the law, in the strict sense of the...' She stopped talking as realisation hit her.

He had given Vallon the doped drinks that led to his death.

Manslaughter. The word came back to haunt her.

So bloody clever Jo Bonnard, playing the Investigative Journalist, always having to prove she was brighter than the men. Jo Bonnard with her scoop of the year. Smart Jo Bonnard with her theory, and the DVD photo-prints probably on their way to the police. Oh God! she thought. What have I done?

She sat with her head bowed. After a long silence she said, 'In twenty days you've ridden three thousand kilometres, four hundred of them up mountains. You've got to ride that stage tomorrow and collect your Best Climber's cheque.'

Dino said miserably, 'I can't face the fans.'

Was he to be pitied or despised? Jo felt like shaking him. 'Oh, grow up, Dino! If it's true you acted for the baby and Carlotta, think of the money as theirs. Bank the cheque immediately—in Carlotta's account. And meanwhile...I can't promise to salvage anything. I can only say I'll try.' He opened his mouth to speak. 'And for godsake don't thank me, because I'll try for the sake of your baby; not for you.'

~

She didn't sleep. All night long, thoughts chased around in her mind.

At six in the morning she got up, took a shower and got dressed. She had to set out early, anyway, to get to Paris in time to cover this last stage. After the broadcast she'd have to hand in the company car...

Twenty past six—a helluva time to phone anyone, but...

She called Paul's mobile phone. He answered on the second ring, awake already, thank heavens, and he was still in Toulouse.

'How far has Niemann gone with my doped drink theory?'

Paul's intake of breath was quite audible. 'I'm not supposed to say anything about it.'

'Paul. Please. I have to know. It's very important.'

He hesitated again before he said, 'Enlarged stills were made from the DVD.'

'Which parts?'

'Nardini handing the carton to Vallon. Vallon drinking from it. Vallon putting the empty carton in the bag. Then Vallon throwing the bag towards the verge. The little boy picking up the bag, and the boy putting the bag under his jacket.'

'What did Niemann do with the enlargements?'

'He forwarded them to La Portette. To the Inspector in charge of the enquiry—Simenon, you said.'

'*Shit!*'

'What's wrong, Jo? Isn't that what you wanted?'

'Yes. But...I've been too damned clever. Oh, Paul, you must feel this is a one-way street. I do nothing but ask favours of you. Can I ask you to do something else for me?'

'Of course.'

'Can you book me a flight out of Paris? It will have to be after seven, at the earliest.'

'To where?' he said, sounding extremely startled.

'Toulouse, or Perpignan...or anywhere within driving distance of La Portette or Font Val—the village where the boy picked up the bag. Can you do that for me?'

'Yes, I can, but. ..'

'I'll phone you after the stage and you can tell me the flight details.' Her mind racing, she said, 'And I've just thought of something else. Can you organise a hire car at the other end?'

'Yes. Yes, all right; but *why?* Try to calm down and tell me what's wrong.'

She told him.

At the end of it all, he said a shocked 'Oh my God!' Then: 'I had a part in this as well.'

'I know. You can't imagine how guilty I feel about involving you in this. I thought I'd been clever, working out Nardini's motives. I didn't think about asking him. My stupidity makes me so angry, because God knows I had it drummed into me at college—*Never assume*—and yet I just assumed it was ruthless greed.'

'So did I. It was a natural assumption. Nardini's a glory-seeker and I doubt if one person in five thousand would have assumed otherwise.'

'I've got to try to undo the damage. His child's life is at stake. If only I could go there right away...'

'But you can't. You'll go tonight, though. Leave it to me.'

STAGE 21

Morning

Henri Beaumont

Henri Beaumont was a big man, slow moving and slow speaking. He was a slow thinker, too; but that didn't mean he was stupid. At the moment he was puzzled, wondering why his ten-year-old son Nicolas was lying to Police Captain Grosbois. Nicolas was not a liar. In fact, he always owned up to any wrongdoing—not that he did much wrong. He was a good kid, so why was he telling lies? Maybe the boy shared his dislike of Grosbois, a big-city smartarse with gelled hair and a daft little triangle of beard between his lower lip and his chin. He was from Toulouse, didn't know a thing about village life.

Grosbois had come to the door asking to speak to Nicolas and adding, 'As he is a minor, I should inform you that you may be present throughout the interview.' Henri knew that, but kept quiet.

In the living room, Grosbois produced a photograph from his attaché case and held it out to the boy, saying: 'This is a photograph of you, taken on the day of that bicycle race.'

That bicycle race. What a clown! The great Captain Grosbois, making out he was superior to a huge international event like The Tour.

Nicolas's spine stiffened, but he said, 'Yes. That's me.'

'You are seen here in the act of picking up a bag from the roadside.'

Nicolas stood even straighter and looked the policeman in the eye. 'It's not stealing. The cyclists throw them away.'

'Where is it now?'

'In my room.'

'I'd like to see it.'

Henri gave a thought to search warrants but dismissed the idea of making much from nothing. He nodded to his son and led the way to the boy's bedroom.

Along with dozens of magazine photos of cyclists, adverts for bikes and a poster, the bag was tacked to the wall. On a shelf were three water bottles with the Tour logo, one with the Mr Chip colours, plus a Chiali glove and an Intapost team cap—all souvenirs from last year's Tour, when Henri had taken Nicolas to watch the Arcalis climb.

Grosbois looked around, raised his eyebrows at Henri and remarked, 'Childhood crazes.'

Maybe it was meant to be sympathetic, but it came out patronising.

'Ah well,' Grosbois sniffed, 'at least it cleans up the litter from the roadside.' He reached out and pressed the palm of his hand over the bag. 'Empty,' he said. 'It contained something, didn't it? A packet.'

Nicolas gave a small nod.

'May I see that packet?'

'I haven't got it.'

And that, Henri knew from his son's face, was a lie.

The officer frowned. 'What did you do with it?'

'I swapped it. For a comic.'

Another lie. And an invention.

'So who has it now?'

'A friend.'

'Here in the village? What's his name?' Grosbois whipped out a notebook.

'Frederic Chantal,' said Nicolas. 'He's gone back home. He lives in Paris.'

Henri hid his amazement. Nicolas and Frederic were friendly, but Frederic was a football fan, and therefore not a boy who would exchange comics for cycling souvenirs, that was certain.

Grosbois sighed impatiently. 'Paris is a big city. What's his address?'

'I don't know.'

The officer turned to Henri. 'What's this nonsense? He doesn't know his friend's address?'

'That's right,' Henri said. 'The Chantal family rent the old Mesnil farmhouse every year for their holiday. But as to where they live in Paris, I've no idea.'

Grosbois drew his lips into a thin line. With a last, disdainful look around the room, he took himself off without so much as a word of thanks for giving me your time.

Henri stood looking down at Nicolas who immediately said, 'It wasn't true. I didn't swap anything with Frederic.'

'I know,' said his father. 'So why invent the story?'

'The cyclists throw these things down.' Nicolas gestured at the bag. 'They know us fans will pick them up. They *want* us to have them. That cop said my collection is *litter!*' His lip trembled and tears began to spill over. '*Litter from the roadside!* Well, if that's what he thinks about it, why should I give him anything?'

Henri sympathised with that, but he was still puzzled. 'What packet was he talking about?'

Snuffling, Nicolas pulled open a drawer. 'I suppose he meant this banana drink carton that was in the bag. Look, Dad.' He held it out. 'It's empty.'

'I know that,' Henri said. It was beyond him to know why Captain Smartarse should want it. 'All the same, son, I don't like this lying.'

'Neither do I, really, but...' The boy's lip quivered again.

Henri patted him on the shoulder. 'Fair enough, son. You've confessed to me, so let's forget it, eh? What time is the final stage on TV? We'll watch it together.'

Inspector Simenon

Police Inspector Sylvain Simenon frowned over the telephone as he listened to Grosbois make his report, ending with comments about people who allowed their offspring to fill their rooms with rubbish and had no idea of who their playmates were. The young Captain seemed to have mishandled things. His attitude wasn't the best for a rural district. He should have spoken first to the child's father, and explained the importance of the carton.

'Type up your report and send it over.' Simenon replaced the receiver with a sigh.

It could be that the child was lying. Children frequently lied.

Second bites at the cherry were never easy, but he would have to try to undo this cock-up. Casual clothes and a friendly approach. Explain to the father. Perhaps talk to the child about cycle racing?

What do I know about cycle racing? Simenon asked himself. Next to nothing. The Tour had given him a huge logistical problem but, apart from that, he was uninterested. He neither watched sports nor participated in them.

Resignedly, he decided to go over to Font Val tomorrow.

Jo Bonnard

The Tour always ended on a Sunday, the only day when the centre of Paris could be closed to traffic. Jo, along with the Chiali and Mr Chip teams, had the longest distance to drive because *Le Jardin* had been the farthest flung of all the allocated hotels. The luck of the draw, Jo thought, had given the two leading riders' teams an additional sixty kilometres to travel before they started their final day. Jo had to get ahead of the road closures, and the only way to do so was to set out at seven in the morning.

The drive gave her time to think and to worry about getting back to the Pyrenees, finding the little boy...Right now, there was absolutely nothing she could do about any of it. Better to close her mind to the impossible, and to think about today's final stage.

Most of the Sunday drivers were heading out from the city. Inbound traffic was less dense. At eight-thirty she was ahead of her schedule and pulled in to a service station for coffee. Someone had left today's copy of *L'Equipe* on the table. The headline *Echo of '89* was a reminder about the final stage of the 1989 Tour.

Fignon entered Paris wearing the Yellow Jersey. At the end of the afternoon he mounted the podium—but only as far as the second step. On the top step stood the American, LeMond, who, on that final day's time trial, had beaten him by eight seconds, the narrowest margin ever recorded in the Tour's long history.

And Fignon never quite got over that defeat, thought Jo. With a fifty-second advantage over LeMond, he had realised too late that his victory was about to be overturned. He had, in fact, collapsed on the finishing line, exhausted and destroyed by the American, to whom a race was a race to be fought, regardless of 'tradition,' all the way to the last metre.

She lowered her eyes to the text again.

In recent years, on account of the time trial coming before-hand and fairly wide time gaps between the leaders, the final stage has been a victory parade. Team cars hand out champagne instead of water, in an atmosphere of fête. But this year, it seems that the closing stage will once again be a competition that could be every bit as tense as that of 1989. Three steps on the podium await three men. But which three?—And in what order?

Jo pondered the same questions. Barring a catastrophe, Marc Martens would win; but would Dino Nardini retain his second place? She had no idea how Dino might react to that confrontation last night. His Best Climber award was safe, but would he now sit back? Or would his rage and desperation make him fight Martens to the finish?

Charreau would surely try to take that second place from Nardini. Jonkers, fourth, would not make the podium unless he caught back six seconds on Charreau, and that also was possible. There was a midway sprint, plus bonus points on the first lap around the Champs Elysées. And, of course, the last mad dash for the finishing line. That was usually a battle between the sprinters although, as recently as 2005, the fighting Kazakh Vinokourov had won it by catapulting himself clear of the peloton with more than a kilometre to go, and by hammering over the cobblestones in as daring and determined a ride as Jo had ever witnessed.

Which of the four leaders was the best sprinter? She reckoned

Marc Martens could cope better than the others if he found himself in a packed bunch of nerveless musclemen thundering over the final hundred metres.

Despite her worries and her anxiety to get to Font Val, she found that she was looking forward to what would undoubtedly be a hard-fought last stage.

She was finishing her coffee when the cafeteria door swung open and a young man came in, talking on his mobile phone. Jo recognised him as Sandy Harris, an eager young reporter from one of the New York papers.

His agitated voice reached her clearly. 'Because my laptop battery's dead, that's why. Just patch me through to the sports desk... Well, somebody who can take copy, for Chrissakes!...Not until *when?*' He looked at his watch. 'Aw, Jeez! Aw, shit!' He turned on his heel and swung out again.

What piece of urgent news had caused Sandy to forget that, in New York, it was four oclock on a Sunday morning? Jo took her mobile phone from her pocket and called her friend Janine, the Press Officer. 'What's the big news today?'

Janine gasped. 'Aren't you on the road? You must have private jungle drums. Anyhow, Leon Jonkers is out of it. He was rushed to hospital at five this morning. Acute appendicitis. It's a crying shame, isn't it?'

It certainly was, but it explained why he'd suffered in the time trial, and why he'd struggled in the *grupetto* yesterday. Jo thanked Janine and grabbed for *L'Equipe* again, to see who was now in fourth position. George Ferrer, for heavens sake! And George was only twelve seconds behind Charreau! She hadn't realised he was so close.

STAGE 21

Afternoon

Jo Bonnard

Jo had been on air for ten minutes, talking about Jonkers's bad luck and adding Race Radio's update that he was out of danger after an emergency operation.

Moto 1 was filming Dino Nardini. Sitting well placed in the front group, he was clearly not going to concede his second place to Charreau. Was he also going to fight Martens for the top step?

'With the unlucky departure of Leon Jonkers,' Jo said, 'George Ferrer is now fourth overall. Although sixty-five seconds down on Martens, he's only twelve seconds away from the third-placed Charreau. Ferrer's form went to pieces halfway through the Tour, but he has fought his way back up the rankings, and today he's riding in the front group.' Good for George, she thought. He deserved success.

'There he is, in dark blue, following the wheel of Jacky Bernard, his faithful lieutenant. Marc Martens and a coterie of Mr Chip protectors are at the head of things, trying to keep a tight control on the speed of the peloton. Charreau's fairly far back, in the middle of the peloton. I reckon Ferrer is going to challenge that third place, and he might get it if Charreau hangs about like he's doing at the moment.'

Charreau appeared to have given up, but Jo barely had time to wonder what was wrong with him.

'One kilometre ahead there's an intermediate sprint, so we'll see some of the contenders for the Sprints Jersey having a go at the remaining handful of points. Claes has ridden right to the front of the group, but Salvatore, Nilsson, Bruno and the other sprinters are not far behind him. Odd though it may seem, Claes is in the least favourable position, because it's much easier to start an attack from several places back. The others will be after Claes in a flash, the moment he makes a move. Watch how Claes is looking over his shoulder, hoping that one of them will initiate the sprint and, in doing so, give him a lead out. Yes, they're all watching each other,' she chuckled. 'This is very cat and mouse stuff, testing each others' nerves and savvy.'

She leaned forward, watching her screen intently. 'It seems there's a bit of place-changing going on, about ten riders back, on the left hand side of your screen. The four big sprinters are on the right, still eyeing each other, and they're probably not aware that somebody's sneaking up on their blind side. It's Ferrer!'

George Ferrer whipped out of the pack and sprinted up the blind-side gutter, and then the picture changed to a helicopter shot. It was replay of the few preceding seconds, and Tony's tech wizardry had put a spotlight on Ferrer as he quietly wove his way toward the front.

The picture switched to Moto 1 and the current action. 'And there goes Ferrer!' Jo exclaimed. 'Going flat out, Vinokourov style, Ferrer has gained a fair-sized gap. Jan Claes was the first to spot him and chase but he, Nilsson, Salvatore, Bruno and Patrick have been much too slow in reacting, and so George has got…oh, here's a caption…eleven seconds' lead on them. The others were out-foxed, and now they're doing the only possible thing, which is to start sprinting for second and third places.'

Ferrer crossed the sprint line and was easing up as the others reached it. Moments later a caption appeared: Bonus points: Ferrer 6, Nilsson 4, Claes 2. 'Well, well,' Jo remarked. 'George Ferrer is heading for third place over all. To quote my veteran colleague, David Duffield: "It's not over till the fat lady sings…and she hasn't sung yet."'

~

The motocameras were doing a marvellous job of filming stage winners, leading lights and personalities for the commentators to talk about, but it was Moto 3 that captured the moment when riders got their first sight of the Eiffel Tower. Heads came up and the pace slowed appreciably. Especially for those riding their first Tour, it was their hour of achievement. But even the old hands experienced the thrill of satisfaction. They'd made it to Paris.

~

They had reached the city centre. Jo exclaimed. 'Oh, I love this shot! No matter how often I see it, this is a classic Tour Moment. Moto 1 is ahead of the riders, waiting to catch them at the top of the steep little climb out of the underpass. Here they come! Bright helmets popping up like bubbles against the darkness of the tunnel.

'And still they come. More bubbles. Up and on to a long straight, past the classical arcades of the buildings. Then they come to the cobblestones of the Opera where they sweep round in wide curves, left and right...They're beginning to string-out now, on the slight up-slope of the Champs Elysées. We'll see this shot again, next time around, but now the helicopter's circling around, treating us to some virtual tourism—the Egyptian Obelisk, the big fairground wheel, the glass pyramid that's the entrance to the Louvre, sightseeing boats on the Seine. Instant Paris,' she laughed, 'and we'll see it all again as the peloton goes five times round the city circuit.'

A new picture came from Moto 1. 'Back at ground level, it's heads down for bonus points at the first crossing of the finish line. The sprinters are in a mad scramble to get to the front of the pack. Jan Claes is there. Nilsson and Patrick have made it, too. These three are getting away clear of the rest. But Ferrer has burst from the pack again. He's flying! And here comes Nardini, right behind him!

'This Tour has not lacked drama, and even now we have Nardini contesting a sprint! He's caught them, and tucks in behind Nilsson, but Ferrer has put himself in the ideal third spot from where he can make another crafty sprint over the last fifty metres...Aha! Jan Claes is ready for him this time...Claes crosses the line first, Ferrer second and Nilsson third. Dino Nardini didn't stand a serious chance. Nevertheless, Ferrer is now well ahead of Charreau, who, for some reason, is still riding along in the peloton, nowhere near the front of the race.'

Now, she thought, catching her breath, everyone should settle down for a while. There were no more points at stake until the final circuit and the end of The Tour. The final charge along the Champs Elysées promised to be a real battle.

At that moment the yellow motorbike came up from behind the leading group and slowed beside Moto 1. The blackboard man held up the board. On it was a drawing of a stork with a bundle suspended in its beak. On the bundle was *Garçon* and, on a label on the carrying strings, was a large 21.

The camera turned to film nearby riders, all grinning and clapping. Cedric Charreau, rider number 21, must just have learned that he was the father of a boy. His lack of commitment to the race was now explained. Jo conveyed the news to her audience.

∼

As the peloton swept over the finishing line for the penultimate time on this Tour, there came another classic shot of a man swinging the clapper of the big brass bell, warning the riders they were on the final lap of the circuit.

'Nilsson of Intapost is going clear. It's a bit early to make a break but it might come off. No, it won't because Claes and Patrick have followed him and…Crikey! Martens is going with them!'

Jo wondered if Marc was making a last-minute tactical error. This was an open challenge to Nardini and Ferrer who would now be obliged to enter the melee of the sprint.

'Claes, Nilsson and Martens have got clear of the pack by a good ten metres. Ferrer is leading the chasers and Dino Nardini is contesting the final sprint as well! He's right behind Ferrer, sitting in his slipstream, but Ferrer's going like a train! He has caught up with the three leaders. Nardini hasn't given up and is still ahead of the main pack. With less than a hundred metres to the line, Claes starts his all-out sprint. Ferrer's right behind him…passes him…and takes the stage! George Ferrer wins the final stage! What a triumph for a man whose form fell apart halfway through The Tour.'

A close-up of a delighted Ferrer came up on the screen. He was quickly surrounded by his *soigneurs* and mechanics, and then by other riders as they arrived in the Control Area. Judging by the handshaking and backslapping that went on, everyone was equally delighted by his victory.

The scene was overlaid by a caption showing the stage results: Ferrer, Claes, Martens, Nilsson, Patrick, Nardini...Then came the overall placings of the Tour: 1st Martens, 2nd Nardini, 3rd Ferrer, and a shot of three flags being hoisted—Belgian, Italian and French.

FONT VAL

The following day

Jo Bonnard

Jo's alarm clock went off. Where was she? She couldn't remember, nor could she think where today's stage finished. Then she remembered there was no stage. The Tour was over.

She saw yesterday's podium as a series of mental snapshots: Marc Martens in the Yellow Jersey, smiling at last...Dino Nardini, unsmiling, not even acknowledging the fans...Intapost, winners of the Best Team prize, and the camera zooming in to see what Chico Montes was holding at face level—a big photo of Danny, the absent member of the team.

Later snapshots—a policeman frantically trying to unsnarl dense traffic...Returning the car to the depot. The taxi to the airport... The plane to Toulouse...Her surprise and relief when she saw Paul and Danny waiting to meet her...The midnight arrival in a hotel at La Portette...A quick shower, and then collapsing into bed like a felled tree, asleep before her head touched the pillow.

Today...Today she had to find a boy, for the sake of Dino Nardini's baby.

~

Over breakfast she explained her mission to Danny. Paul had apparently not told him the full story.

'Analysis of that Frutactiv carton might incriminate Dino. I was instrumental in telling the police about it. Now I have to beat them to it.' Jo gazed into her coffee cup as though it might hold the answer to her problem. 'Assuming the little boy kept his souvenir, how on earth can I talk him into parting with it?'

'What age is he?' asked Danny.

'About nine or ten.' She looked up and smiled. 'I can still picture him in his bright red waterproof, standing at the roadside with his hair dripping wet. He must be a real fan.'

And at that moment—like the light bulb in a cartoon—an idea came to her.

An article about young fans...What attracted them to cycling? Did they practise the sport? Would they like to make a career of it? What did they most admire in their heroes? It would make a great article!...Or was she rationalising, justifying a devious scheme?

~

Paul had kept Jo's car, of course, and was driving it. Danny sat in the back, his plastered leg stretched out and a map open across his knees. Jo sat in the front, looking out unfocussed at the green slopes of mountains that were veiled by a fine mist. How was she going to find the boy?

Suddenly Paul said, 'Here we are. Font Val.' He pulled up in the almost deserted village square. 'Where do we start looking?'

'The school would be the likeliest place,' said Jo, 'but of course they'll be on holiday.'

'That's the school over there,' Danny pointed across the square, 'and it's open.'

Jo got out of the car, crossed to the building and followed the sound of voices. Through an open doorway she saw a squad of painters draping sheets over furniture.

A tall man, stooping and grey-haired, emerged backwards from the room, saying irascibly, 'Careful with that bookcase!' Stepping between paint-pots, he almost collided with Jo. 'Oh! Sorry. Ah... Are you looking for someone?'

'I'm looking for the head teacher.'

'You've found him. Still on duty, thus disproving the public's conception that we have the same holidays as the pupils.' Over his shoulder, he said, 'Don't break the glass.' He turned to Jo again.

'Apprentice painter's a former pupil. Careless lad. Don't suppose he'll ever change...Now then, young lady, why are you looking for me?'

'My name's Jo Bonnard. I'm a cycling journalist and commentator for Eltsport TV.' She took her press card and Tour accreditation from her bag and held them out.

The headmaster inspected them and handed them back. 'Well now! I've read some of your articles and I always thought Jo Bonnard was a man!' He laughed and shook her hand. 'And you commentate on TV as well, eh? Can't say I watch Eltsport, but I'm delighted to meet you. I'm Fabien Legrain. So, what brings you here to look for me?'

'I want your help, Monsieur Legrain. I'd like to talk to a boy who, I guess, is one of your pupils. He's a big cycling fan. Well, not all that big—physically, I mean. About nine or ten years old, with a mop of black hair. He wears a red cagoule in the rain.' She put on a hopeful expression and crossed her fingers.

Legrain looked thoughtful. 'We have quite a few cycling fans. Can't be Robert; he's tall and fair. Red cagoule, eh? Ah!' with sudden enlightenment, 'It'll be Nicolas. Nicolas Beaumont.'

'Could you tell me where he lives? I really would like to talk to him. A word with his parents would be helpful as well.' She mentally pleaded with the man, willing him to agree.

'Hmm,' he said doubtfully. 'Helpful in what way?'

She explained her idea for an article about young fans. This was the truth—but not the whole truth. Did her explanation amount to dishonesty? Legrain didn't seem like a man who'd be easily deceived.

Legrain said, 'Interesting idea,' without much enthusiasm, still protective of his pupil.

Jo thought of Dino's baby girl who might grow up confined to a wheelchair—or might never grow up because Dino, charged with manslaughter, might have to refund the prize money. And all because Jo Bonnard had been too clever...That was not something she wanted to have on her conscience, so to hell with mild dishonesty. She had to persist. 'When The Tour came through the village, the TV camera picked out this little boy—Nicolas, you said? He was waiting by the roadside in that terrible downpour, so he had to be a real devotee. I remarked on him to the viewers.'

The headmaster appeared to reach a decision. 'The Beaumonts live outside the village, about three kilometres in the direction of Haut Val. The boy's father is a carpenter. You'll see his yard beside a grey stone house.'

Jo thanked him sincerely, said a rapid goodbye and hurried back to the car.

~

'You want to see Nicolas? What about?' Madame Beaumont was a tiny, bird-like woman, especially compared with her husband who towered behind her in the doorway.

'He's a cycling fan, isn't he?' Jo repeated her explanation about seeing him on TV, and launched again into her idea for an article. She did not enjoy this dissembling, but forced herself to go on with it.

'His headmaster told me where you live, so we thought we'd take the chance to talk to him since we're in this part of the country.'

Madame Beaumont looked up uncertainly at her husband.

He was still studying Jo's press card. He spoke for the first time. 'First the police. Now the press.'

The police had already been here! Jo tried to hide her shock.

The big man frowned at her. 'You said 'we.' Is somebody with you? It's not that Grosbois again, is it?'

Jo had no idea who was Grosbois. 'I'm with friends,' she said. 'Paul and Danny Breton.'

A tousle-headed boy shot out of a room and cannoned into his father. This was Nicolas, the boy on the DVD, staring at her and saying, 'Danny Breton! You're kidding.'

She grinned at him. 'No I'm not. He's in the car. Would you like to talk to him?'

'Really? For really real? It's not a joke?'

Jo was halfway down the path, calling, 'Danny! Extract yourself. Come and meet Nicolas.'

The decision seemed to have been taken out of his parents' hands.

Danny Breton

'Is your leg sore? You can sit on the bed if you like.' Nicolas was quivering with excitement.

'Thanks.' Danny sat, propped his crutches beside him and looked around the boy's room. 'You've got quite a picture gallery.'

'That's you.' Nicolas pointed to the poster.

'So it is.' Danny recognised it as a centre-fold from a magazine that had run a short article about him. *Danny Breton, the son of cycling legend Paul Breton, will be the youngest rider in this year's Tour. ..* He felt embarrassed and changed the subject. 'That's a good shot of Marc Martens on his time trial bike. Who else is up there?'

Nicolas put names, dates and places to his display of photographs, ending: 'That's Paco Ribero on his mountain bike. Did you see him two days ago, going down that hill? Whee-ee!'

'I saw,' Danny said grimly. The kid was grinning, so he added: 'Don't even think of trying it. I thought he was totally crazy, risking a fall. Bad enough when it's accidental.'

'I saw you falling into the river. Were you scared?'

'I guess I was. I didn't really have time to think about it.'

'I'm going to be a cyclist,' Nicolas said. 'I want to be like you.'

Embarrassed again, Danny joked. 'With your leg in plaster? Better to be like Marc Martens and win The Tour.'

The boy shook his head. 'I'd rather be like you. You're my favourite. Imagine really talking to you! This...' He took a deep breath. 'This is the greatest day of my life!'

'Thanks, Nicolas.' Danny looked at the kid's starry eyes. It was the first time he'd met hero-worship. He'd thought that only footballers and pop stars were idols but apparently he, Danny Breton, was a role model for this little boy. It was a mind-boggling thought.

'Look,' said Nicolas. 'This is one of your team hats, and there's this bag. I wish it was yours, but it's not. I got it when you came through the village last week. You were nearly in the lead. I called and waved to you, and you smiled at me. Do you remember?'

Danny didn't remember. Kids were always shouting and waving. Seeing the anxious look on the boy's face, Danny recalled Jo's description and said, 'You were wearing a red waterproof. Right?' An evasion, but worth the look of joy it produced. He'd smiled, had he? Circumstances permitting, in future he would smile at kids. 'Come on, show me the rest of your collection.'

There was a school exercise book with press clippings pasted on its pages—that magazine article and several paragraphs about Danny Breton. *Second place in Normandy's stage 3 was an early-season success for Intapost's young rider...*and so on. Then Nicolas opened a drawer, saying, 'This is nothing much, really, just a carton. That stuck-up Captain Grosbois wanted it. I don't know why, because he said it was just *litter.*'

Captain Grosbois had to be a police officer. Danny held his breath. The carton was the reason they were here. How could he get the boy to part with it? He was a nice little kid. Danny didn't want to con him. Genuinely curious, he asked, 'Why did you want to pick *that* up?'

'I didn't actually pick it up. It was in the bag. I thought I might swap it, but nobody wanted it. I don't specially want it either, but I wasn't going to give it to Captain Smartarse. Oops!' He put a hand over his mouth.

Danny laughed. 'I won't tell you said that.'

The little boy hung his head. 'I told him I *had* swapped it. It was a lie. My dad's not pleased.'

A weight dropped from Danny's conscience. 'You really don't want this? How about turning the fib into the truth, then? You could do a swap with me.'

Nicolas went wide-eyed. 'That would be great!'

'Anyway, you deserve a better souvenir.' Danny retrieved his crutches, levered himself to his feet and went to the door. 'Dad!' he shouted, and his father appeared at the door of the big cosy kitchen where they'd all been invited when they'd come in from the car. 'Dad, can you bring my Tour Guide? It's in the back of the car.'

A few minutes later, Nicolas sat holding the thick book. Inside was written: *For my friend Nicolas Beaumont. Good luck. Danny Breton.*

Blinking back tears, Nicholas said, 'I'll keep this forever.'

It struck Danny that the boy spoke with total sincerity. He had a sudden image of Nicolas ten years from now, showing the book to a friend...and the friend would say: *Who's Danny Breton? Never heard of him.* There and then, Danny made a decision. He would make a true effort to ride himself into the fame that Nicolas expected of him. He knew he had the ability. Few riders had his privileged background.

Perhaps that was his problem. He just hadn't *tried* enough, or *cared* enough about winning. From now on, his dilettante attitude was going to toughen up.

He cleared his throat. 'Now come on, Nicolas. Do the swap.'

Nicolas solemnly handed over the drink carton. 'It's perfectly clean,' he said earnestly. 'There was still some sticky stuff in it and Mum thought it might go mouldy, so she helped me to wash it out dead carefully with hot water and bleach. Five times.'

Danny looked into the carton. Its foil-lined interior was, indeed, perfectly clean.

~

They joined the others in the kitchen. Danny caught Jo's eye and gave her a barely perceptible nod.

Madame Beaumont turned. 'Has Nicolas been chatting your head off?'

'No. We had an interesting talk. I've learned a lot, in fact.'

'So have I,' said Jo. 'The point of view of a young fan's parents. I'm definitely going to write that article.' She put her notebook into her bag and spoke to Madame Beaumont. 'We've taken up so much of your time, and I'm very grateful for your help, but we have to get back to Paris. I've got to catch a plane tomorrow night.'

'Aw!' said Nicolas. 'Are you going already?'

'Nicolas!' His mother turned. 'Don't make a nuisance of yourself.'

'I didn't, did I?' he appealed to Danny. 'Look what Danny gave me' He held out the book. 'Well, not exactly *gave* me. It's a swap.' He giggled. 'Guess what for? The carton that Captain Sma...Grosbois wanted. You know? The *litter*.'

Henri Beaumont directed a frown at Danny. 'Why?'

'Nicolas had a bad conscience for telling a fib.' Danny grinned conspiratorially at his new young friend. 'So we turned it into the truth. And I've got a souvenir as well, to remind me of a boy I've been proud to meet.' As he held up the carton, he had an idea. 'I'll get this carton flattened and sealed in tough plastic. It'll be my mascot.'

He'd ride with it in his pocket to remind himself of this little boy, to remind himself to be less bloody soft in future, and to go for victories. *Second place in Normandy's stage 3*...He could easily have won that stage—and several others—if he'd made a genuine effort.

Inspector Simenon

An hour later, Inspector Simenon, wearing casual clothes, leaned his elbows on the wall. Through the open doors of the workshop, he could see Henri Beaumont skilfully working with a plane, smoothing a piece of wood.

There was an exchanged *Bonjour,* and after a moment Simenon said chattily, 'Don't know how you do that. Looks easy, but when I try it I always dig the blade in.'

'Takes practice.'

'Is your son learning the tricks of the trade?'

Beaumont kept at his task. 'Ten years old. A bit young yet.'

'Going to be a carpenter, is he?'

'Says he's going to be a cyclist.'

Simenon felt encouraged. He'd reached the subject quickly. 'Oh? They make good money, do they?'

'More to life than money.'

Don't get into philosophy, Simenon warned himself. He'd thought out a reasonable approach. 'I never knew much about cycling, but when The Tour comes through your town you get more interested. Closing the roads is a problem, of course. Causes a lot of disruption.'

'Causes a lot of litter, too, eh? Cyclists throwing things onto the roadside.'

Hell and damnation! Grosbois had plenty to answer for.

The big carpenter straightened his back. 'Your Captain was here yesterday, asking my boy about litter. If you're after the same thing, Inspector, I'm telling you once and for all—there's no carton from the roadside in this house. The boy swapped it. I'll repeat that with my hand on the Bible, if you want.'

Henri Beaumont

Simenon went away and Henri resumed his work. What could be so important about a carton that had brought the Inspector, no less, chasing after Captain Smartarse? Maybe there was something wrong with the stuff that had been in it. You heard these stories about food poisoning; things being taken off supermarket shelves because they were contaminated. He nodded to himself, pleased

208

to have worked out a likely reason. A good thing Yvette had disinfected it before letting Nicolas put it in his collection. She'd told him about it, laughing that the boy was worse than a magpie. A good thing Nicolas had genuinely swapped it now. Henri Beaumont wasn't a liar either, and he hadn't had to lie to Inspector Simenon.

And young Nicolas was happy. Never seen him happier in his life, meeting his hero Danny Breton—a decent lad, just like his father. Henri remembered Paul Breton in his heyday. Never have thought he'd be such a nice bloke, no swank or arrogance whatever, asking him and Yvette to call him Paul. He'd advised them to let Nicolas join the local cycling club as a junior, but not to lash out money on an expensive bike until he was older. If the boy had talent, Paul said, it would show itself; but Nicolas would have to win plenty of amateur races before a professional team would take him on.

Madame Bonnard had added, 'Make sure he learns a trade, though, or has a qualification for when he's in his thirties. A long way ahead,' she'd laughed, 'but cycling's a short-term career. Only a few cyclists make enough to retire on.'

She'd mentioned satisfaction and enjoyment from your work. Henri understood what she meant by that. He ran his hand over the smooth surface of the wood. He reckoned it had been a satisfactory day.

MILAN

Three days later

Jo Bonnard

Jo had said *Au revoir* to Paul and Danny in Paris, and had caught her flight to Milan, to report on the latest high-tech in the Cycle Exhibition. In Milan she had phoned Claudia and been warmly invited to visit. On arrival, she had found Claudia playing with her blue-eyed baby son in this rather luxurious flat, and had told her the upshot of their joint investigations, ending with the search for the carton.

'Washed out?' Claudia leaned back in the deeply cushioned chair and began to laugh weakly.

'With hot water and bleach. Five times,' said Jo. 'So, even if the police had taken it, there'd have been no trace of amphetamine. For the sake of my conscience, I'm glad I didn't actually tamper with potentially incriminating evidence.'

'What did you do with it?'

'Danny kept it. It's going to be his winning mascot, he said.'

Claudia retrieved a toy from the floor and returned it to the baby. Then she reached for the coffee pot and refilled their cups. 'I had a phone-call from Dino yesterday.'

Jo was greatly surprised. 'I thought he wasn't speaking to you. What's happened?'

'I could scarcely believe it, but he apologised for treating me so badly. He said it was because I had a perfectly healthy baby and he couldn't bear the unfairness of it. I didn't know what he was talking about. Then he told me about his little girl. I was terribly shocked.' Claudia shook her head. 'It's astonishing that he managed to keep everything so secret. He says that *you* know?'

'Yes. He told me.'

'Oh...He wanted to know if I had your phone number. When I said you were coming here, he asked if he could come and talk to you.' She looked anxiously at Jo. 'I said he could. I hope you don't mind.'

Jo sighed. 'He knows I alerted the Federation to his ownership of Publichiali. No doubt he wants to ventilate his fury. I can take it.' She sighed again. 'I was too hasty. I didn't think of questioning his motives. He acted in desperation because he needs a great deal of money.'

Claudia tossed her hair. 'He was incredibly stupid.'

A buzzer sounded in the hallway. 'Entry-phone,' Claudia explained, getting to her feet. 'That could be him now.'

Minutes later, Dino stood in front of Jo, looking as she had never seen him before—sheepish was the word that came to mind. He shook hands and then they sat in awkward silence while Claudia, the urbane hostess, went to fetch wine. It was a relief when she returned with a bottle and glasses on a tray. She handed a corkscrew to her cousin.

Dino filled the glasses and took a visibly deep breath. 'Carlotta and I are getting married next month.'

Jo was the first to recover her voice. 'Congratulations. Is your father pleased?'

Dino nodded. 'He's religious, you know. He says I've been "living in sin." But now he's giving me five hundred thousand dollars on interest-free loan. I can make up the rest, and Carlotta's going to America with the baby in October. It's all arranged.'

'That's very good news,' said Jo.

Claudia said prosaically, 'A loan?'

'You don't need to tell me,' Dino said grimly. 'It'll take a long time to repay it.'

'What are your assets?' Claudia asked.

Jo thought once again that Claudia was wasted as a society girl. She was a businesswoman to her back teeth.

'The Publichiali group of companies,' said Dino, 'which includes sponsorship of the Chiali team. But I can't ride in it,' he added wretchedly. 'I'm banned from pro riding for two years.'

'My advice,' said Jo, 'would be to appoint an experienced *directeur sportif*—preferably a former cyclist—and build a team around Salvatore, Bruno and whoever else still has a contract. And get rid of Fiarelli. He's done you a lot of harm.'

Dino still looked miserable. 'A two-year ban. That means I've had it, you know. And I can forget about appearing in adverts.' He heaved a sigh. 'It's an awful thought, not being able to ride.'

Claudia scoffed. 'Don't sound so tragic! You can still ride a bike, if that's what's important. Your 'awful thought' is not being able to stand on the podium, waving to your worshipping fans. You're just like Harry was. Grow up, Dino.'

Jo kept her head bent as she heard her own angry words echoed in Claudia's stinging comments, but Dino made no reply.

Claudia's tone became businesslike again. 'The Publichiali group brings in a steady income.'

Dino stared miserably into his wineglass. 'A company director, sitting in an office. I'll hate it. Cycling has been my life.'

Claudia made an exasperated sound in her throat. 'Really, Dino, you are so dim! You already have a CEO, so make your shares over to Carlotta.'

Dino's mouth dropped open. 'Carlotta?'

'By doing so, you would no longer be a shareholder. Then, although you can't ride in it, you could remain involved with the cycling team.' Seeing Jo's stunned expression, she added, 'It's legal.'

Jo knew that cyclists were rolling adverts, wearing the logos of their sponsors who put up the money, provided that increased brand-awareness justified their outlay. Advertising was the name of the game, and cycling was a business that depended on publicity, especially through TV exposure. Apart from marathons or triathlons, no other sport took place on the open road. The public paid no gate money, bought no tickets, watched the spectacle for free. Jo knew that her commentating job was dependent on all those commercial breaks. Money did indeed make the wheels go round. But listening to Claudia, Jo felt like a financial babe in arms.

'Claudia,' she said. 'I've been thinking since I met you, you're wasting your talent. You should go into business.'

'Oh, I will,' Claudia said airily. 'Next year I'm joining a firm of business consultants.' She flicked a glance at her cousin. 'Perhaps Carlotta will be one of my clients.'

'And what will I do?' Dino asked, evidently accepting her superior knowledge.

Claudia gave him a pitying look. 'Jo handed you some advice, if you've the brains to take it.'

TOUR DE FRANCE.

The following year

Jo

'Good afternoon, viewers, and welcome to this ninth stage of the race. As you can see, it's a beautiful day here in the Pyrenees. The riders, still in a compact bunch, will soon be tackling the big climb of Trois Têtes. This famous ascent was included in last year's Tour and, if any of you were watching on that day, I'm not surprised if you don't recognise it now. But you may remember the rainstorm. It was an unbelievable downpour, and I was commentating on a race I could barely see.

'If this were a theatrical production—which it is, in a way—I'd be saying: same scenery, different lighting, some changes in the cast. I'll try to pick out some of the principal players for you. Those of you who've watched the first eight stages will know who's leading the race: Cedric Charreau, on the left of your screen. Behind him is Marc Martens, following that Yellow Jersey like a shadow, hoping to get it back. Marc wore it for the first four days, having ridden a record-breaking prologue time trial.

'Beside Marc is the tall figure of his mentor, Bob Rothman. There were rumours that the American might retire, but here he is *'one more time,'* as he said at the pre-race press conference. The two appear to be having an argument.' Jo laughed. 'They do that but believe me, they're the best of friends

'Charreau took over the Yellow Jersey on stage five, but will he still be wearing it tomorrow? Martens is only fourteen seconds behind him, and two of the climbers are within a minute of his time.' Handily, a close-up camera shot gave her a cue. 'Here's one of those climbers now—David Vauban riding for GSG in the team that used to be sponsored by Intapost. David rode brilliantly in the Giro, the Tour of Italy, earlier this season. His team-leader shouldn't be far off. There he is. Paco Ribero, wearing number fifty-one on his back.'

'Each team has a number, and riders with something-one are the team captains. In the green outfit of the Chiali team is Salvatore, number twenty-one. So we know that Salvatore is Chiali's main rider, and coming into the shot is number twenty-two, Guido Fiorenzi, a top-class climber who transferred from Rotoral to Chiali early this season. The team also has a new *directeur sportif*—Dino Nardini, last year's King of the Mountains, now retired from active competition.'

When the commercials came up, Jo thought about Dino. Today was his daughter Gina's third birthday and, eight months after her operation, the doctors were predicting that it would prove a complete success. Jo had got that information this morning from Chiali's website, which was one of the best and constantly updated—owing to Claudia's influence on the management, no doubt.

A Chiali team car drove into camera range. In the back seat was Dino Nardini.

Dino had lived on and for the cheers and adulation of his fans. To be deprived of the limelight, relegated literally to the back seat, was a kind of poetic justice.

The advert break ended. The climb had not yet reached the steepest part, and Jo continued to chat about the riders.

'That's George Ferrer, thirty-four years old and still going strong, wearing the white-and-blue colours of Fromages du Nord this year. George used to be with AFA who are here with only four of last year's squad, including Jacky Bernard who's promoted to captain under a new *directeur*, Alex Hubbard.'

Newcomers had filled the places of Harry Vallon and Nat Arnold. Arnold had not, apparently, been given a contract by any top-ranked team this season. Neither had Tom Dash. Jo knew what had happened to him...But she was a cycling commentator, nothing more, so she'd say nothing about him.

'Now there's a definite movement towards the front of the pack as the climb gets serious. This is where the climbers, apparently defying the law of gravity, usually leave the ordinary mortals behind. But this is an extremely long climb of more than twenty kilometres, twisting up and up, so it needs endurance. Who might be first at the top? Let's recap if you want to make little bets amongst yourselves.

'Pure climbers—Vauban, Ribero and Fiorenzi. Endurance men—Charreau, Ferrer, Rothman and, of course, the incredibly strong Marc Martens.

'And don't discount Danny Breton, yesterday's stage-winner, another strong all-rounder. Last year he was injured in a fall, but he's back fighting fit, and with a new fighting attitude. He's showing every sign of following in the footsteps—or rather, the wheeltracks—of his famous father, Paul.'

At that she smiled, recollecting Danny's joke when he'd sat at the breakfast table a couple of weeks ago, reading *L'Equipe*. 'I'm always *Danny Breton, son-of-the-great-Paul*,' he'd quoted, laughing. 'Hey, Dad, how would you feel about: 'Paul Breton, father of the great Danny'?'

And Paul had roared with delighted laughter and told Danny to make his wish come true.

The Eltsport Company frowned on personal observations. No way was Jo going to tell the viewers she was talking about her husband and her stepson.

Acknowledgments

This book was completed thanks to Alex, a fellow cycling enthusiast who became my friend, and then my 'cyber-son'. From his computer in distant Romania, his daily e-mails have been supportive in many ways. Regarding the book, it was his encouragement and insistence that kept me at the keyboard.

Graham Watson, who I'm proud to call a friend, and whose photographs of cycling have inspired me for many years, told me he has 'no problem' with his brief appearance in the story.

David Duffield gave me permission to use his name in connection with an opinion.

Janet, my friend and computer expert, patiently answered my questions about transmitting the DVD.

Dr. John Day, friend and editor, noted every misplaced comma and, because he knew nothing of Tour terminology, made helpful suggestions about clarifying the jargon.

My friends and colleagues Carmella, Sandra, Bob, Thomas and Greg, read the first draft of the novel and enjoyed it. None of them was into cycling but, when three of them became Tour-watchers, I was encouraged to keep going.

To all of these people – my sincere thanks.

L.C.